HOOK, LINE, AND SINKER:

The Seventh Guppy Anthology

PREVIOUS GUPPY CHAPTER ANTHOLOGIES

Fish Tales (2011)
Fish Nets (2013)
Fish or Cut Bait (2015)
Fish Out of Water (2017)
Fishy Business (2019)
The Fish That Got Away (2021)

HOOK, LINE, AND SINKER:

The Seventh Guppy Anthology

Edited by Emily P. W. Murphy

Wolf's
Echo
Press

First Edition
Trade Paperback Edition: February 2023

Wolf's Echo Press
PO Box 54
Amasa, MI 49903
www.WolfsEchoPress.com

This is a work of fiction. Any references to real places, real people, real organizations, or historical events are used fictitiously. Other names, characters, organizations, places, or events are the product of the authors' imaginations.

Cover Design by Emily W. P. Murphy. Cover images are used under license from istockphoto.com. Individual image credits are: Goldfish: ChrisGorgio, Shark: id-work, Magnifying glass: Passatic.

ISBN-13 Trade Paperback:	978-1-943166-35-0
ISBN-13 e-book:	978-1-943166-36-7
Library of Congress Control Number:	2022946740

Printed in the United States of America
10 9 8 7 6 5 4 3 2 1

CONTENT WARNING:

Sisters in Crime is committed to creating safe and welcoming environments at all gatherings, in its communications, and in its publications. This includes being sensitive to topics which may cause emotional or physiological distress in readers, listeners, and/or viewers. In providing this content warning for *Hook, Line, and Sinker: The Seventh Guppy Anthology*, the Guppy Chapter of Sisters in Crime is intentionally creating an inclusive space that respects the myriad lived experiences of the many individuals engaging with our chapter. Please note that this book includes the following instances of sensitive content:

Abuse
Ageism
Alcohol intoxication
Blood
Body hatred and fat phobia
Child exploitation (nonsexual in nature)
Death or dying
Drug use
Homophobia and heterosexism
Kidnapping and abduction
Mental illness and ableism
Miscarriage/abortion
Murder or attempted murder
Nudity and sexual situations
Sexism and misogyny
Swears or curses
Theft and robbery
Torture

Use of deadly weapons including firearms, knives, and toxic substances
Violence (verbal and physical)

If any of these topics would compromise your health, well-being, and self-care, please do not read beyond this page.

TABLE OF CONTENTS

INTRODUCTION

SUSAN VAN KIRK

Con artists getting their comeuppance, liars, psychics, online dating liars, identity thieves, grifters, and frauds. These dark crimes and shadowy people inhabit *The Seventh Guppy Anthology*. This collection of stories is written by Guppies, more formally called members of the Guppy Chapter of Sisters in Crime.

"Truth Be Told," "Americanization of Jack Mackenzie," "Manual for Success," "Trailblazer," "Capone's Chair," and "Just Another Shot in the Dark" are a few examples of the stories. These titles reflect a multitude of mystery subgenres including cozy, hard-boiled, humorous, dramatic, historical, contemporary, and suspense. All are variations of the fish who takes the bait—hook, line, and sinker.

Why Guppies? The Guppy Chapter of Sisters in Crime (SinC) is a 1,100+ organization of mystery writers, from beginners to published authors. The chapter began as a group of writers who wanted to share ideas and support each other. Today, the chapter has grown significantly, but the mission remains the same: "to create an environment in which members can share information, knowledge, opinions, motivation and inspiration without fear of ridicule or rejection." While SinC has many land-based chapters, the Guppy Chapter is wholly online with classes, manuscript swaps, critique groups, a listserv, and a sensational newsletter. The Guppy anthology, published every other year, is an opportunity for Guppies of all writing experiences to see their words in print.

I'd like to recognize the people who brought this project to fruition. Emily P. W. Murphy edited the anthology. Carol L. Wright and Debra H. Goldstein coordinated the project. The judges who chose the stories were non-Guppies from the writing world who are experienced in short story and mystery writing.

We'd like to thank you for taking an interest in reading our stories. You've fallen for our bait—hook, line, and sinker.

Susan Van Kirk
President of the Guppy Chapter

TRUTH BE TOLD

C. N. BUCHHOLZ

I PREDICTED EVERYTHING WOULD GO to hell once Kennie the Con weaseled her way into my psychic business, Truth Be Told, but I didn't foresee danger and demise. Not even halfway through my Over Sixty Séance Special, she had my longstanding customers—the Loon State Ladies of Today—scared out of their red babushkas and ready to cane it back to their senior center bus, where I was willing to bet their driver, Sid Shapiro, was asleep behind the wheel.

Kennie had switched my meditation music to a cranked-up selection of Gregorian chants. "Oh," she moaned and groaned into the microphone, adding to the holy horror. The chandelier lights blinked off—ahead of my schedule—and her evil laughter permeated the room. The ladies gasped. I gritted my teeth.

My mind drifted back to our childhood. I knew Kennie like the freckles on my face—the ones that let our parents tell us apart. Growing up on Minneapolis' North Side, we were known as the Kleinbaum twins: Kendra and Kandice. Our classmates dubbed Kendra "Kennie the Con." Every morning, she'd stop at the drugstore and power shop for candy while I waited outside and shuffled my feet, hoping she wasn't shoplifting. Again. Because believe me, the last thing you want is for a girl with your face to get photographed stealing. Again.

At school, she operated her sugar business out of her locker, marking up the loot for twice the price and schmoozing the kids out of their dollars.

Being the good twin, I tried to stay out of Kennie's schemes, despite her offer of a sweet piece of the proceeds. I knew her unsavory business methods would only lead to trouble—the kind that resulted in several visits

3

to the principal's office, Mother's sharp voice, and Dad's belt. I didn't want any part of those goodies.

In high school, Kennie ventured into beer and cigarette sales, and dealings with her new best friend, Mary Jane. "Only a dope smokes dope," Dad often grumbled. I didn't care for Mary Jane, either. After our graduation, when a robbery and car theft landed Kennie in a luxury room with steel bars at Hennepin County's finest, Mother began referring to me as her only daughter.

Sprung five years later, Kennie stood on my doorstep, estranged from our parents. "Got room to spare? I promise I won't cause a problem."

Right. I caved and motioned her inside my duplex. She dumped her meager belongings on the couch and fast-talked her way into working behind the scenes as my psychic associate. "It'll keep that damn parole officer off my ass."

I walked her through the dining-room-turned-psychic-room with its vintage bohemian-themed furnishings and pointed out the peephole, hidden camera, chandelier lights set on a timer, and ceiling grate with a fan—operated with a handy-dandy clicker—placed behind it. With a bored expression, Kennie pulled out a switchblade, opening and closing it several times.

I blanched at the sight of the knife but kept my cool. "Must you?"

She sighed and pocketed the weapon.

"Check this out." I directed her attention to the séance table. A college engineer gal pal had rigged a lift to the base to make the tabletop rise and fall—even shake—and had wired the foot pedal control beneath the table skirt. "One push forward or backward announces a spirit's arrival."

Kennie smirked. "Who's the con, now?"

I stiffened. "My customers believe in a spiritual world. I don't force that upon them. They want to see their loved ones, and my job is to make that happen."

"Sounds effed up. Like the legal system."

"Hmph. I wouldn't know." I turned and motioned her to follow.

In the hallway, I opened a closet door and waved her inside. The small space shared a common wall with the psychic room. I had set up a laptop computer to play soothing music and voice recordings through surround-sound speakers in the other room. A projector lens peered through the peephole to cast ghostly images on cue.

Kennie spun in the chair. "Is this where I get to be the Great and Powerful Oz?"

"Powerful, yes. Great, not so much." I explained that I could operate most of the controls at the table, but it would help to have a hand with the lights and recordings. "With you manually working some of these controls, every séance can be spot on and more ethereal than ever."

"Ether . . . what? Is that even a word?"

I stared at her long and hard. "Just promise that you'll follow my directions and do exactly what I say. No more. No less."

"Kandy baby, you can trust me." She patted the switchblade in her pocket. "I got your back."

Yeah. That's what I was afraid of.

I shifted my mind back to the four Loon State Ladies seated in darkness around my table.

What are you doing? I wanted to scream as the lights flickered again. *Follow the script!* It was just like Kennie not to wait for my cues but instead devise her own agenda.

"That . . . that never happened before," Alma Abrams squeaked in the dark. Her voice was high and cute, like Betty Boop. Not at all what you'd expect from an old Jewish lady in her late 80s.

I struck a match and lit the candelabra in the center of the table. Across from me, Alma clutched her arthritic hands against her chest. The ladies leaned in closer to the flames.

"Maybe that was your *meshugge* mother-in-law," Margo Machkowsky rasped, her smoker's voice wrapped in a thick Yiddish accent. "She's coming back to haunt you." Margo's voice was *exactly* what you'd expect from an old Jewish lady in her 80s. I often thought Margo and Alma could start a podcast based on their voices alone.

"*Shah!*" Alma said. "She might be listening."

Bevie Berkovitz, who was hunched over in a wheelchair, snorted. "Her crazy mother-in-law and mine. God help us both."

Margo laughed, following up with a bout of dry hacking coughs. Alma giggled.

"Ladies, let's concentrate." I pointed to three objects that lay next to the candelabra: a black-and-white photo of a young bride, a pearl necklace, and a bottle of Shalimar perfume. Frannie Friedemann, the smallest and most frail of the Loon State Ladies, had supplied them before the session in the hope that we could contact her mother, the bride in the photograph. Frannie made a sucking noise through her false teeth and stared at her mother's photo.

The women knew the spiel. Before a séance or reading, clients gave me personal items that belonged to their dearly departed. "I have to prepare the room's aura," I had told them. "It'll help open a door from our world to the Otherworld." During the séance, we held hands and focused on the items, conjuring up the spirit of the day.

What they didn't know was that I scanned the photos and downloaded them, blurring images and faces to later display with my projector. I soaked perfumes onto cardboard swatches and taped them behind the ceiling grate, so the hidden fan would blow the fragrances into the room. The vocals— soft, gloomy, distorted voices claiming to be loved ones—were pre-recorded by yours truly.

"Francine?" Kennie's voice whispered from the speakers, stretching out the two syllables. "Francine?"

Frannie sat rigidly. Her jaw dropped open, and I worried her dentures might fall out. She grabbed my hand and reached for Alma on her other side.

I cleared my throat. "Everyone, please focus. Don't break our meditation circle. Let's *all* hold hands."

The lights blinked on and off again, leaving only the candles aglow. Bevie elbowed Margo's side. "I'm glad I wore my padded panties." She laughed with such force that her wheelchair shook.

Margo nodded. "Me too."

"Francine," Kennie repeated. "Help me." A slight cool breeze drifted around the room, carrying with it the mixed scents of bergamot, iris, and vanilla.

"Mother!" Frannie cried. "That's the smell of my mother's perfume. Shalimar—her favorite."

"*Feh!*" Bevie chirped, pinching her nostrils. "She was what? A lady of the night?"

A stronger gust of wind blew across the room and snuffed the candles' flames. We sat in complete darkness. Frannie's tiny hand trembled in mine. "*Oy vey.* If the rabbi only knew—"

"Table up," I began to chant. The others sang along. With my foot, I pressed the floor pedal. I felt the table begin to shake and slowly rise. The hidden projector switched on, bathing us in eerie light.

"Look!" Alma squeaked. A blurry image of a woman floated near the ceiling. "That has to be your mother, Frannie. She's wearing a bridal gown."

Bevie sighed and rocked in her wheelchair. "To be young again. We should be so lucky."

The image disappeared, and we sat in darkness once more. I felt a slight brush on my arm and, a few moments later, the chandelier lights flickered back on.

"*Oy gevalt!*" Margo pointed at the table. "Frannie! Your mother's necklace!"

"It's gone!" Frannie sobbed, her teeth threatening to escape.

My eyes shifted toward the adjoining wall and back to the women. "Check your pockets. I'll be right back."

I burst into the closet and grabbed Kennie by the shoulders. "Did you take the necklace?"

Kennie smiled. "Hell, yeah."

I shook my head. "What's wrong with you? You're screwing up my show. These women might never come back."

Kennie's eyes narrowed. "What's wrong with *you?* Apparently, you need the Great Oz to spruce up your dead-people routine with a little excitement." She pulled the necklace out of her pocket. "They ain't ruby red slippers, but these pearls can get us some good cha-ching at the pawn shop."

I grabbed the necklace and shook it in her face. "Stealing is *not* what I do. Now, I'm going back in there and—"

She lunged out of the chair and pinned me against the wall, her face an inch from mine. "You're wrong, Kandy baby. It's what *we're* gonna do. One thing I learned in the big house—you're either with me or you're not."

"Get your hands off me," I hissed.

"Or what? You gonna call the babushka police in here for help?" She looked over at the computer screen displaying the view from the hidden camera. The screen showed Alma patting Frannie's bony shoulder, Bevie wheeling around, pointing left and right at the carpeted floor, and Margo crawling on all fours. Kennie laughed and loosened her grip. She stepped back and turned up the computer's volume. "I gotta hear this."

"Stop already!" I shoved her hand away from the keyboard. "I want you out of my house. Now."

For a moment, Kennie stared at me, her right eyelid twitching. "You always thought you were better than me," she said. She cocked her hand back and swung her fist. The blow landed with force, breaking my nose with one loud crunch. I dropped the necklace on the floor and covered my face. Blood dripped from my nose onto my hands, and I struggled to breathe.

"Please," I whimpered, my eyes watering. "Just leave."

Her next blow was to my temple, another to my jaw, and then one to my eye. I fell back into the chair.

Kennie breathed hard. "You're lucky I didn't use my knife. And that's only because you're family."

She ducked out of the closet, and I tried to get my bearings. My head pounded, my nose was a wet mess of throbbing pain, and my eye was swelling shut. Dazed and disoriented, I stared at the computer screen, trying to make sense of the images and voices in the other room. I leaned forward and saw Kennie standing in the psychic room.

"Did you find the necklace?" Alma asked her as she comforted Frannie.

"My God," Margo cried as she struggled to her feet, one hand on the table, the other gripping her cane. "What happened to you? There's blood on your clothes and you look—" She started to cough.

"Never mind how I look." Kennie pulled out her switchblade and waved it around. "Put your purses on the table. And hurry!"

"What?" Bevie about fell out of her chair. "Are my eyes and ears—"

"Move your asses!" Kennie snarled.

Brows furrowed. The women dumped their heavy purses onto the table.

Frannie adjusted the dentures in her mouth and waggled a crooked finger at Kennie. "You sure have a lot of *chutzpah* stealing from helpless, old women."

"I tell you," Margo wheezed, still clutching her purse, "she's gone crazy, this one. It's a *shande*."

Kennie snatched the purse away. "The only crazy ones here are the lot of you." She began to dig through each purse, shoving cash and credit cards into her pockets. "Spending your money on contacting the dead. Hah! Should've called yourselves the *Looney* Ladies." She jerked her chin at Margo. "Now sit your *tuchus* down before you fall down."

"Yes, Margo," Alma squeaked, her voice trembling. "Sit your *tuchus* down."

Margo remained standing. "And here we thought you were such a nice lady." She slapped her palm on the table. "All this time coming here. Now you want to rob us, you *goniff*? That's *fakakta!*"

Kennie shrugged. "Think of it as a nice big tip for my expert soul-searching skills."

"Skills-schmills." Margo turned and yanked open the blackout drapes covering the window to the parking lot. Sunlight spilled into the room. She banged her cane against the windowpane. "Help! Help!"

The others joined in. "Help!"

Kennie dropped the purse she was holding. "Knock that shit off! All of you!" She reached over, grabbed the cane from Margo, and jabbed the end into her stomach.

"Oof," Margo cried, collapsing into a chair and gasping for air.

Kennie threw the cane out of the room. It rattled on the wooden floor in the hallway. "Next time, it'll be my knife."

"That's enough!" I shouted at the computer screen, adrenaline recharging my brain. I snatched the necklace and pulled myself out of the chair. With blood still dripping from my nose, I stumbled into the hallway and grabbed Margo's cane from the floor. I entered the psychic room, cane held high in one hand and the necklace in the other. "I'm calling the police! First you steal this woman's pearls and then you threaten our lives!"

The women looked back and forth between Kennie and me. Bevie rolled her wheelchair back against the wall and began rummaging under her seat.

Kennie laughed. "The good twin and the bad twin, eh? We make a good act."

I shook the cane at her. "I'm through with your games. Give them back their purses before—"

9

"No can do, sister." Kennie thrust the knife at me, aiming for my heart.

I twisted out of the way, and a deafening shot rang out. The acrid smell of gunpowder filled the room. Kennie—wide-eyed—stared at Bevie, who was sitting straight up in her wheelchair, gripping a revolver with both hands.

Alma rocked back and forth. "Oh, my, oh, my, oh, my."

Kennie dropped the knife and clutched at the red stain on her shirt. She staggered backward and pressed two bloody palm prints on the wall. "I can't believe . . ." Her eyes fluttered closed and she collapsed.

The front door slammed and Sid's shoes pounded across the wooden floor. He leaned against the doorframe, out-of-breath and holding his side. "What happened? I heard yelling and then . . ." He glanced down at Kennie and the knife on the floor, did a double take at my bloody swollen face, and then noticed the gun in Bevie's hands. "Uh, oh. What did I miss?"

Bevie lowered the revolver and spun the cylinder, counting the remaining bullets.

Margo smiled. "A little *mishegoss*, but nothing we ladies couldn't handle."

Bevie nodded. "Truth be told, I've been *schlepping* this fancy-schmancy thing around for years. Finally got some good use out of it." She shoved the gun back under her seat and adjusted her red babushka.

SENIOR DISCOUNT

LIDA BUSHLOPER

MARGARET CARRIED HER MEAGER SACK of groceries to her car. She had originally planned on a major shopping expedition, but the money situation worried her. As a result of her nagging anxiety, she had scaled back her purchases, settling on just enough to get them by for a few more days: bananas, milk, and chicken salad from the deli. Instead of paying cash, she had used her debit card. She knew her partner, Scott, would understand.

Now, not wanting to push the shopping cart with its inevitable wonky wheel out to her car, she was glad for the manageable weight of the bag. At her age, she was grateful for any lightening of life's loads.

Margaret had trained herself to be always aware of her surroundings, but this time, preoccupied with her vague sense of unease, she didn't notice the car parked next to hers. As she unlocked her car door, she was startled by the sudden appearance of a man by her side.

"Here, let me help you with that," he said, reaching for her groceries.

Margaret didn't need help. In fact, she bristled at any hint that her age was showing. Plus, he was standing too close to her. But on further inspection, the man, good-looking in a vaguely middle-aged way, was so charming and had such a kind smile that for once she didn't mind. He shifted her grocery sack onto the passenger seat, then swung the door wide to make room for her before handing her in. She was about to thank him as he swung the car door closed, but then something went wrong. Instead of closing with a solid chunk, there was a metallic "clank" and the door bounced back on its hinges. Her door wouldn't close. She pulled her seatbelt away from the door and buckled herself in. The man tried again to close the door, only to produce that same loud "clank." Margaret was

11

confused, then puzzled. The car was old, but well maintained. The man's brow furrowed.

"Something seems to be wrong with your car."

Now Margaret was really confused. "There shouldn't be anything wrong with it. I just drove it here, and it ran just fine."

Margaret was starting to worry. She had left her cell phone at home. How could she call for help? Plus, she knew she had parked out of range of the security cameras attached to the supermarket building. Trying not to be too obvious, she studied the man. Margaret's instincts had been honed during many years of people watching. She was rarely wrong about her conclusions. And while there was no one nearby, it was still broad daylight in a public place. Besides, there was no question that she needed some kind of help.

The man scratched his head. "Why don't you step out for a minute and let me take a look? Maybe I can figure out what's wrong." Margaret unbuckled her seatbelt and did as he asked. She watched as he burrowed under the dashboard. A few seconds later, he sat up, hauled himself back out of the car, and stood facing her.

"I think I know what your problem is. I'm actually a mechanic, and I specialize in this make of car. In fact, I even drive the same car myself. See?" He gestured to the car parked next to Margaret's. Margaret peered over his shoulder. Sure enough, his car was the same brand as hers, just many years younger. When she looked back at him, he held out his palm. "See this chip? This is from under your dashboard. It controls some of your car's workings." Margaret peered at the tiny square of black plastic embossed with her car's logo. She had never seen anything like it.

"See how frayed the edges are?" He indicated one side. "See all those scratches? That needs to be replaced right away. In fact, you're lucky you got here without breaking down on the road. In this condition, your car's not safe to drive." The man reached into his pocket and produced an almost identical object. "Look, I just happened to have a brand new one with me. This is what it's supposed to look like. Not all worn like yours is." The second piece of black plastic he showed her also had her car's logo stamped on it, but appeared shiny and new. Margaret's face fell. "Well, mine certainly looks messed up. But what do I do now?"

"Well, you could have the car towed to the dealership for repairs."

"But it's Sunday. The repair department won't be open."

The man shrugged helplessly. As the silence lengthened, their mutual discomfort increased.

Finally, he sighed. "Look, I could get into a lot of trouble for this. But since I happened to have this brand-new chip with me, I could replace it for you right now. You'd only have to pay for the part. And you'd save the cost of the labor charge at the dealership."

Margaret's eyes widened. "You can do that? I mean, right here in the parking lot?"

The man hesitated. "I could . . . but like I said, I'd get fired if anybody found out about it."

"I'll never tell a soul, I promise. But how much would I owe you for the part?"

"I hate to tell you this. It's expensive. $80.00. And that's with your senior discount."

Margaret's face lit up. "Well, that's no problem." She took out her wallet, stuffed with bills, and showed it to him. "I have money. I can certainly pay you. And gladly since you've been so kind."

Still, the man hesitated. "Oh, I don't know . . ."

Margaret knew it was her turn to be the convincing one, and she was up to the task. She also was not without her charms. "Oh, come on. You seem like such a nice man. Heck, I'd rather give the money to you. This way, you won't have to share it with your bosses at the dealership. And you wouldn't leave a lady stranded, would you?"

The man gave a little chuckle. "Well, I guess you're right. I can't leave a lady in distress." He paused, then said, "You might want to stand back a little. Don't want to get those nice clothes dirty."

Margaret was tempted to roll her eyes, but she kept her face neutral. He was laying it on a little thick. Her clothes were anything but nice. She always dressed down when shopping. But she went along with his gallantry and took a step back. From this angle, she couldn't observe what he was doing under her dashboard. Still, she wasn't concerned. She was sure everything was under control. Scott would be able to figure out whatever jiggery-pokery sleight of hand the fellow had used to disable her car door.

After a few minutes, the man emerged from under the dashboard, ostentatiously wiping grease from his hands with a shop rag.

He opened and closed her car door several times. It now worked smoothly.

Margaret carefully counted out four twenty-dollar bills from her bulging wallet. As she pressed them into his hand, she quelled her slight temptation to give him a hug. As nice as he seemed, they had spent quite enough time together. No need to draw any more attention to their interaction, just on the unlikely chance that any of the other shoppers had noticed them. She contented herself with an expression of warm gratitude.

"Thank you. Thank you for saving a lady in distress."

When Margaret got home, Scott was waiting anxiously for her. "I was getting a little worried when you took so long. How did it go?"

"I didn't do it. Something felt hinky. It didn't feel safe. You know what I mean?"

"Totally. You did the right thing, trusting your instincts. No need to take a chance if you think it's risky. Better to walk away if you have a bad feeling about the situation."

"But I think I may have ended up doing us a favor."

"What do you mean?"

Then she told him about her encounter in the parking lot. Scott smiled.

"You old devil. And don't worry about the $80.00. There's plenty more where that came from, right?" They practically split their sides, laughing.

A few days later, the TV news confirmed Margaret's suspicions. A teaser during the evening's newscast flashed onto the TV.

"Local man caught trying to pass counterfeit $20.00 bills. His story— that an elderly lady in a parking lot gave him the money—seemed improbable to law enforcement. More details on this breaking story later in the broadcast."

Margaret was outraged. "Elderly, my left cheek. I've got a ways to go before I'm 'elderly.'" Scott smirked at her. "Serves him right for trying to scam an 'old lady.'" Margaret hit him playfully with the throw pillow. "Who're you calling 'old?' You're no spring chicken." She paused, then said, "Hey, I just thought of something."

"What?" Scott asked, muting the TV.

"That guy did us two favors, not just one."

"How ya figure?"

"Well, not only did he draw attention away from anyone who might be looking at us, but he accidentally provided us with some quality control."

"Explain," Scott said.

"If he couldn't pass those bills, there must be some reason. Maybe we missed something. Maybe we're losing our touch. We should take another look at those plates."

Scott looked at her with admiration. "You always were the smart one. Come on, sweetheart. Let's go make us some money. Or maybe some whoopee."

She hit him with the pillow again. "Later, you lecher. Right now, we've got work to do."

The Americanization of Jack Mackenzie

Susan Daly

I ANGLED MY BEAT-UP TACOMA into the Town Hall parking lot. And braked hard.

Borden Kennedy had done it again. His oversized Buick sat smugly in my allotted space, which was clearly marked "Mayor." With barely a sigh, I reversed into a spot in the far corner.

Walking toward the Town Hall, coffee in hand, I paused as always to admire the statue of Jack Mackenzie: local hero, war artist, and Canada's most famous landscape painter. The memorial depicted him in rugged outdoor clothes, standing with a palette in one hand and brush in the other, addressing a bronze canvas attached to a real rock.

This August morning, Jack wore a sparkly pink bow around his manly bronze neck.

Loretta Beamish, the town clerk, stood there scowling. "Disgusting," she informed me.

So what if Jack was celebrating Pride Week? With the changing seasons, he sported knitted scarves to keep him warm, or a variety of hats to ward off sunstroke. All through the pandemic, he'd been protected with a series of colorful masks, courtesy of local quilters.

Jack was well-loved in the town, and these expressions of concern and celebration did no harm. Certainly Alison Bellamy, Jack's sculptor, didn't mind.

"Good morning, Loretta. Borden's parked in my spot again." Parking was her jurisdiction.

"I'm sure there's no need to get in a snit, Julie—I mean, 'Your Worship.' He just forgets. After all, he was mayor for twelve years."

"And he's been ex-mayor since December." But there was little point in arguing with Loretta. She turned and entered the elegant old building.

I've always loved the well-preserved Town Hall. Having somehow evaded the swing of the developers' wrecking ball in the 1960s, it's now the pride of November Falls.

I sat down on the bench facing the statue to finish my coffee.

"Hey, Julie!" Damn. The booming voice of my nemesis. I turned to see the big, blonde, balding former mayor coming toward me.

"Good morning, Borden. What's up?"

He sat down and brandished the book he was carrying. Borden? With a book? "Have you read this?"

The Winds of November.

"Yes." Everyone in November Falls had read it. In fact, just about everyone in Canada. It's been a perennial classic since 1951.

"You have? Did you know it's about Jack Mackenzie? And November Falls?"

"Yes." Really? Even someone whose reading tastes begin and end with golfing bibles must have heard of it. "Did you like it?"

"Well, it's a bit soppy, but here's the *big thing*. In a word: Hollywood North."

Due to advantageous tax offers, the strength of the US dollar over our own currency, and legions of talented film professionals, Canada has been Hollywood North (actually two words) for decades. Jobs and hospitality flourish, with every corner of Canada masquerading as America: from New York and LA to small towns where jaded city women discover the True Meaning of Christmas.

"Someone wants to make a movie of it?" So far, November Falls had avoided the dual-pronged attention of location scouts.

"Exactly! Some lady director. She makes romances, chick flicks. Swallow . . . Templeton?"

"Skylark Temple?" Okay, now he had my attention. She'd received an Oscar nomination last year for her latest project, *Island of Blue-Eyed Girls.*

She hadn't won, of course, Hollywood still being mired in Old World Masculinity.

"Yeah, her. You and I are meeting her for lunch at the Laughing Loon."

THOUGH *THE WINDS OF NOVEMBER* is a Canadian classic, it was written by an American, Mary Louise Lambert.

In the late summer of 1932, she came to Ontario to visit friends in November Falls. Here, she met Jack, the enigmatic up-and-coming painter, and they fell in love. Or so the story goes. Her story. She was 18 to his 27, and how involved they'd really been is anybody's guess.

The book describes deep mutual passion and highly romantic episodes. September, canoeing on the still, northern lakes. October, with long walks in the glorious fall color. Making love by the fire in the late autumn chill.

Then came the cold winds of November. Her parents insisted she return home to Sacramento. Heartbroken, she left her love behind.

The following year, she married a dentist.

Mary Louise always kept a secret place in her heart for "the man who taught her the meaning of love." She followed Jack's career from a distance: his growing fame as an artist, his part in the Spanish Civil War. When she learned of his tragic death in 1939, something broke inside her.

In 1951, after her husband died, she dipped into her past and wrote a heart-rending memoir based on that significant time in her life. With embellishments.

The Winds of November couldn't find an American publisher. They had no interest in non-American stories just then. So, she tried a Canadian publisher, who snapped it up.

It hit the public at just the right moment and became a bestseller. For years it was on reading lists and publishers' reissues of Canadian classics, and it continued to sell moderately well for the rest of the twentieth century.

* * *

I HAD TO ADMIT, BORDEN had worked fast. He'd met Skylark two days ago, when she'd arrived in town and mistaken him for mayor based on where he'd parked.

At 12:30, the three of us sat with beer and burgers at the Laughing Loon. I was intrigued to meet the promising young director.

"First off, let me just say, I love *The Winds of November*." Skylark held up her own copy, a hardcover with a worn dust jacket. "I found it in a charity shop in Vancouver for a quarter."

She explained that after her success with *Island of Blue-Eyed Girls,* she'd been given *carte blanche* by a big studio to cover her next project—something equally romantic.

"It's a story for our time, a story the world needs right now."

"But doesn't he die in the end?" Borden sounded unsure.

"Yes! And *that*'s what makes the story so uniquely poignant. Not just his death, but his life leading up to the inevitable tragedy. And it's all true."

I nodded. "Parts of it, yes."

"It's such an essential story. They meet, they love, they part. In 1937, Jack goes off to fight with Franco in the Spanish Civil War to help topple the oppressive Fascist regime." Her eyes were shining, no doubt seeing it all. "He becomes an unofficial war artist, depicting the suffering of the Spanish people—"

"But Skylark—"

"When the war is over, he returns home, bitter and broken."

"Um, actually, the Fascists fought under Franco. They overthrew the elected Republican government. Jack was fighting *against* Franco with the International Brigade—"

Borden kicked me under the table and Skylark looked confused, then picked up the thread. "He's losing his sight due to a wound he suffered in Spain. Before he goes completely blind, he paints one last picture—Mary Louise as he once knew her. Then, when his sight is nearly gone, he disappears into the wilderness he loves and is never seen again."

I didn't correct her this time. Another of Mary Louise's flights of fancy was that all the women in Jack's paintings were really variations of his lost love. A complete fabrication. Except for the broken, betrayed people in Spain, Jack had never painted human figures.

But yes, he *was* going blind. In late fall 1939, he went canoeing in nearby Algonquin Park with two friends. Their third day out, they'd made camp and settled in for the night as usual. In the morning, Jack was gone. He'd left a note for his friends. *I'm sorry. It's better this way.*

His remains were discovered the following spring on the rocky cliff overlooking Harriet Lake, one of his favorite painting locations.

SKYLARK DECIDED NOVEMBER FALLS WAS the perfect setting. While offering modern attractions and comforts, the town still held the charm of its late-Victorian and early twentieth century roots. It had everything: restored buildings along the banks of the November River, old houses on winding streets sloping up from the water, and a backdrop of evergreens with endless hills beyond.

She'd taken one look at Jack's statue in front of the Town Hall and discovered the focal point of the film.

Borden was her number one cheerleader. Since the town had no process in place for granting film permits, it would have to be passed in council. I told him to put a proposal together and present it for consideration.

Borden did his homework, put together a case, and presented it to council. There were six members of the town council and each had opinions to offer. The one opponent to Borden's plan was Eric Klein, my old history teacher.

"We don't need movie production people taking over the town," Eric said. "Parking their giant polluting trucks and equipment everywhere, blocking the shops and businesses, harassing the tourists—"

"It will mean jobs," Borden interrupted.

"Sure, for film production crews from Toronto, and actors from the States."

"They'll be staying in our accommodations, buying meals, spending money. It will put November Falls on the map."

"We're already on the map. We're tourist central for Muskoka."

This was true. November Falls offered three-season getaways, including skiing, ice-fishing and snowmobiling, plus every imaginable summer pastime on and off the water. With color tours and hunting in the fall, that left black-fly season in spring as the only dead period.

Add to that, we had a thriving arts community of writers, painters, and musicians, along with several art galleries, museums, and festivals.

And Jack Mackenzie. Neither the town nor Jack needed more publicity to put us on the map.

Nonetheless, it seemed an attractive proposition, even after Eric reminded us of the Deerwood disaster a few years back. A US production company, filming some spy story, had burned down that town's landmark historic hotel.

The motion was made, seconded and passed in council, 5-1. Borden was appointed the official Film Liaison Officer.

November Falls joined the ranks of Hollywood North.

IN LATE SEPTEMBER—THE START of fall color season—the movie people arrived. They filled the hotels, B&Bs, and bars—space that might be said to belong to legitimate tourists. They were all over the streets, bringing a new kind of excitement—the anticipation of star sightings and freely flowing money.

The first intimation of trouble came the morning before filming began. My friend Alison, Jack's creator, called me as I was driving into town.

"Meet me at the Algonquin Hotel."

Had they burned it down already?

When I first parked in front of the elegant old hotel, located on the river near the edge of town, I didn't notice anything. Alison walked up to my truck and pointed to the sign on the front.

Craigdarroch Hotel, est'd 1901

"Okay, so they've given the hotel a different name." I wasn't concerned.

Alison shook her head. "Craigdarroch is a town in Washington State."

I was trying to connect the dots when my phone rang. Ron, the chief of police.

"Anyone know why the signs on County Road 3 have been changed to say Washington State Highway 5?" he demanded.

Another incoming call. Eric.

"I'll get back to you, Ron." *Click.* "Hi, Eric."

"Your Worship." His voice dripped with foreboding. "Is there some reason why there's an American flag flying in front of Town Hall? Did Canada get annexed overnight, and no one thought to tell us?"

Oh shit.

It was the old, old story. Canada playing the never-ending role of Somewhere in America.

Worse, that discomforting tradition of taking a Canadian story and shipping it south.

"*Blue-Eye Girls.*" I muttered, ending the call.

Alison looked at me.

"Skylark's version of a charming Scottish story. She lifted it wholesale from nineteenth century Orkney and relocated it to the North Carolina Outer Banks in the 1950s. I should have guessed she'd do something cute like that with *The Winds of November.*"

I drove down River Street (probably now State Street) toward the Town Hall. Sure enough, the US flag flapped on the pole directly behind Jack's statue. I caught sight of Skylark and Borden, deep in conversation with Eric, who seemed on the verge of a stroke.

They all looked up when I joined them.

"Oh, Your Honor," Skylark greeted me, tugging her apricot silk jacket tighter around her as though it were mid-December. "The *very* person I need to see."

"We all do." Eric sounded more than usually curmudgeonly. Borden plunged into some mansplaining, but I cut him off.

"What's going on?" I demanded. "Craigdarroch? Washington State Highway? *That?*" I pointed to the flag. "What world are you setting this movie in?"

Skylark ignored the question. "We were just wondering how to get this sign put up over the City Hall doorway. Councilor Klein here doesn't seem very happy about it."

A sign stood propped up against the bench. *Craigdarroch Town Hall.*

"I'm not. Julie, I hope you'll remember I was against this from the start." I assured him I did.

23

"Okay, Ms. Temple, let me guess. Somehow, you decided the concept of a Canadian artist wouldn't cut it with your American audiences." I levelled a look at Borden, who had the grace to look uneasy. Skylark showed no remorse.

"Oh, Julie, I want audiences to *love* it. To embrace it as their own. Can't you see why it *has* to be an American story?"

"No." I turned to our Film Liaison Officer. "What did you know about this, Borden?"

"Now just calm down, Julie. Skylark and I have been talking about it, and it all makes sense. It is, after all, a book written by an American. About an American woman."

Eric jumped in. "*And* a Canadian artist. A man renowned for his *Canadian* landscapes—the Prairies, the Rockies, the Arctic. Here in Ontario." He waved his arms to represent the vast scope of Jack's work. "How are you going to rework that?"

"We're making him a West Coast artist." Her eyes lit up. "But that's a *great* idea, Councilor. Our hero can travel all over America, including Alaska and the Rockies. And of course, the forests of the Pacific Northwest. Jack's paintings will be *perfect.*"

"Don't even think about it." Eric was looking strokey again.

Skylark ignored his ominous tone as she grabbed Borden's arm in excitement. "Wait . . . Borden? That stunning painting hanging in the Town Hall? What did you call it?"

"*Winter's Approach on Harriet Lake.* It's Jack's most famous, most iconic landscape."

It is all that. A sweeping landscape from a high point overlooking the lake. You can just feel the wind blowing in from the west, whipping up the surface of the water below and the iron-gray clouds above. You know it's about to snow.

The place where Jack had gone to die.

There are copies everywhere—public schools, libraries, plus the inevitable posters, mugs, and t-shirts.

"Jack's masterpiece?" Skylar looked ecstatic. "Excellent! We'll use it in our promo material."

"Not so fast," I said. "That painting belongs to the town, and we control the reproduction rights." It's always been a nice source of income, especially gratifying since in 1934, the town council had grumbled about spending $350 on a local artist, no matter how up-and-coming he was.

Skylark looked unperturbed. Borden, on the other hand, seemed uneasy. "Uh, actually, Julie . . ."

In far too many words, he explained that as Film Liaison Officer, he had the authority to sign all agreements with the film company, including those involving town property use and public images. And he had done so.

I took a few calming breaths. They didn't help.

"Really, Borden? And just how did you get all that authority?"

"Oh, at a special town council meeting to deal with some film-related matters. I think you were in Toronto that day at some mayors' conference. The council agreed they didn't want to hold a meeting every time something came up, so they gave me full signing authority on all film matters."

"Let me guess. Five to one?" I didn't dare glance at Eric.

Skylark gave me a sweet smile. "Oh, Julie, don't be angry. Can't you see this is a win-win for everyone? Even with our teensy little changes, it's going to be wonderfully advantageous for November Falls. Imagine the increased tourist flow."

"Hardly. As you pointed out, Ms. Temple, you're convinced that your audiences just want to relate to American stories, American lives. That they can't see beyond their own borders."

"But think of the publicity we'll bring to Jack Mackenzie too. We're going to make him into a famous artist. Imagine what that will do for his reputation. The sales of his paintings. Americans will adore them."

"Oh yeah?" Eric overcame his stroke symptoms. "Well, for your information, Jack Mackenzie already *is* a famous artist, and his paintings command huge prices at auction. He doesn't need some cheesy little movie like yours to throw new light on him."

"Oh? Really?"

"And frankly, the art-buyers of Canada don't need to bid against foreign billionaires for our own paintings. The last thing we need is another Hollywood personality hyping another Canadian artist."

"Although the way you've disguised his legend," I said, "your audience won't know him from Norman Rockwell."

25

A veil of hostility crept over the director. She straightened her shoulders.

"Well. Let me point out we still plan to feature the statue in the movie. It's an excellent symbol and will add significantly to the romance of the story. It will be our logo."

Before I could retort, or Eric could explode, she added, "*That's* in the contract too."

ERIC AND I MET ALISON at the Laughing Loon at noon to drown our sorrows and look on the dark side.

"*Harriet Lake*," Alison said. "She'll prostitute it. Turn it into American apple pie."

"She has to be stopped," Eric declared.

I shook my head. "Borden's tied it all up in the contract. We'll just have to let them make their movie and go home."

"You don't get it, Julie," Eric's voice held an ominous tone. "Location tourists. They're gonna love it."

Alison and I stared at him.

"It's a *thing*. People obsess over a movie or TV show, and they get fanatical about the location. Look at Albuquerque. Throngs of crazed fans throwing pizzas at Walter White's house or trying to buy drugs at the carwash."

"Damn." Alison turned pale. "Bird Girl."

Eric nodded. "*Midnight in the Garden of Good and Evil.*"

Right. The charming sculpture of a girl feeding birds, made über-famous, first in a book, then in a movie.

"The Savannah cemetery became ground zero for the wing-nuts," he went on. "The city finally had to move the statue into a private gallery to keep marauding hordes from making off with it."

Alison sighed. "I love it when people put scarves and flowers and things on Jack. It's a tribute. But . . ."

I could see her imagining rape and pillage.

"Okay," I said. "Let's not overreact here. Those shows were filmed where their stories took place. *If* the movie's a hit, *if* it becomes a cult classic, and *if* fans decide to worship at Jack's feet, well, clearly, they're not going to look for our boy in November Falls. They'll be swarming Craigdarroch, Washington."

"*If* it had a statue," Eric said.

"He's right." Alison said. "If Skylark makes the statue a cornerstone of the movie, they'll find Jack. And us. The Internet is a powerful tool."

"That *Blue-Eyed Girl* movie?" Eric said. "It was huge. Fans overran both the filming location in North Carolina *and* what they thought was the original house on the island of Hoy. Idiots."

We ordered another round of beer.

Eric sank lower. "You can bet she won't have him go to Spain with the Mac-Paps."

Alison looked puzzled, but I'd paid attention in Eric's history class. "The Canadian volunteer battalion that fought in the Spanish Civil war," I explained.

"Named for two of our most famous rebels," Eric said. "William Lyon Mackenzie and Louis-Joseph Papineau. I don't know what they're teaching you kids these days."

"Oh, right," Alison said. "Them."

"She'll put him in the Lincoln Battalion," I said, heedless of Eric's despondency.

My prediction, however, had the opposite effect.

"Damn it!" Eric slammed his beer glass on the table. "There's no way we can let this film be made."

"I hear you, Eric." I dabbed his beer off my jacket. "But thanks to Borden, we have no legal way of stopping her."

A glow of rebellion lit up his eyes. For the first time in weeks, I saw him smile. Grin, even.

"In that case, we'll just have to do something *illegal.*"

BY THE FIRST OF NOVEMBER, Skylar had filmed the earliest scenes, capturing the brilliant October colors, along with plenty of footage to incorporate later into the more intimate shots. Also ahead were the interiors and Jack's death in the late fall, as well as the scenes in Spain, to be portrayed by Southern California.

For today's shooting, the weather was cooperating, with ominous gray skies and a feisty autumn wind swirling the fallen leaves. Perfect setting for one of the most poignant scenes in the script. Mary Louise Lambert—now an old woman—returns to Craigdarroch for the unveiling of the statue of her one-time lover.

All around were crew members with their equipment, performers, and a few police officers on location duty. Eric, Alison, and I stood in front of the Town Hall with a crowd of locals. Everyone was comfortably wrapped against the incoming chill. Alison's nephew was on the crew and kept her informed of all the daily filming schedules. We weren't going to miss this.

Skylark was in full director mode, issuing terse commands while shivering her butt off in her skimpy Los Angeles designer jacket. Borden stood nearby, looking important. As Film Liaison Officer, he was responsible for coordinating any use of municipal property. *Especially* Jack Mackenzie.

The statue was covered in a sheet, awaiting the unveiling. The idea was to have Mary Louise arrive early—alone—to give herself a few private moments with Jack. She'd whisk off the sheet and gaze in aching silence as a tear trickled down her face.

"Okay, let's do it," Skylark called out. All the usual camera and action stuff started up, and Mary Louise stepped up onto the rocky base surrounding the sculpture. She stood still for a few moments, then grasped the edge of the sheet and pulled it away to the ground.

With a clang, Jack's head came with it.

Skylark cried "*Cut!*" Mary Louise went into semi-hysterics. A lot of yelling from the crew, a chorus of horrified dismay from the crowd, both extras and spectators.

Alison ran forward and confronted Skylark in a fury.

"You stupid, egocentric . . . *American*. That is my master work—not only a work of art, but a work of love, a memorial to a great artist, *and* a huge attraction for tourists and art lovers. Jack Mackenzie is a *god* in this town—all across Canada. Not only have your people desecrated his memory with your stupid movie, but now you've destroyed a national treasure."

Skylark stood still in defiant silence. Borden, next to her, stammered helplessly.

Eric and the police did their best to quell the angry crowd, now threatening to turn into a mob. Alison was right. Jack was their god.

Alison turned away and picked up poor Jack's head. She cradled it for a moment like a Greek tragedian. Then she placed it gently at his feet and threw the sheet over the statue. She sat down in front of him, hugged her knees to her chest, and sobbed.

I went up to Borden and Skylark, righteous anger driving me.

"What the *hell* happened there, Borden? You're supposed to be on guard against that kind of damage. I'm making you personally responsible for getting reparations from this production company." I turned to Skylark. "And *you!* I'm revoking your film permit as of this moment. Borden will deal with the particulars."

Skylark nodded, speechless for a moment, then she gathered up her ego.

"Fine. I'm sick of your smug little Canadian town and all this worshipping at the feet of your pathetic home-town Canadian hero. *And* your ass-freezing Canadian winter weather. We're out of here."

To her retreating form, Eric called out, "Come on back in February."

THREE DAYS LATER, THEY WERE gone, leaving barely a trace behind— except for the state highway signs, which our roads department would have to take down. The production company went home to the real America.

Eric, Alison, and I sat on the bench near Jack's statue, warming ourselves with lattes. More than a hint of snow hung in the leaden afternoon sky; winter tourist season would soon begin. November Falls once again belonged to its citizens.

Jack was still surrounded by the plywood housing the Town Hall maintenance staff had put up within an hour of the disaster.

Borden approached us and stood there looking pleased.

"Well?" I said. "How did it go?"

"Everything I demanded, and more. Since the contract included a severe set of conditions about damage to town property, *especially* heritage property, which goes beyond intrinsic value, they were facing a massive sum for reparations." He looked at Eric. "You see? I was paying attention that day in council when you mentioned the Deerwood Hotel fire."

Eric expressed grudging appreciation.

"What are they on the hook for?" I asked.

"The studio's insurance will cover all the property rental for the entire time of the original leases. Full pay to *all* the actors and film production hires, including make-up, costume, set building, cameras, accommodation. The works. Even the extras among the citizens. They're all getting paid as if the full eight weeks of production had gone ahead."

We expressed approval all around.

"Though I guess some people are grumpy about losing their big moment on screen."

"What about damage to my sculpture?" Alison asked.

"I said they'd hear from us. We haven't finished assessing the replacement value."

"I don't see how it can be replaced," Eric said.

As we spoke, I was keeping an eye on the workers removing the makeshift plywood housing. As the last sheet came down, I looked at Alison, who now wore a broad smile.

"It doesn't need to be replaced," she said, and indicated Borden should look behind him.

He turned and emitted a cry of surprise.

Jack Mackenzie was back in his rightful place, head and all, still holding the bronze palette and facing the bronze canvas.

"It's repaired already?"

"It was never broken," Alison said. "The figure who lost his head over Mary Louise—I hope she recovers from that, poor thing—was an early prototype. I used it when creating the sculpture ten years ago. It's been in a shed behind my workshop ever since. I gave it a wash of bronze paint, then removed the head and stuck it on with wax."

"But how did you—?" Borden didn't look ready to believe us yet.

"I got help from Eric and Julie." She didn't mention her nephew.

"The middle of the night," Eric said, "we shielded the area with some of those damned ubiquitous trailers they use, then we backed Julie's pickup truck right up to the edge of the rocks. Alison installed it originally, so she knew how to remove the bolts, and move it safely."

"We replaced it with the fake," Alison said. "No one was going to look at it closely, since it was covered up."

Borden stood there looking stunned.

"We returned it last night, once we were sure the enemy had left town."

"I'm sorry we had to deceive you, Borden," I said. "But we figured you'd do a much better job of intimidating Skylark if you didn't know."

Borden was still uneasy. "But—but that's illegal. We're getting outrageous sums from them for, uh . . ."

"Perpetrating a scam?" Eric looked pleased and unworried. "Yeah, I guess we are."

The workers had cleared away the plywood, so we got up and walked over to admire Jack. Other people noticed too and started coming around to stare in wonder and delight at their hero.

"You did a great job with the restoration, Alison." Eric was playing to the audience. "You'd never know there'd been any damage at all."

Borden wasn't finished. "But damn it, Julie . . . Eric. We can't do this. It's fraud. Criminal, even."

I'd never before seen our former mayor so concerned over a legality.

"Is it?" I said, while Alison wrapped a colorful hand-knit scarf around Jack's neck as protection from the coming winter—and from people inspecting the repair too closely.

Borden couldn't seem to find a response.

"Well, if you feel that way, Borden, I guess you can go back to the production company—and their insurance provider—and explain how it was all a mistake."

I could see him imagining the scenario and watched as he came to a decision.

He nodded slowly. "Maybe you're right, Your Worship. After all, it *is* for the good of the town, isn't it?"

"Absolutely, Borden," I said. Alison and Eric murmured agreement.

"Oh, and speaking of that . . ." Borden began to look his old confident self. "Skylark said she never wants to hear about that damned book again. So she's given the town the movie rights to *The Winds of November*."

Well. I had underestimated our former mayor.

Maybe I'd let him keep his old parking spot.

CRIME AND CONVENIENCE

STEVE SHROTT

I AMBLED INTO TWENTY-FOUR-SEVEN, 7-ELEVEN'S illicit cousin, and said hello to my boss and proud American, Amir Constantine.

He sat behind the front counter, rubbing the furry black thing under his nose, which he called a moustache and others might mistake for some crawly insect, and gave me a perfunctory nod.

"Got new shipment, Tostitos, Cathay."

I told Amir about a zillion times, my name was Cathy, but he always added the extra vowel. I kinda liked it. Gave it an international flavor. "Good about the Tostitos, Amir. But why are you telling me?"

He rolled his eyes. "You ate four bag last week, never paid. And still owe for box of Count Chocula."

"Right. Right. Sorry Amir." I slid out my new leather friend, which I had recently acquired by not entirely legal means, and took a gander through it. I was shocked at all the hundreds. Good score. I handed one to Amir.

He took the bill and rubbed it, then he held it up to the light, rubbed it again. Then blew on it. Yes, we had really built up trust between us. Considering how I obtained it, I guessed he was right. He put it in the cash register and was about to give me change when the door sprang open and the chunky man with the black hair and large nose whom I had extracted the billfold from burst in.

Now I'm not normally afraid of stockier guys 'cause usually most of their stockiness is soft, full of potato chips and donuts. But now, looking at him, I realized he worked out at the gym and could probably lift me up like a Pop Tart.

33

I quickly hid behind one of the metal shelves that just happened to have many bags of Tostitos. Hey, a girl's gotta eat.

Big Nose held up his phone and showed Amir a picture. "You seen this girl? She stole my wallet."

Oh my God, the creep took a photo. I felt all the moisture in my body dry up like I was in menopause—even though I'm only twenty-eight—give or take.

The problem was that Amir had never told a lie in his life. This was going to end badly.

Amir looked at Big Nose a moment, then sputtered out, "No, never see girl like this."

My lungs blew out air like someone released the nozzle on my Aunt Sadie's oxygen tank. I couldn't believe it; the dude saved me.

Big Nose left and Amir yelled out my name. I wandered over to the counter where he gave me a look as if I were a piece of veal that had gone rotten. "You see man?"

I nodded.

"I lie to him." He wiped his eyes. "What you do, Cathay?"

"Nothing. He's just some blowhard in the neighborhood trying to make trouble and . . ."

"He say you stole wallet."

I gave him big eyes. "Me?"

"Your face show guilt like cat after eat pet bird."

"Look Amir, we're buddies right?"

He just stared, not saying anything.

"Okay, you are a real nice boss. But I don't make enough here to live on, and my rent is due. So, I . . ."

"Steal."

"Borrow."

"You're going to pay back?"

"Yes. Uh, not exactly. See, I just took a little cash, but only because he can afford it. He wore a Rolex. You know a real one, Amir. Not one of those from a table full of Gucci purses and 'Louis Vuitton' luggage sold on some street corner."

"Uh huh."

"Later, I'll slip the wallet with all the ID and everything into his mail slot. See, I'm not a bad person, Amir. Just trying to survive."

He tapped his foot on the floor like a father outraged his daughter had arrived late from prom with two buttons on her blouse undone. "Is first time?"

I nodded, maybe a little too enthusiastically.

"It is wrong, Cathay."

"We can agree to disagree."

His stony face indicated we would never in a million millenniums agree. Oh well, you win some, you lose some.

"You know what, Amir, you're right." I lowered my head to my chest. "I will never do that again." I crossed my fingers behind my back.

He grunted out something, then put me in charge of making the Smurpees for customers. It's pretty much the same recipe as Slurpees only with more sugar.

When Amir's shift ended, his brother-in-law and wife took over. I left, Amir following me out the door. "We go now."

"What?"

"We go drop wallet off."

"Yeah, I'll go do that."

"No, both." He opened the door of his seventy-nine Ford mustang whose body had a lovely coat of rust and maybe more rust on top of that rust.

"Really, Amir, I will do it. Tonight's not really convenient. I have an appointment with my dentist." Big smile. "Too many Smurpees."

"Get in car. It take five minutes."

I was stuck. "Fine."

I slid into the torn front seat with the stuffing pushing through. The dashboard was cracked, but standing on it was a six-inch high plastic Jesus who stared into my eyes as if confronting me about all my transgressions. I tried to look away, but he was good.

Amir started the vehicle and we were off.

"What address?"

I took out one of Big Nose's IDs and read the address to him. "Twenty-seven Crescent Lane."

We didn't say much to each other in the twenty minutes it took to get there, which was fine by me. I was busy trying to get Smurpee gunk off my blouse.

The house was in a wealthy area of town known as West Haven. CEOs, entertainers, politicians lived there. The house was several stories high and looked like a mansion.

Amir walked me to the front door like he was my jailor. I took out the wallet and was about to throw it into the mail slot when he grabbed my wrist.

"First, I put in hundred you gave me from wallet." He reached into his baggy pants and pulled out a C-note, then stuck it into the wallet. "Two, you apologize to man for taking."

"What? No, that's not a good . . ."

Unfortunately, Amir had already knocked on the door. I was screwed.

But strangely enough, the door opened by itself.

We walked into the house and found papers, books, pictures cluttering the floor and a desk that had been toppled over.

"This guy needs Molly Maids bad."

In addition, there was a horrible smell. But then I looked on the floor and saw why.

Big Nose lay with a knife in his chest.

I screamed.

Amir appeared calm, like he was lying on the beach wearing his Speedo. I immediately tried to erase that cringy image from my mind.

"Blood on stairs and door indicate man crawl from other room, then die as open door."

"Let's get the hell out of here, Amir."

I started toward the door, but he didn't follow. Instead, he started looking around in some of the other rooms. A few moments later, he came back. "Wallet not his."

"Of course it is. You saw the ID. He's Cleveland James and he lives here."

"He like you."

"I don't think he likes me. He's barely flirted since I came in the door." I laughed at my joke. Amir turned to me, stony-faced again.

"Cathay, man dead. Give respect."

"Sorry."

"What I say is he stole wallet too. He not Cleveland James."

"How do you know?"

"Look at place. Expensive. But this man not rich. See chain around neck, shoes."

I stared at the cheap chain and the old, battered running shoes.

"But he wears a Rol . . ." I looked down at his arm and saw that the Rolex was gone.

Amir spread his hands. "We need phone police, Cathay."

"I don't think that's a good idea."

His brow crinkled. "Why not?"

"Look, I never told you, but I have a bit of a record. I can't get mixed up in something like this."

"I ask when you hired if have record. You say no."

"That could be interpreted many ways."

He didn't say anything to that, just kneeled next to the body. "Get man's phone."

I rolled my eyes. "You want me to reach inside a dead man's pants?"

"If not want police, it only way of figuring out what happen."

"Figure out? Amir, you're not Captain America. You run a damn convenience store."

"Good deed make heart grow larger."

"Where'd you get that from? *How The Grinch Stole Christmas?*"

"Get phone, Cathay."

I was too tired to argue. I blew out air, closed my eyes, and reached into the man's pants, careful not to touch any other dead parts of his body. I handed the phone to Amir. He scrolled through it for a few moments.

"This man really Jonathon Walters. Has boat down at docks."

"So, why would he impersonate the other man?"

Amir shrugged. "We need see boat."

"No way. I need to go home."

He gave me a funny smile. "Your dentist live with you?"

Oh, right, forgot the dentist story. "Yes. It's very convenient." I had a feeling he didn't believe me.

When we arrived at the Marina Office, we asked the elderly man in charge which boat belonged to Jonathon Walters. He told us slip number forty-two.

It was a smaller, older blue-and-white pontoon like my uncle had, but this one seemed in good shape. There was a big sign on the side, saying, "Boat Tours."

Beside it was another pontoon. The man on board in shorts and a dark tan seemed to be watching us. Amir walked over to him. "Hello, you know who with this man last time he here?"

I could see the man's eyes narrow, as if he was suspicious about something.

I interpreted. "What my friend wanted to know is if you've seen the owner. He was supposed to take us out today."

"Oh. Nope, haven't seen him for a day or two. I was worried about him after he took out that mob guy."

I felt my eyebrows rise like rockets about to take off. "Mob guy?"

"I think his name is Cleveland something or other. I recognized him from some article in the paper. Bad dude. The rumor is when he's around, you'll find dead people."

AMIR AND I SAT AT a nearby coffee shop drinking our lattes. After I heard who the real Cleveland James was, I started shaking like one of those milking machines they use on cows. Wouldn't be so bad if I could make cheese. I love cheese, and of course, Tostitos. "How are you so calm, Amir?"

"Used to have bad customers who try to rob every week. Some have guns."

"Wow."

"But once they hear stories, they stop." He spread his hands.

"What stories?"

"No need to tell. You see bat with blood."

"I thought it was from the tomato sauce leak."

He put his finger to his mouth. "Keep under coat."

"That's hat, Amir. Look, I think we've done enough. We can call the police anonymously and let them handle it from here on in."

"You involve me. I must see end."

"Jesus H Christ."

"Don't swear Cathay. Not ladylike."

I held up my leg with the purple Crocs. "Like wearing these is."

"I think Walters killed by this man Cleveland James."

"Because he stole his wallet?"

"Must be more." Amir began scrolling through Walter's phone looking for answers—or else he was going to order a deep-dish Za.

A moment later, his face turned sad.

"What's wrong?"

Amir handed me the phone.

It was a message that Walters had written.

> You are the perfect daughter. Sorry, I wasn't the perfect dad. You're my anchor, Jane. You must find a way out of this mess before it's too late.

I'm not the most sentimental gal, but that got me misty-eyed.

"Terrible pain for daughter to find dad dead."

"She may not know yet."

He nodded. "My father die when fourteen. I get over. Sister never did. She end up hospital." He stood up and took out his phone. "Be back in minute."

I had a feeling Amir left to call his sister. Although he said he got over his dad's death, I could tell by his wobbly voice that he hadn't. Death is something no one gets over easily, and sometimes you never do.

Amir was right, we had to see this to the end. Maybe just for Jane.

He came back a few moments later and sat down. "I just think of something. James messed up house but didn't find what looking for. Then killed dad for it. What if he think daughter have this thing?"

At that moment, we both knew we had to get to Jane's place fast.

We found the address in Walter's phone and a few moments later we were at her apartment complex.

We knocked at number four and a young girl who looked about nineteen answered. She had frizzy blonde hair and the bluest eyes I'd ever seen. Right now, there were tears in them. Lots of tears.

Amir smiled at her. "We came check on you. Dangerous man might come and—"

Before he could finish, a bearded, wrinkly faced man appeared at the door with a gun.

"Too late. The dangerous man is already here."

He escorted us in and made us sit on the floor. "Cleveland James, at your service. You don't have to tell me who you are. I already know. I've been following you, hoping you'd take me to the money."

I felt like I might keel over. Of course, I was already on the floor, so it wouldn't make much of an impact. Amir didn't look so good, either.

James turned to Jane and pointed the gun at her.

"Let me explain why your old man died. He got greedy. He heard the phone call between me and the Han organization on the boat. Then he stole my wallet, my watch, but most importantly, my meth. He made a deal with Han pretending to be me. I asked him nicely, but he wouldn't say where the money was. Said it was for you. He wanted to do one last good thing. So, I had no choice but to work him over." He smiled. "Maybe a little too hard."

Jane rubbed her eyes.

"But you know where the money is, don't you, honey?"

Tears rolled down Jane's face. "No, I don't."

"I don't want to hurt that beautiful little body of yours, but I will. You know, even if we don't kill you, a shot through your leg can be pretty painful."

"I told you I don't know."

"I warned you." He aimed the gun at Jane.

I was frozen. I wanted to reach out and strangle him, but I couldn't move.

Suddenly, Amir rose from the floor and stood in front of Jane. "She said she not know."

A shot rang out.

Amir dropped to the ground.

My heart beat like crazy and I couldn't catch my breath.

"Tell me now, Jane, or someone else gets a bullet." He moved the gun between me and Jane.

Watching Amir's courage had given me some. I knew I had quick hands from all my wallet lifting, so I grabbed for the gun. But he wouldn't let go.

Using all my strength, I was able to point the gun toward the ceiling. It went off and plaster fell down and hit him on the head. It wasn't a great look for him. I thought it would knock him out, but it didn't.

I held tight to the barrel of the gun as I kicked him. After a few hits on his left knee, he fell, pulling me down with him. I was on top of him now and starting to weaken.

At this point, I wished I had kept up with my weight training, or even gone to the gym once. He was in great shape and grabbed the gun away from me. He pointed it directly at my chest.

I looked at him and wondered if this was the end.

The gun flew out of his hands. Someone had kicked him.

I turned and saw Amir. He was alive.

He pummeled Cleveland with his legs and arms, jumping around as if he were a Ninja. I'd never seen anything like it. The guy ran a damn convenience store.

He eventually pushed some nerve or something in James' neck, and he went unconscious.

Amir was barely out of breath as he walked over to me and Jane. "You okay." Both of us nodded.

I stuttered out the words, "The bullet hit you. How did you . . .?"

"Bullet-proof vest just in case bat story doesn't work."

"Right."

Jane got us some rope and duct tape and we tied him up.

Amir called the police and told them the whole story about Cleveland James. We waited until they picked him up. Then we took Jane to her cousin's place. She thanked us and gave us a tearful goodbye.

When I got in Amir's car, the Jesus on the dashboard continued to haunt me. This guy never gave up.

I thought we were done with everything, but Amir headed back to Walter's boat.

"Why are we going there?"

"Something bothering."

A few moments later, we stood at the stern of the pontoon. The skies were sunny and there were lots of seagulls in the air, which was strangely peaceful considering the evil we had just witnessed.

"Do you remember text Walters sent Jane?"

"Yes, he said he wished he was a better father."

"Other part. She was his anchor. I think he give clue to Jane. He want her to have money."

"Okay. So, where is the money?"

"You not listen? On anchor." Amir began pulling up the boat's anchor. "Help please, Cathay."

I grabbed the chain next to Amir's hands and helped him lift the anchor onto the boat. Personally, I think I did most of the work myself, but I guess he helped a little. As the anchor came up, we saw that a small suitcase was attached to it. We opened it up. Amir had been right; it was filled with cash in a plastic bag.

While I waited in the car, Amir gave the money to the police at the station. They offered us a substantial reward for capturing a major drug trafficker. We both agreed that Jane should get the money.

The next day at Twenty-Four Seven, I had all kinds of questions for Amir about how he learned to fight like he did. But he wouldn't answer any of them. All he said was I still hadn't paid for the Tostitos and the Count Chocula.

42

Gutted, Filleted, and Fried

Kait Carson

"IT'S FOR THE BEST, BABY. Ya gotta admit, we weren't working."

Not working, darn straight. He wasn't supposed to leave. Not yet, anyway. My husband's eyes probed mine so deeply that I wondered for a moment if he was putting on a show for the neighbors. But no. This was no act. Warning bells sounded in my head. What had I done wrong?

He hoisted his leather duffle to his shoulder. Bally. Nothing but the best.

The heels of his boots tapped loud and harsh as he strode to the back door. I chased after him. "Don't leave me!" The roar of his Harley drowned out any hope of a reconciliation. "Matt!" I wailed, heedless of the neighbors next door, clearly visible through their open window. I retreated back into the house, slumped into a kitchen chair, and buried my face in my hands. Tears seeped between my fingers. What was happening? How could he end everything just like that? It was way too soon. Now everything was in shambles.

My Maine coon, Zoe, leapt into my lap and curled into a soft ball against my stomach. I scooped her up and rubbed my nose back and forth against hers.

"How the hell did this happen, Zoe? What is he thinking? How am I supposed to manage on my own?"

Breakfast remains covered the table. I pulled my coffee mug closer and looked for the future in the bitter dregs. The past filled my memory instead.

* * *

43

NOBODY TELLS YOU THAT CHARLESTON, South Carolina on the Fourth of July is hot, muggy, sticky, and so humid, you can stir the air with a spoon. Not a whisper of a breeze stirred the full skirt of my bright yellow sundress. I almost regretted my spur-of-the-moment decision to treat myself to the Patriot's Point fireworks. It was too late to get bleacher tickets. Blankets and towels covered the entirety of the grass at Waterfront Park. Even if I could find a bare patch of grass, scrubbing grass stains from my skirt was not high on my list of things to do. The evening sky turned deep peach as I headed toward a sidewalk café. Might as well grab a snack before I returned to my hotel and put the finishing touches on my PowerPoint presentation. This was a business trip, after all. Armed with an iced coffee and warm croissant, I eyed the sea of full tables clustered on the outdoor patio. A man sitting solo at a two-top pushed back his wrought iron chair and waved me over. I squinted and wondered if he'd been at the meet and greet held for early arrivals last night.

"Please, ma'am. I'd appreciate it if you'd join me." The Tom Selleck dimples that creased his cheeks set my heart racing. I'd have remembered him for sure. He bent from the waist in a courtly bow. Not too surprising in a guy who looked like he could have stepped from a Ralph Lauren catalogue. His light blue polo shirt was the perfect counterpoint to his sharply creased, cream-color trousers.

"I don't want to intrude." Oh, yes, I did. This guy had that well-heeled look I found devastatingly attractive. A breeze, first I'd felt in an hour, belled my skirt and blew my hair into my face. Nearly blinded, I placed my coffee on the table and used the hand to flatten my skirt before modesty became a memory.

The man reached for my napkin-wrapped croissant and placed it next to my drink. "See, kismet." He stuck out a hand. "Matt Tremayne and I'm pleased to meet you."

I've always been a sucker for men whose eyes crinkled at the corners when they smiled. Matt's not only crinkled, they were the same color as my favorite childhood crayon. Turquoise.

Laughing, I took his hand in mine. "Allison Rivas, thank you for rescuing me." He tucked the chair beneath me and returned to his seat across from me at the table.

"That's what I do, Ms. Rivas. Rescue damsels in distress. You know that Charleston is a very unique place. Magic happens here. It's the birthplace of the Atlantic River."

My drink paused midway to my mouth. "Excuse me? Atlantic River?"

"Some call it the ocean. You're a visitor?" That killer smile lit his face.

I nodded, broke off a corner of my croissant, and nibbled it. "From Miami."

"We have Florida in common. I'm living in Delray Beach. Born right here, though." He gestured vaguely toward the water. "Well, on The Battery anyway."

I mulled that over for a nanosecond. Battery birth and Delray, a playground of the rich and not so famous, spelled wealth. I wondered if Florida traffic rendered us geographically undesirable. "Tell me about the Atlantic."

"Everyone knows the Ashley and Cooper rivers meet here and form the Atlantic."

I nearly choked on the bite of my pastry. When I saw his impish grin, I couldn't help myself. I laughed, and geography be damned, knew I'd make it work somehow. My head spun with hopes and dreams for our future.

Soon after we returned to Florida, he moved into my house. Our wedding followed a few weeks later. Whirlwind to some, it fit right into my plans.

THE DOORBELL PULLED ME OUT of my reverie. I leaned back in my chair and spotted the letter carrier through the glass partition in the front door. She swiped her arm over her face. Even at this hour, the south Florida heat was a killer. I caught a flash of green on the letter clutched in her hand. Certified mail, then. Divorce papers? No, that would involve a process server. He wouldn't dare. Even Matt wasn't that stupid.

I wiped my eyes, doubtless smudging my mascara, and rose from the table to answer the door.

"Everything okay, Ms. Rivas?" our letter carrier asked, concern evident on her face.

I must look worse than I thought. "Yes . . . no. I don't know." I sniffed and took the envelope from her outstretched hand. It was from the bank. *Matt, you've really messed up this time!* I looked back up at her kind face. "My husband just left me. Completely out of the blue. I think he's lost his mind."

She looked like she didn't know what to say to that. I couldn't blame her. Hands shaking, I slit the envelope and read the letter inside. There was no way she could miss the big red "NOTICE OF INTENT TO FORECLOSE" stamped across the letter inside.

I gulped in a breath and scanned the letter, my anger building as I did. I had thirty days before the bank filed a mortgage foreclosure complaint. My stomach sank as I began to suspect what he'd done. The mess up wasn't Matt's, it was mine. A hot tear coursed down my cheek. "This isn't possible. I don't have a mortgage on my house. An equity line, yes. But it has been years since I've accessed it."

The letter carrier's mouth dropped open.

"Matt and I keep separate accounts." I babbled on. "He pays . . . I guess paid . . . the bills, but I put most of my salary into the joint account for our living expenses." Too much information, but I couldn't stop myself.

"I need to call him," I said, fishing my cell from my pocket. The letter carrier nodded and retreated from my doorstep as I pressed Matt's speed dial. The Florida housing market was hot as the weather on a late August day. The house represented a significant asset. *My* significant asset. I'd bought it before he was a glimmer in my eye. The only reason I put him on the deed was to assure him of my undying love and to build trust. At the time, it seemed like cheap insurance.

He didn't answer. Maybe he was still on his motorcycle going— wherever he was going. I left a detailed message on his voicemail, then sent him a text message for good measure.

The tight timeline in the letter left me little choice. I needed to do some damage control, and for that, I needed information. I flipped through the pages of the letter. Banks didn't threaten foreclosure for one missed payment. And why was there even a payment to be made? Rather than call the bank, I changed from my running clothes into a sleeveless shift and hopped into my car. The fuel light flashed a warning as I pulled out of the driveway. Frustrated, I scribbled another item on my mental to do list. Today definitely was not going as planned.

The bank vice president ushered me into an office cold enough to serve as the fresh produce room in Costco. I perched on the edge of the chair, wished for a sweater, and pushed the folded letter across the desk toward her. "I got this in the mail today. There must be a mistake. I don't even have a mortgage." I fished in my purse for a tissue and daubed my eyes, knowing they were still reddened from this morning. A look of compassion filled her face as she read the contents. She pressed a few keys on her computer and entered some information.

Her eyes widened as she read the screen. "I am so sorry." Her words gave me comfort. I expected her to agree that it was an easily rectifiable mistake. Instead, she said, "I don't know what we can do. Your entire line of credit has been withdrawn, and nothing has been repaid.

A hot flush of shame mixed with anger crept up my cheeks. *How dare he do this to me? Who does he think he is?* I pressed my hands on the cool surface of her desk and took a slow, deep breath. "That's not possible," I said. "My husband pays the bills and I'm scrupulous about transferring the money to our joint account for anything I charge on my credit cards. I hate paying interest to carry a balance." I peeked up and the bank vice president nodded, an expression of understanding on her face. "Can you please check our joint account? Move the funds from there?"

The clack of the keyboard sounded loud as a rifle shot. "No, I'm afraid there's only a hundred dollars in the account."

There was helpless pity in her eyes. "My husband left me this morning," I whispered to her across the desk. "I didn't see it coming at all. I have no idea where he went." She reached across the desk and placed a hand on mine, whether in solidarity or comfort, I wasn't sure. "Can you please check my personal account? I need to know how bad things are." This was not the way I envisioned my future. He'd gutted me.

She squeezed my hand, then returned to the keyboard while I read off the account numbers from my checkbook.

"This account has less than five hundred dollars." She looked as upset as I felt.

"That's not possible." I kept my voice at a low whisper with effort.

"That's *my* account." I stood and pushed back the chair under me with enough force to send it flying against the wall. "I'm the only one who . . . No." I smacked myself in the forehead. "I added Matt early in our relationship. I trusted him. What has he done?"

The vice president said something, but I didn't process her words. I turned and stumbled blindly to the door.

THE FLASHING LIGHT ON MY dashboard reminded me that I had better fill up. I pulled into the gas station and slid my credit card into the slot. The readout told me the card was declined. "Damnit, Matt!" I screamed at the gas pump. Desperate, I pulled my backup credit card from my wallet. The one tied to Matt's brokerage account. That too came back declined, as I knew it would. It was foolish of me to even try. I searched my purse and found forty dollars. I marched into the gas station and forked over the last of my cash. It wouldn't go far, but it would get me home.

My teeth worried the inside of my lip at the thought. He'd really screwed me over. The sight of Zoe in the window when I turned onto my street brought wrenching sobs. This wasn't supposed to happen. I wasn't ready. I stopped the car in the driveway and rested my head against the steering wheel. The warm touch of leather brought comfort. I sniffled desperately and searched for a tissue.

I scooped Zoe up as I walked into the house and buried my face in her soft fur. The Maine coon tabby looked massive but weighed little more than a cat half her size. It took less than five minutes on my computer to confirm my credit card was cancelled and Matt's brokerage account was reduced to a whisper of its former glory. I fought back a smirk. There's more than one way to fillet a fish.

I pressed the number for Matt's speed dial again. This time, a recording told me I'd reached a disconnected number. Pain pierced my heart and something else I recognized as anger. He wasn't going to get away this easy. With shaking fingers, I pressed 911. The operator chided me for using the emergency number, but put the call through to our local police. The officer who answered asked me to come to the station.

* * *

"MY HUSBAND DISAPPEARED THIS MORNING. He drained all my accounts and now his phone's been shut off. He stole from me." I said in a rush once I was seated at one of the desks in the police station.

"What would you like us to do?" The officer sitting across from me looked like she'd graduated from the academy the day before yesterday. Her brown hair slicked tightly into a bun, her face dewy with the glow of youth. Even the nametag that identified her as Officer Anderson looked shiny and new. I eyed the page of printed notes on the pad before her. Heck, she couldn't even write in cursive.

"Find my husband." I almost added a duh, but I restrained myself.

"Did you want to report him as missing? He's an adult. There's nothing we can do yet." She paused and cocked her head to the side. I could almost hear her thinking. "Is he incapacitated or endangered? We have alerts for that."

"No. I want you to get my money back." Anger I couldn't show fizzed in my veins like champagne. I debated what response would give me more credibility. "He's not acting like himself." My voice trailed off. She could draw her own conclusions.

Officer Anderson touched the keyboard in front of her. "No Matt or Mathew Tremayne in our system. Did he go by another name?"

I shook my head. "Not that I know of."

She nodded. "I was afraid you'd say that. Is there a history of mental illness?"

My hand flew to my mouth. "Can you check his VA records? He was in Iraq."

She pushed back from the desk. "They would be confidential, but you can try if you know where he sought treatment. It's possible a sympathetic doctor might share some insight." Her eyes filled with compassion. "Legally, he didn't steal from you. From what you've said, his name was on the accounts. It was his money too."

"But—"

"I'm sorry. It stinks." She paused. A series of expressions chased themselves across her face. "Be careful, ma'am. If he's not acting rationally, you don't know what he might do. Do you have any idea where he might have gone?"

I shook my head and left the police station. He might not have legally stolen from me, but he'd broken every law of love. Legalized theft. Great defense.

If the cops couldn't help me, I'd help myself. I drove home and stopped the car in the driveway just before it would have blasted through the garage door. I slammed into the house and headed for the den. There had to be answers here. I'd find him, and I'd make him pay.

I pawed through the files in the den. The weight of my thoughts nearly crushed me. What an idiot. I pounded my fist on the top of a metal cabinet in frustration. This was so not happening. A paper fluttered from the file I held. I scooped it up and realized it was in Matt's handwriting. *Meet me at our place.*

Our place. An abandoned building site in far southern Miami-Dade County. Early in our relationship, I'd taken him there and told him about the round flying saucer houses that used to populate the property. I'd always wanted to live in one. They'd been torn down years ago, but he'd promised me he'd buy the land and build me a flying saucer house. He'd cut a hidden hole in the fence. We'd sneak in and picnic. That was where he'd asked me to marry him. An idea formed as I smoothed the undated note.

I changed from my dress into jeans and a long-sleeved T-shirt, grabbed my keys and bounded out to the car. I had an easy two-hour ride ahead of me. I hoped I had enough gas. Just in case, I emptied the lawn mower gas can into the car. That should do it. It would be just like Matt to hole up there.

Our place sat on a lightly traveled road that ran through the last of South Florida's farming country and ended at the Everglades. Not much out here to create traffic unless you were a farmer or a teen looking to hook up. It was the perfect place to hide.

The abandoned homesite came into view as dusk was giving way to full dark. Palms and slash pines waved in the breeze and cast eerie shadows along the verge. Matt once estimated the vacant land covered ten acres. Most were wooded. Now it looked lonely, and a bit scary. I parked right in front of the hedge that concealed the hole in the fence. My car was the only vehicle in sight. My heart pounded as I slipped from the car and pulled aside the tangled branches of Surinam cherry hedge. In the gathering gloom, I couldn't tell if the ground in front of the hole was disturbed. I knew I was. I clicked on the penlight I kept in my handbag and ducked into the property. Longing for the comfort of another voice, I pressed Matt's speed dial number. Maybe he'd had a change of heart. Instead, the voice repeated that the phone was no longer in service.

I let the thin shaft of light guide me to a cluster of white bird of paradise plants. The thick fan of their branches concealed our picnic place. My penlight died as I pushed past the sticky boughs. Darkness closed in. I stifled a scream as a bird cawed harshly and took flight from a nearby palm. The only other sound was the chirping of the crickets.

Fear clenched my chest. I waited for ten minutes to let my eyes adapt to the velvety darkness. Every creak of a branch and whisper of leaves sent frissons of fear through me. Each shadow looked like the Florida Man monster who'd haunted my youth. Matt wasn't there. I had to leave before I scared myself to death.

I made my way back to the car, tripping over branches as I went. Sweat slicked my skin as I slid behind the wheel. A feeling of exhaustion washed over me as I drove home. Who was the man I knew as Matt Tremayne?

I pulled up into my driveway. This time, I hit the button to the garage door opener and parked inside. I hopped out of my car and noticed that the alarm panel light flashed a breach. I backed away from the door and out of the garage, planning to go to my neighbor's house. They were new in the neighborhood, but I knew he worked for the Florida Drug Enforcement Agency. He'd come with me to make sure the house was secure. The last thing I wanted was to find Matt inside.

I passed around the front of my house and discovered Zoe huddled in the weak beam of the pole lamp that illuminated my walkway. Panic and fear set in. Zoe never went out.

I looked from the walkway to my front porch. The front door stood open. I scooped up the cat, dialed 911, and ran next door. There were no lights in their house and no response to my pounding on the door. I stood on the neighbor's porch, clutching my cat to my chest, and waited for the police to arrive.

* * *

MY HEART LEAPT WHEN OFFICER Anderson emerged from the patrol vehicle. I ran to her as I would to an old friend. At her direction, I remained on the front lawn with Zoe. At the open door, Officer Anderson drew her gun and shouted, "Police. Show yourself." After a brief pause, she entered with her partner. Not five minutes later, she reappeared and beckoned me into the house.

"If this was a burglary, it's the neatest one I've ever seen." We stood side by side in my living room. Nothing seemed out of place. "Can you confine the cat to a cage?" She ruffled the fur on the top of Zoe's head. "Don't want her to disturb any evidence."

"What if it was Matt? His prints are everywhere. Mine too." She followed me to the garage, where I took Zoe's kennel from the shelf and encouraged her to enter. She went in willingly. Unusual for her. I couldn't blame her for being disoriented. I felt a wave of guilt wash over me. Poor girl deserved better.

The officer took my elbow and led me back to the house. "We didn't see anything out of line, but you might. Where were you?"

I fished the note from my pocket and handed it to her. "This was in our den." I studied my feet and explained the significance of our place. "I hoped he'd be there. Tell me this was some kind of joke."

She handed me back the note and we walked from room to room. The house was in perfect order. Moreover, there was no evidence of forced entry. "You told me earlier today," she said as she thumbed a few pages in her notebook, "that your husband had cleaned you out financially." When I nodded, she continued. "So, why would he come back? Is there something else in the house that he could turn to cash?"

She spoke to me, but her gaze was on her partner. What did she mean? I wracked my brain. "No. Nothing." I drummed my fingers on the table.

"You were upset today, the note from your husband . . ." She raised a hand to stop the interruption that flew to my lips. "Understandably, it upset you more. It looks like you left the house with the door open." She flipped her notebook closed. "Are you certain you set the alarm? You had a lot going on.

"Listen." Officer Anderson spoke to me in a soft voice as her partner returned to the car. "If Matt was in the house, he didn't actually break any laws. He can argue that it is still his home. But I know how these men can be, and I'm worried about you." She handed me a business card. "If he comes back, this is my personal number. I want you to give me a call right away."

An empty feeling filled my heart as I watched the officers go. I was truly alone. I retrieved Zoe from her captivity and hugged her hard. To make amends for her terrifying evening, I filled her treat bowl with her favorite canned food and set it on the floor. At least my cat loved me. As I watched Zoe scarf down her very expensive designer cat food, I poured myself a glass of pinot noir, glad Matt left the wine. He had good taste.

I scooped up Zoe and went to the office. Once there, I keyed in Matt's name. Officer Anderson was correct. He had no internet presence before our marriage. I wracked my brain. How could I find out who he was, and what he was? I remembered reading stories about solving crimes with familial DNA tests. Not an option in my case. As far as I knew, Matt hadn't taken one. My fingers hovered over the keyboard. I uploaded a recent picture of Matt into a Google image search.

I spotted Matt's face as I scrolled through the image results. It was a Georgia mug shot of someone named Michael Tenneson. His height, weight, age, and personal particulars matched Matt to a tee. I dug deeper and found he'd been convicted of identity theft, fraud, and conspiracy. The dates of incarceration and probation jibed with the dates Matt told me he'd been in the military serving abroad. He'd been serving all right, but not the way he led me to believe.

I sent the pertinent information to the printer. Then I fished Officer Anderson's card from my pocket. I figured this was as close as I'd get to Matt coming back.

BACK AT THE STATION, OFFICER Anderson keyed in some information from the mug shot I'd found. She printed off a fingerprint card and five pages of additional data. "Do you have anything of his with you that we can use to prove this is the same guy? Something with his fingerprints?

They say everyone has a double, and the names are different, even though you're sure it's him."

Could it really be that simple? "I have the note. Otherwise, we can go back to the house." I wanted this guy. Needed to know where he was and why. I had plans to make.

The officer made a call and handed over the note to another officer while I stewed and doodled the name Matt Tremayne. When Officer Anderson approached, I crumpled the paper and shoved it into my purse before someone realized my doodle was more than a reasonable facsimile of Matt's signature. An eager light shone in her eyes when she told me Matt's and Mike's fingerprints matched. I hadn't been Matt's greatest love. Instead, just his latest mark. The thought renewed my anger.

"Are you willing to press charges?" Compassion filled the cop's face while I felt mine heat with the blush of shame. "Given his record, and the marriage under a false name, there's a good case for fraud here."

"Can I? Didn't you say the money was his too?"

"Yes. It would be up to the State Attorney to charge him, but looking at the evidence, and the facts as you've told me, I'd say it's possible."

I gave myself a mental shake. He deserved this. All his lies. He'd be sorry. "Yes. And I hope he goes away for a long, long time."

"We'll get him."

"Do you know where he is?"

"We do now." She chuckled. "He might be a brilliant con, but he stinks at common sense." She turned her monitor to face me. "Michael Tenneson filed a change of name in Lee County. It showed up when we ran his fingerprints."

"Today?"

"No. The hearing was last week. He's had this in the works for a while. It won't look good for him."

"Were we even married? I mean, if he lied on our marriage license?" This was getting better and better.

"I don't know. Maybe not."

* * *

54

SIX HOURS LATER OFFICER ANDERSON'S call woke me from a deep sleep. "He's in custody. They should be here in a few hours. Do you want to see him? It's not protocol, but it can be arranged if you happen to be here."

A shiver of fear, anger, and disgust coursed through me. What a naive bunny I'd been. He'd taken me. Now it was my turn to return the favor. "I do have a few words for him."

Zoe rubbed her face in mine and made biscuits against my arm. "We're safe, my girl." I glanced at my watch. If I was going to confront Matt, I better get going. "Breakfast for you, coffee for me, and then . . ." I lightly tapped her pink nose. "The adventure begins."

The duty officer buzzed me in. Officer Anderson met me in the hall. Her eyes held a distinct glint of enjoyment. "I'll have to stay, and there are people behind the mirror."

I nodded. "Has he said anything?"

"He claimed it was all your idea. Cash out the equity, empty your accounts, then disappear."

My eyebrows flew so high at her words I could feel them tangle with my hair. "My idea? Why would I do that?"

Officer Anderson touched my shoulder with a compassionate hand. "He's a con man."

Matt's mouth dropped at the sight of me. He sprang to his feet. The cuff around the wrist that secured him to the table pulled, and he yelped. "You. This is all your fault. Tell them this was your idea. I'm not taking the rap for you." The face I'd once thought handsome contorted into a mask of hate. "They've arrested me."

I moved to face him, careful to stay out of reach of his one unrestrained hand. I rested a hip against the side of a plastic chair and looked at the man I'd married and said, "It's for the best, Babe. Ya gotta admit we weren't working out."

I spun on my heel. Someday I'd get my money back. In the meantime, it didn't matter. The cash from his investment account was safe in my Cayman bank, and it was all mine. One old saying was true. There is no honor among thieves. They were wrong about not being able to con a con. The one behind me was gutted, filleted, and soon to be fried. Best of all, there'd be plenty more fish in the sea where I was headed.

Man Up in the Air

Judith Carlough

TEMPTATION DOESN'T ALWAYS TAKE THE form of a serpent with an apple. Sometimes, it looks like a knockout blonde with curves that beckon like a country road.

I had just boarded the plane, heading home to Savannah. The emergency meeting with my regional team to make peace with a disgruntled client had gone over like a teetotaler preaching at Mardi Gras. My team wanted to fire the client—he was a colossal pain in the ass—but my company had posted its worst-ever earnings last year, and I couldn't afford to lose this client. I eventually won over the team with dinner at a rib joint over endless rounds of beer and promises of an additional week of vacation.

Waking up that morning, I had felt like twice-hammered whale shit, but I virtuously dragged myself to the hotel gym where the twenty-something trainer asked if I wanted to join their Senior Stretch class. Christ, I'm only forty-seven, but I must have looked seventy. I silently cursed the trainer and his seven-percent body fat, then doubled my usual weight load to show the boy wonder I could still deliver the mail. On my third set, I pulled a muscle in my left shoulder, and the trainer had to help me off the weight bench. He added to my humiliation by offering a sling, but I wanted to look tough. "I'll just rub a little dirt on it," I said with a laugh. Man, that was stupid.

Now, as I slipped into my seat in first class, my back and shoulders felt like I'd been carrying King Kong. The Aleve hadn't kicked in. My left shoulder throbbed, and my fingers were swollen to the size of carrots. I clenched and unclenched my hand as I tossed my backpack on the empty aisle seat, praying it would remain vacant.

I closed my eyes and exhaled deeply, grateful the trip was over and we were going to keep the client, yet dreading my homecoming. It was my fifteenth wedding anniversary, and my wife, Barbara, had given me holy hell for the last-minute trip. I'd told her to make reservations at Le Chevalier, the most pretentious French restaurant in Savannah. I hated everything about the place except the wine list, which I would put to good use.

The twins wouldn't be excited to see me, either. I had failed to get them tickets to a sold-out performance of Billie Eilish, and fourteen-year-old girls don't easily forgive. But if I toppled from my paternal pedestal, so be it. I wasn't paying a scalper five hundred bucks a pop, not with my business on the skids.

The flight attendants were busy in the galley, and the thought of a drink perked me up. I debated ordering a double bourbon, needing some hair of the dog to put the last twenty-four hours behind me. Then one flight attendant emerged from the galley—creamy skin, a tawny blonde braid down her back, firm breasts that strained her uniform jacket—and all thoughts of business evaporated. Don't get me wrong, I've never been unfaithful to Barb, but I'm not blind, and lookin' ain't cheatin'.

"Would you like a beverage?" Her smile was brighter than noon in the Sahara. A name tag read: Ashleigh.

"Uh, scotch," I said, my voice raspy. "No, I mean bourbon."

Her eyes twinkled. They were a light blue, the shade of my favorite jeans. "I have both. Maybe one of each?"

"Just bourbon, rocks. I don't really drink scotch." I couldn't have sounded more stupid if a script writer had prepared my lines.

"Perhaps a double?" she asked, reading my mind.

"Uh, no. No thanks, not a double." No way did I want her thinking I was some old boozehound, even though I had no reason to care what she thought.

Ashleigh took other orders in first class, disappeared into the galley, then brought the drinks, including a generous bourbon. "You visiting Savannah?" she asked.

"I live there."

Her megawatt smile intensified. "So do I! Just moved in a couple months ago from Jacksonville. What a great town." She leaned in to lower my tray table and came dangerously close to a gut that spilled over my seat belt. I sucked it in so fast I gasped and had to pretend it was a cough. "Once I finish serving drinks, you'll have to tell me the best restaurants," she said. A strand of hair had escaped the neat braid and brushed my cheek like a caress. She gave me another dose of her killer smile before walking to the next row.

I busied myself with a paperback and drank my bourbon, but my concentration was shot. Ashleigh's perfume lingered—a light citrus scent— and I wondered what her long, blonde hair looked like unbraided and swinging across her shoulders. It brought back a memory from my fifth anniversary, when Barb and I took a long weekend at Hilton Head because we couldn't afford Maui, our dream vacation. I had watched her run on the beach in a bright blue bikini, her mahogany curls bouncing in a ponytail under a baseball hat. I was so turned on, we made love twice when she got back. Sadly, I couldn't remember the last time we'd had sex twice in a day. Or a week.

I checked my cell phone; there was no out-going service at the moment, so I couldn't call the florist and order flowers. I had asked the twins what I should buy Barb, and they said a Birken bag, which I had never heard of. When I saw they cost over ten grand, I wondered how teenage girls knew about stuff like that. Damned Internet. I wound up buying Barb a five-hundred-dollar Visa gift card at the local CVS. Let her pick out whatever she wanted; I didn't have a clue. My phone pinged and I saw three bars, so I called the florist and ordered fifteen red roses, which I'd pick up on the way home. Mission accomplished. If she liked the roses and gift card, I might get lucky tonight. Then a text pinged from Barb, and it was a real buzzkill, nagging me to order fish or chicken tonight if I had eaten red meat on my trip. Of course, I had eaten red meat—a full rack of baby back ribs— but I'd never admit it. I'd order what I damn well pleased. I was paying for it. I texted her back, using a couple of choice words about chicken and fish, before chucking the cell phone onto the vacant seat, resenting that I'd be dropping a ton of dough on a meal I wouldn't enjoy, and feeling extorted by the need for gifts like Birken bags. Not for the first time, I saw myself as a human ATM for my family. It made me glad I had done something for myself a couple years ago and bought a Porsche. 'Course I didn't know my business was about to nosedive. Still, I kept the car; a man has to keep up appearances.

My stomach growled. I wanted a bacon cheeseburger, and *god* I could hear Barb accusing me of eating like a teenager. She's fitter than me, always has been, and looks great for her age, but she had become the food police, getting on my case after my annual checkups started trending in the wrong direction for cholesterol, lipids, and high blood pressure. Jesus, that happens to all men in middle age. Does it mean we have to stop living? She should understand that a man has certain basic needs, and beef is one.

Sex is another. I looked up to see Ashleigh coming down the aisle to take lunch orders. She gave me a finger-wave. I felt my equipment stirring below the belt. That didn't happen as easily with Barb anymore. It's difficult to get aroused after seeing the same landscape for fifteen years. An unpleasant flashback reminded me of a couple times when Barb felt frisky and I couldn't rise to the occasion. I shook it off at the time, blaming too much to drink. She never brought it up again it. Maybe it didn't bother her, I thought, as I finished my bourbon.

Ashleigh returned and replaced my empty glass with a fresh one. She recited lunch options, and I chose the turkey club. She lingered, settling her cute butt on the arm rest of the vacant aisle seat. "So? Did y'all make me a list of restaurants?"

I promised I'd make a list if she told me what kinds of food turned her on. I immediately worried that only old farts said *turn you on*, but she giggled and said, Italian, Thai, and sushi, then sighed. "It's so difficult for a single lady to eat alone; men get the wrong idea."

I was already getting all kinds of wrong ideas as Ashleigh moved to the next row.

I made a list of restaurants and thought about all the times I'd eaten alone: on the road, at the office, even in my own home since Barb had started a part-time job. Two times a week, I was expected to take care of the girls while she ran all over hell's half-acre, doing renovations and remodeling for a big interior design firm and having drinks with colleagues. I didn't give a rat's ass about decorating, and the job didn't pay enough to even cover our property taxes, but she loved it, so I went along. That should have scored big points in the Good Husband Department, but now her job was all Barb talked about. Instead of listening to me when I tried to share my client problems—which she had always been interested in before—she interrupted with stories about *her* clients. And lately, she had been pressuring me to renovate our house, which had been perfectly fine until she took this fool job.

I upended my second bourbon just as Ashleigh materialized. "Is this seat taken?" Her tone was mischievous, conspiratorial. "I have a few minutes before lunch."

"Sure, siddown." My tongue felt thick as I cleared away my backpack, spilling its contents onto the floor like an oaf. I kicked the debris under the seats in front of us.

She sat. Her skirt rode up, revealing toned thighs. She pointed at her name plate. "I'm Ashleigh, as you can see, but y'all don't have a name tag, so I'll just guess. Matt? Brian? Horatio? Gimme a li'l hint."

Her playful flirting was hitting me like catnip. "My given name is Macon, but everyone calls me Mac."

"I've never known a Mac before. You're my first."

It sounded provocative. Or was that the bourbon? "I hope I don't disappoint you," I said. Then I winked before I could stop myself. I was coming on to her like a sleazeball lounge lizard.

"I doubt that's possible." Ashleigh reached over and tapped my shoulder, sending an electric current directly to my sweet spot.

I showed her the restaurant list and described each place; each one seemed to delight her.

"Now, tell me about your job, what kind of work you do?" she said.

I talked easily about my company, bragging a little, omitting the recent downturn.

Ashleigh asked how often I traveled, to which cities, and hung on my every word. No beautiful woman had paid me this much attention in years. "I hope you don't mind all these questions. I just find it fascinating what folks do for a living."

Mind? I couldn't get enough, but I know when to turn the tables. "What about you? What do you like to do when you're not working?" I asked.

She rattled off yoga, running, shopping, and tennis.

"I used to play a little tennis," I said, smug. "Club champion three times."

Ashleigh *oohed* and *aahed*, and I felt guilty since my trophies were for mixed doubles with Barb, until I blew out my knee and had to give it up.

"I'll bet you'd be great at pickleball," Ashleigh said, excited. "Do you play?"

"Not yet," I said. Barb had been bugging me to try it, but I thought it was a step down from tennis. Pickleball was for old folks, but if gals like Ashleigh played, maybe I should reconsider.

"What's fun to see in Savannah?" Ashleigh asked.

I named the usual attractions—Forsythe Park, River Street, Mercer House, Bonaventure Cemetery, the Forrest Gump bench—and she proclaimed each idea *great, terrific, super.* Then Ashleigh frowned—a cute, pouty expression—but it made me willing to wrestle a wolverine to win back her smile. "It's so hard when you're alone and new in town, and you don't know which places are safe to go to as a single lady."

I swear it was a bald-faced invitation to whisk her around Savannah, and god help me, I nearly volunteered. I was saved when the other flight attendant interrupted and told Ashleigh they had started lunch prep.

She got up immediately. "Duty calls," she said with a little shrug. "See you after dessert."

What the hell was happening? I'd never strayed beyond a lustful imagination, yet I was contemplating a rendezvous with this gorgeous stranger. It felt so damn good to be on the receiving end of a beautiful young woman's undivided admiration.

Ashleigh brought my turkey club with another generous bourbon, then served the other passengers. My novel lay in my lap, a prop, as my reptilian brain worked on ways to show Ashleigh around Savannah without doing anything more. I failed. Every scenario started with me lying to my wife and ended with Ashleigh and me in a tangle of white sheets, an empty champagne bottle nearby, and Marvin Gaye playing in the background. In my fantasy, I still had all my hair, a tapered waistline, and a tan. I regretfully considered my flabby reality, and swore I'd start working out.

My third bourbon was half gone when Ashleigh cleared my plate and asked why I hadn't eaten my square of carrot cake. "Don't you like sweets, or are you sweet enough?"

Carrot cake was my favorite, so I lied. "I'm more of a cognac guy." I rarely drink cognac, but it seemed like a James Bond thing to say.

"Good to know." She disappeared into the small galley.

Good to know, why? My reptilian brain answered, *Because she wants you, man. She's gathering information for future reference.* When that part of my brain starts guiding me, it's a sign to lay off the alcohol. Instead, I gulped more bourbon.

Ashleigh patrolled first class, attending to everyone, stopping by long enough to drop off a snifter of cognac. She winked. "I love watching a man enjoy himself."

My intuition had been right; she *was* coming on to me. Strong. I spent the remaining minutes before landing trying to compose what I should say. Should I offer to show her around Savannah? Ask her for her number? *Someone like Ashleigh comes along once in a lifetime*, I told myself. *The sand is running through the hourglass*, my reptilian brain added.

Before I could determine the right move, the captain asked us to please store our tray tables in their upright, locked position, yadda yadda. I had never been more nervous about a landing, and it had nothing to do with the plane. What should I do? *Fortune favors the bold.* I handed the empty snifter to the other flight attendant.

The plane touched down. Ashleigh remained seated with the other flight attendant in the galley jump seats. As we taxied the short distance to the gate, I knew it was the moment to take action or regret it forever.

The plane stopped before we reached the gate and Ashleigh suddenly unlocked her seat belt, slipped back to my row, and sat. "I hope you won't think I'm too forward." She kept her voice low and leaned in. "There's something I've just got to ask you."

I took in her unlined face, her full, perky breasts, her hair more luxurious than sable. Every ounce of my testosterone was on full alert. My heart raced. I felt a tumble of emotions: lust, guilt, confusion, hope, and a truckload of macho pride that I still had what it took to attract the hottest female of the species. And finally, sadly, I felt the deep conviction that I could not pull this off.

Ashleigh's face glowed with anticipation. "May I have your cell number, because . . ."

I held up my hands to stop her. I bet she'd never been turned down before, but I had no choice. "Thanks, Ashleigh, but I'm married." I tried to sound kind, but the bourbon and cognac made my voice fuzzy.

Poor Ashleigh didn't have a poker face; distress overtook her expression like storm clouds defiling a blue sky. "But you don't wear a ring," she said.

"I hurt my shoulder working out this morning and my fingers are swollen." I dug into my pocket and found my ring, as if I needed evidence.

"Sonofabitch," she said, her disappointment replaced by pure annoyance and a frown that wasn't cute, just businesslike. "You were so perfect for my mom. I really wanted to hook you two up. She's been so lonely since we got to Savannah."

Ashleigh kept speaking about how her mom needed to get out more, but most older guys were creeps, and her mom loved pickleball, and travel, and blah blah blah. None of her words registered. I was the one who needed a poker face, but my feelings no longer mattered. I was of no further interest—or use—to Ashleigh.

The plane had reached the gate and Ashleigh was back at her job, smiling and chatting with passengers as they left. She gave me a curt, *Nice to meet you, Mac,* as I passed into the jetway. I tried to keep a neutral expression, but my humiliation burned.

Once in my car, I called the florist and increased my order to thirty roses and asked if he had a printer. He did. When I arrived, I sat in his parking lot and used my cell phone to make an online purchase. I used the florist's printer to make a hard copy of the online receipt, put it in one of the florist's envelopes, and tucked it into my jacket pocket.

At my front door, I heard Jimmy Buffett playing, one of my all-time favorite artists. I opened the door to spectacular aromas; I could swear carrot cake was among them, but it had to be a cruel trick of my overstimulated imagination. In the kitchen, I stopped short. Barb was in jeans and a skimpy tee shirt, cooking. She looked fantastic.

"What about Le Chevalier?" I asked.

She brushed a curl from her damp forehead. "I don't know what I was thinking. You've had a difficult trip. After I read your text—you sounded so tired and grumpy—I picked up ribs from Smokin' Piggy's, with the

Tennessee bourbon glaze you love, and sent the girls to Mama Jo's for the night. I hope that's okay."

Barb looked more gorgeous than ten Ashleighs.

"I'd throw you over my shoulder and carry you upstairs to show my gratitude, but I pulled a muscle this morning at the gym," I said.

She turned and gawked, like who-are-you-and-what-have-you-done-with-my-husband? Then she dipped her eyebrows and said in a very sly tone, "If you want a little action, I seem to remember our couch has been highly satisfactory in the past."

An hour later, I uncorked a great bottle of Barolo. We sat down to ribs and carrot cake with fifteen candles, and Barb cried when she opened the envelope and found the receipt for tickets to Maui.

Manual for Success

Sandra Benson

Krystal Markham danced from one foot to the other while two men carried a gleaming mahogany coffin through her front door and around the corner into her living room. "Just put it there, on the coffee table," she called. "I've got it all cleared off. All the books are put away and everything. That never happens in this house," she added, in case they thought she was the sort of mother who didn't encourage her child to read.

Quite the opposite. Madison, now sixteen, was an excellent student. Too bad she took after Krystal's ex-husband, Dan. He was about as thrilling as a pair of sensible shoes. Maddie was staying with him for the weekend. The two of them were probably making a spreadsheet or something.

But Krystal had found brochures in Maddie's room from Stanford. Stanford! Was her practical girl secretly yearning for California, and a famous college that neither Krystal nor Dan could afford? It gave Krystal's heart a little tremor of hope to think her daughter might be imagining a life that held . . . more.

That's where the coffins came in.

One of the delivery men approached her with a clipboard and a pen. "That's everything," he said. "Sign here."

Beaming, Krystal signed her name with a flourish, swinging back her long hair, which was currently a rich chestnut brown. "Thanks very much," she called after them with a smile and a wave as their heavy shoes tromped through her front door and down the concrete stairs to the yard. She'd dashed out to their truck while they carried in the cherry coffin—or was it the oak one?—and had placed pamphlets with her new business cards tucked into them on the driver's seat.

EverRest: Make your final arrangements now! No pressure! Great quality! Contact your EverRest representative today to schedule your own home party! Prizes and discounts for EverRest party hosts and hostesses!

Every person you meet is a potential customer! (EverRest Manual for Success, Page 3)

Krystal bounced lightly on her toes as she looked around her living room. The mahogany coffin was balanced neatly on her coffee table. Two more coffins stood propped up against the wall at either end of the brown leather sofa. She draped a fluffy blanket over the corner of the sofa to hide the ripped leather where the cat liked to scratch. Since he was already confined safely upstairs, she opened the lid of the Deluxe Model Solid Oak Eternity Casket to show off the shiny silver PermaLoft quilted lining.

Glancing approvingly at the living room one last time, she gave her dining room another quick check. A stark white coffin glistened against the wall where she usually stashed her half-completed projects. The coffin was almost the same finish as her kitchen cupboards (different handles, of course), and another casket with a clear black lacquered finish stood beside it. She tilted her head to one side, then nodded in approval. The contrast made for a touch of drama, and all the home décor sites said drama was important in the dining room. Memorial accessories were strategically positioned on the sideboard. The table displayed a carefully arranged assortment of cremation urns, hors d'oeuvres, small plates with napkins, and her best wineglasses. *Serve wine to relax your guests and help them enjoy your party! But not hard liquor! Remember, hard drinks create hard customers! (Page 4)* Her order pad and credit card reader were sitting, ready for action, on the hall table.

Everything was perfect.

Krystal ran lightly up the stairs to do her makeup and change into her new red silk dress. *Create excitement in your party environment! Remember, red is a selling color! (Page 9)* "A touch of class results in cash," she chanted softly while she swiped mascara onto her lashes, then looked critically at the result. She smiled, finding a bit of lipstick on a front tooth and rubbing it off with an index finger. Better. Moving to a bigger mirror, she twisted from side to side, checking her reflection. Would you buy a coffin from this woman? She practised a reassuring smile and admired herself for another moment, then swept downstairs. She'd just started pouring the wine when her first guest arrived.

The only sure things are death and taxes! (EverRest Manual for Success, Page 2)

KRYSTAL SAT ON HER LEATHER sofa, high-heeled shoes askew on the carpet. Her feet were propped up on the mahogany casket, and she swirled a half-empty glass of shiraz in her left hand. In her right hand was her order pad with four—four!—orders from tonight's party. There had been a slightly disappointing preference for cremation urns, which generated far less money than the caskets, but she had sold the white lacquered coffin to elderly Mrs. Baker from next door.

"Oh, I just love that one!" Krystal had said when Mrs. Baker asked about it. "It's almost the same as my kitchen cupboards!"

Mrs. Baker had helped herself to more wine and said, "My cupboards are maple. That's why I'm buying this model. The last thing I want is to spend eternity in a box that looks like my kitchen. It would be like going into the afterlife to wash dishes. This one," she arched an eyebrow, "looks more like my boudoir. That sounds like much more fun."

Krystal had smiled and put through the sale. Now, as she admired her order pad, she tallied up the total for the night's sales. With the coffin, three cremation urns, two memorial albums, and five key codes to download copies of dignified but upbeat musical selections, she'd managed to sell a total of $7,842.58. Just a few more parties until she would be able to quietly replace the $25,000 she'd taken from Madison's college fund to pay for the inventory. Maddie's dad always reconciled the accounts at the end of the month. If she replaced the money before then, no one would know she'd borrowed it. Once she started really making money at EverRest, she would be able to afford any college her daughter wanted.

She took another sip of her shiraz and decided to call her regional manager to share the good news. Leonard Hunter was about her age, in his mid-thirties, but he was already a big wheel in EverRest. He drove a very sexy red convertible painted with the EverRest logo on the doors. When he interviewed her at a local coffee shop for the job, he'd pointed the car out to her—not that it was inconspicuous—and told her it was his reward for having the best sales team last month. They'd met there again when she signed the contract to buy her start-up inventory.

Krystal checked her hair in her phone's camera before starting the video call. Her phone bleated a few times, then Len's face, with startling dark blue eyes fringed by thick black lashes, filled her screen. "Krystal! I was thinking of you tonight."

Her stomach swooped. "You were?"

"Of course. You had your first party, right? How did it go?"

She steadied herself. This was business. "Fabulous!" she crooned. "I sold over seven thousand dollars." She beamed at her phone.

"Okay," he said. "Well, that's a good start. I mean, not bad for your first one." Krystal felt her mood start to deflate like a leaky balloon. "But did you get any new recruits? Are any of your guests interested in joining the EverRest family?"

"Well, no." Leonard watched her silently with those remarkable blue eyes. Krystal waited, but the silence only grew. Had she not done well enough on her first party? "I mean, I only invited people who already have jobs, because they're the ones who can afford to buy stuff, right? So, they weren't looking for another job."

Tiny creases appeared between Len's well-groomed brows. "Krystal, this isn't just employment. It's an opportunity to free yourself from the confines of a nine-to-five grind. It's a choice to take control of your own destiny. If you don't offer that to people, you're stifling them. You're stifling yourself. You are the only one who can make your dreams a reality, Krystal. But to do that, you have to bring other people into the EverRest family.

"Besides," he added, "after four recruits, you become their manager and get a cut of their profits. And when they bring in new people, you get a cut of their cut too."

"Right, yes, of course. That would, um, certainly grow my own business faster."

"Much, much faster, Krystal. That is what you *must* do to grow your business."

"Yes, I understand." Krystal injected more brightness into her voice. "Well, but I did do fairly well tonight. For my first party and everything."

"Uh huh." Leonard looked away from the camera and held up a finger briefly, then looked back at her. "Okay, well let's think of this as a dress rehearsal. And you can always contact each of your guests as a follow-up and then talk to them about joining EverRest."

"Oh! Oh, yes, that's a good idea." Krystal flicked quickly through her guest list in her mind. She couldn't imagine any of her rather dull neighbours bringing the poise and sparkle that you'd need to be a successful EverRest representative. And really, wouldn't it be counterproductive to have more competition?

"Splendid!" Leonard's voice had an ending-the-call tone to it. She hastily interrupted before he could disconnect.

"Um, so once the sales go through, how long is it until I get my commission?"

"It's about two weeks to get everything processed."

Her eyebrows rose. "Two weeks?" Her pulse began to pound uncomfortably at the base of her throat. She took another sip of wine.

He smiled warmly. "Yes, as I say, the commissions are a nice bonus but what you really need to get some traction going is to build a network of representatives. As soon as you have four of them, there's a $25,000 bonus payment for you."

"That much?" That would replace the college fund. "Just four people?"

"Four people who purchase inventory collections, that's right. But you have to make sure they come into the company through you, Krystal. That's very important. You can't just refer them to EverRest, you must be on record as their recruiter. Just like I'm on record as yours. Do you see?"

Krystal stared at her shiraz. "I think so. So if I bring in four, I get a bonus. And . . . do you get a bonus then too?"

Leonard smiled, showing sharp white teeth. "You bet I do! Just like you will when your four recruits bring in recruits of their own. In fact, the higher up you get, the bigger your bonus."

"Right. Of course," murmured Krystal. "Okay then, thanks for clearing that up for me. Sorry to have bothered you."

"No bother, Krystal," purred Leonard. "I will always have time for my favourite recruit. I see great potential in you." He ended the call before she could respond.

Krystal drained the shiraz, drumming her fingers on the coffin on her coffee table. Then she took her empty wineglass into the dining room to see if there were any more open bottles that she could finish off.

The quality! You won't believe your eyes! (EverRest Manual for Success, Page 6)

MADISON STOOD AT THE ENTRY to the living room, her jaw slack. Her backpack slipped from her hands and landed with a thud on the floor. "Mom, what have you done?" She stepped into the room tentatively, as if she was barefoot on broken glass. Her gaze travelled from the mahogany casket on the coffee table to the deluxe oak one leaning against the wall, its lid now closed to protect the satin lining from the cat. It didn't seem to gleam quite as brightly in the daylight, Krystal thought.

"Are you going goth on me?" Her daughter's eyes were wide. "Or have you been reading too many vampire romance novels?"

Krystal forced a laugh. "Don't be silly, Maddie. This is my new business. I'm an EverRest representative now."

Maddie tightened her ponytail, her face drawn into a suspicious frown. "You're a what? And why is all this creepy stuff in our house?"

"An EverRest representative. I'm taking control of my financial destiny," Krystal said, raising her chin. "And it's not 'creepy stuff.' These are premier quality furnishings for first class memorial services."

"If this is first class, I'll fly economy," muttered Madison. "This is literally the weirdest thing you've ever done, Mom. And you've already set the bar pretty high for that." Krystal thought that was unfair. She was not boring and predictable, like Maddie's dad, but that did not make her weird. She was . . . creative.

"Sweetheart, this is going to be a whole new chapter for us. You know how you've been thinking about going to college in California? I'm going to be able to make enough money so that we can afford it. And get you a new computer. And if I make enough sales, they'll even give me a convertible. What do you think of that?"

Madison folded her arms. "A convertible? What do you have to do for that, a little graverobbing?" She peered around the corner to the dining room, where Mrs. Baker's white enamelled coffin still stood beside its glossy black counterpart. "Mom, this is too freaky. I am not living in a funeral parlour." She stuffed her hands into the pockets of her jeans. "And I don't need to go to that college. It was just, I dunno, a fantasy. If I can earn a scholarship, that's great. If I can't, it doesn't matter. I'll go to school here. It's fine."

Krystal's lips tightened. She threw her arms around Maddie, rocking her from side to side. "No baby, it's not fine. I want you to have the very best. I'm going to make that happen for you." She felt her daughter stiffen and shake her head.

"Mom, seriously, I literally don't care. But no way is this stuff staying here in the house. Can we at least move it out to the garage? Please?" Maddie pulled back to look at Krystal, her face imploring. "I can not have any of my friends over while this stuff is here. It's too weird."

Krystal pulled her back into a hug. "Okay. Give me a hand and we'll carry everything out there. But you'll see, it will all work out. Here, let's start with the deluxe oak. Be careful now, this one is top of the line." Her admonishment was met with an eye roll, but Madison moved forward, her face in a moue of distaste, to grasp one of the brass handles on the coffin.

Between them, they lowered the casket close to the rug and maneuvered it slowly around the furniture in the living room. "Careful!" called Krystal. "We don't want to scratch it. I wonder whether we should have started with one of the less expensive models. Maybe we should set it down."

Madison huffed impatiently, raising her end of the coffin so it wouldn't knock over an end table. "No, let's finish this one first. How many of these are there, anyway?" She edged it around a corner, walking backward, and stopped at the front door. "Wait a sec, I don't want to bang my knuckles."

"Is it too wide?" Krystal tried to recall how the delivery men had carried the caskets into the house. She'd been so excited, she hadn't really been paying attention. "Let's turn it sideways so the handles are on the top.

Careful! Don't let the lid fall open!" Madison rolled her eyes again but followed her mother's lead in rotating the coffin and began stepping down the concrete stairs.

Krystal followed at the top of the stairs, an ornate brass handle grasped with both hands. The casket hung down sideways from the row of handles, swinging slightly as they moved in sync down each step. "Okay, now if we hold it like this, we should be able to—" She was interrupted by a loud screech as the weight of the coffin pulled away from the handle's screws. She watched as the Deluxe Model Solid Oak Eternity Casket with PermaLoft silver satin cushioning fell away from her in slow motion and shattered on the concrete steps outside her front door.

Krystal stood near the top step, the ornately curved brass handle still clutched in both hands. She looked in horror at the splintered remains. Madison, her eyes round, let go of her end. The disjointed wood and satin teetered for a moment, then slid down the rest of the concrete steps like an unbalanced toboggan and shot down the walk, coming to rest at the base of a large red rosebush. A thin branch snapped and flopped down across the remains of the coffin, scattering it with scarlet petals.

"No! No, no, no!" cried Krystal.

Madison's face tightened. "I didn't do anything! It fell! It was already broken!"

Krystal ran down the steps past her daughter and crouched by the shrub. She lifted a piece of the coffin. Staples showed where it was still attached to its silver satin lining. "It's ruined," she whispered.

Madison squatted beside her. "Mom? I'm sorry. It was my fault. I shouldn't have said we had to move them." Silence stretched out between them. "Mom?" Her voice caught.

Krystal seized her daughter's hand and raised it to her lips to kiss it quickly. "Don't be silly. It's not your fault. Not at all." She made a wry face. "And I'm sorry I shouted. I was . . . stressed. I need to sell these." She tried hard to smile. "Not this one, though."

Madison gulped and nodded. "Nope, not this one," she said, a little too heartily. "What should we do with it?"

Her mother sighed. "Good question. Firewood? Jigsaw puzzle?" She lifted two pieces of the demolished casket, twisting them in the air as if trying to piece them together. Her hands stilled. "What the f—um, fudge?" She turned the pieces over. "Maddie, look at this."

"What?"

"This wood. This deluxe premier quality solid oak freakin' coffin. Look!" She flipped the two pieces back and forth. The flat surfaces showed a pattern of oak, considerably duller and more scratched than when it had been on display in her living room. At the ragged edges of the break, she saw crisscrossing layers of wood. "That's plywood. That's freakin' plywood with an oak veneer!" She flipped them over again, hardly able to believe what she was seeing.

"What do you mean?"

"I mean this extremely expensive top-quality casket is made of plywood with a picture of oak glued to the outside. It's a fake. It's all fake. And I paid $25,000 for all this stuff."

Madison laughed. "Mom, come on. Where did you get $25,000? You didn't really, did you?" Her words slowed. "Mom? Where did you get that money?"

Krystal's mouth worked soundlessly for a moment, then she dusted off her hands and seized her daughter in a quick hug. "Don't be silly, Maddie, you know we don't have that kind of money. I meant that the inventory was *valued* at $25,000. You know, for insurance purposes. For goodness' sake, as if I'd spend that much money on anything," she scolded. Madison relaxed and hugged her back.

"Now," Krystal continued, "why don't you help me finish hauling these pieces around back to the garage? They're not doing a thing for our front garden. Then we'll carry out the rest of them, *not* sideways. And then let's have some ice cream for all our hard work, all right?" Madison smiled and stood up, dragging the remains of the casket across the lawn toward the small freestanding garage that stood in the back yard.

Krystal waved at her encouragingly and bent to gather up fragments of the broken coffin from her garden bed. For just a moment, she let a wave of panic rise through her chest before firmly pushing it back down. Shaking out her arms and taking a deep breath, she pasted a smile on her face and followed her daughter with an armload of splintered plywood, ripped satin, and torn fragments of a picture of oak.

* * *

Take control of your money and your life the EverRest way! (EverRest Manual for Success, Page 2)

TWO WEEKS LATER, KRYSTAL'S GARAGE still held four caskets, seven cremation urns and an assortment of black-edged cake toppers, thank-you cards, and black balloons that she hadn't been able to sell. Despite the advice on page 7, *Everyone you meet will need EverRest products!*, she hadn't been able to gather enough people to host a second party. No one she met seemed interested in hosting one either, not even when she told them they could get valuable discounts and win exciting prizes.

Her phone pinged with daily reminders from Len. "Got any recruits?" followed by dollar signs and smiley emojis. Any day now the message would be from Dan, demanding to know what had happened to the money in Maddie's college fund.

The red silk dress hung limply in her closet. She had tried to take it back to the store, but the clerk had noticed the small wine stain on the bodice. Never had such a vibrant colour made her feel so miserable.

It was precisely thirteen days since she'd had a full night's sleep.

Krystal backed her aging Mustang out of the garage and drove Maddie to Dan's house for the weekend. While dropping her off, she asked if he had any propane tanks she could borrow. "I'm having a small barbecue this weekend," she explained, "and I kind of forgot to fill my tank. Actually, it looks rusty and I'm not sure it's safe. Do you mind?"

He had two full tanks (of course he did, no one was more reliable than Dan. It's one of the reasons the marriage didn't work out) and was happy to share them. Krystal drove the tanks home and lugged them into the detached garage, stashing them against a wall near the caskets. After moving her car out to the street, she hoisted up her old propane tank, which was heavy with fuel, and fastened it to the rickety gas grill. The burner tubes were rusted through in places, and it looked like spiders had been making nests in the jagged metal gaps. Satisfied, she wheeled the whole assembly across her yard and pushed it up tight outside the garage against the wall.

She called Leonard. "Hey there! I've got some good news for you."

"I love good news. What's up?"

"I think I've got my four new reps. Isn't that great?"

She could hear his intake of breath. "Really? All four? Are they ready to sign?"

"Well, that's just it." While they talked, she lined up her stash of canned cocktails, comparing their alcohol contents. "I think they're all really close, but I want to make sure I get this right. I was hoping you might be able to give me some advice. Since, you know, this will give both of us quite a boost."

"Absolutely. What do you want to know?"

"Gosh, there's so much to think about. Do you think you'd be able to maybe come around? I thought I'd put some steaks on the grill tonight to celebrate. Maybe you could join me, and we could go over how to wrap up the new reps?" She smiled coolly as he accepted and went to the kitchen to marinate two steaks that she couldn't afford in brandy and oil. Lots and lots of brandy and oil.

Krystal waved the EverRest convertible into the garage when Leonard arrived. "This sun is so hot!" she said. "Your beautiful paint job is going to fade, and there's loads of space. The grill's over here in the shade, nice and cool. How about a drink?"

She opened a cooler and brought out the canned drinks with the highest kick, which she set out with a plate of salty snacks. Leonard cracked open his can and raised it in a toast to her new recruits. She sipped cautiously from her own drink while watching his disappear, then smoothly refreshed it with another open cocktail. Finally she brought out the raw steaks, still submerged in a heavy glass casserole dish full of marinade, and set the dish on a table. She'd loaded the dish full of mushrooms, peppers, and onions in addition to the meat. It was a nice job; you could hardly see the marinade. She opened the gas lines to maximum and flicked at the ignition button. "That's funny," she said. "It doesn't seem to be lighting. Do you know how these things work?"

Leonard set down his can and peered into the gas grill. "Smells like it's working," he said. "Is there a spark when you push the button?" He pressed the ignition and the grill flared to life with a loud *whoomp*. "Whoa!" He stepped back, laughing. "That was close!"

Krystal smiled. "Thanks, Len. We'd better get these steaks and veggies started. Would you mind?" She handed him the heavy casserole dish and a short pair of tongs. "I really need to water these petunias. Oh hi, Mrs. Baker!" she called across the fence.

"Hello, dear. Having a barbecue, are you? Ooh, with a man. He looks rather yummy."

Krystal lowered her voice confidingly. "Actually, he's my boss. We were supposed to be having a business meeting but between you and me, I think he's had too much to drink. And of course he wants to take charge of the grill."

Mrs. Baker winked at her. "I think he's cute. Maybe that grill won't be the only thing that gets hot tonight. Good luck, dear." She wandered back toward her lawn swing. Krystal picked up the end of her garden hose and turned the water on. The hose was aimed at her flower bed, but her eyes were locked onto the leaky gas grill.

Leonard balanced the unwieldy dish in his left hand and tried to pick out a mushroom with the flimsy tongs. He frowned in concentration. Brandy and cooking oil dripped from the first mushroom as he lifted it clumsily from the marinade and held it over the open flame. The drips flared as each one landed in the grill, and he jerked his hand back. "You got any better tongs?"

She shrugged. "Sorry, no. Hey, why don't you just tip the dish over the grill and let everything slide out? It's the EverRest way, Len. If you're gonna do something, do it big." She cranked up her smile to full wattage, as if she was working on a sale.

Grinning in return, Len lifted the heavy casserole dish over the cracked burners and tipped it to pour the contents onto the grill. Flames shot up through the brandy and oil. "Holy crap!" he cried, stumbling backward as the fire overtook the top of the barbeque.

"Here, Len! Put the fire out!" She handed the streaming garden hose to him. Leonard aimed the hose at the grease fire and blasted the flaming oil up the garage wall, engulfing it. The roof caught next. It took all of two minutes for the extra propane tanks to blow. A black-rimmed thank-you card floated gently across the back yard and landed in the damp petunia bed, where one edge of it smoked daintily.

"My EverRest convertible." Leonard stumbled further back, tripped over the hose, and sat down hard on the grass.

"You had insurance for it, right?"

Leonard shook his head miserably. "It's the company's car. They let you use it if you've got the month's top recruits. I didn't think I'd need insurance."

"Oh, that's too bad. My ex, Dan, he was always really careful about things like that. He got me to insure everything at our house. I still do. Good thing we're covered for fire. This is such a terrible accident."

The flames roared through the garage. Krystal imagined she could hear the distinct sound of the plywood coffins crackling as emergency sirens came nearer. Mrs. Baker, who had seen the whole thing (or enough of it to be a witness), stood in her own yard. Her paperback romance novel lay on her lawn, its pages slowly rolling closed. She was staring, mouth slightly open, at the flaming structure as the first fire truck arrived.

Krystal smiled. She still loved fire engine red.

TRAILBLAZER

SALLY MILLIKEN

"THOSE MEN ON THE DATING apps are all duds. Why would anyone look for a partner there? All they want is sex." I sighed.

"People do it for a reason, Brie. And I would have thought you'd have an open mind by now." My friend and co-worker Cathy was perpetually trying to help. She was happily married with a kid and fretted about me as badly as a mother hen: albeit a badass hen that looks like Meryl Streep in *The Devil Wears Prada.* She'd grabbed my phone as soon as I mentioned I'd joined a new dating app. "And it reflects a certain optimism. You would benefit from stepping out of your comfort zone too, you know."

I grimaced. Cathy had both hands on my phone now. I wouldn't have it back for a while.

"What about this one? He has potential." She glanced at me to make sure I was listening. "Thirty-five years old, clean-cut. Says his trail name is Trailblazer. In his bio it says, 'Mountain man ready for our next adventure.' I'm telling you, he has potential."

"Maybe . . ." I'd scrolled through too many potential profiles to have any such optimism. I pushed my shaggy brown bangs out of my eyes—I'd spent the last month growing them out after a rash decision to cut them— and took a bite of my hummus and lettuce sandwich.

Cathy and I were taking a break in the company cafeteria of our Chelsea office, across the Mystic River from Boston. Most days we ate at our desks, swapping jibes over our shared cubicle wall, but at least once a week, we tried to eat lunch together.

"You can do this," she said. "Ignore the negative voice in your head." She opened her well-used Tupperware container and began to dress her salad. "Don't roll your eyes. You have to have patience. All you do is flit from man to man. It may take more than one date to get to know a person."

I shrugged. "One date is usually enough. Sometimes it only takes thirty seconds."

"Well, this one fits the profile you're looking for. He loves to hike. It says here that he's done the AT. Why anyone would want to hike from Georgia to Maine is beyond me, but at least you know he'd have some interesting stories to tell." She grinned and waggled her eyebrows at me. "And he'd be very fit." She swiped at the screen. "He's good looking too. Here . . ." She held the phone out for me to see.

I squinted at the screen. "Do you think that's really his photo? He's too handsome."

"Brie, take a risk." She poked her salad fork toward me. "All you do is work anyway. Who knows? Maybe you'll have some fun."

"I like my work." I sipped my hot tea, grimaced at the bitter taste, and stirred in a spoonful of honey. "And you know the hours we have to put in to climb the ladder. It's all part of my five-year plan."

She'd returned to scrolling. "He's perfect. Just what you're looking for." She slid my phone toward me across the table. "Contact him. Now."

I sighed and tightened my ponytail. My straight hair was perpetually slipping out of its elastic. "Fine. Fine." I supposed Cathy was right. He was out there, somewhere. Maybe even here and now.

Without overthinking my decision, I texted a response to his dating app post: *Hi Trailblazer, I'm B. Heart.*

He answered immediately: *Hi! B. You can call me TB, like Tom Brady, the GOAT.*

Off to a rocky start. I'm more of a Bruins fan, but I shrugged it off, knowing New Englanders are passionate about their Pats. I didn't follow the team much but knew enough that it hadn't been the same since TB, TB12 that is, left the team.

And, hey, at least he replied. Nine times out of ten, or rather, ninety-nine out of a hundred, they didn't. I texted back: *K, TB. Great to meet you. I'm more of a hockey fan myself.*

What else? After thinking for a moment, my eyes landed on my messenger bag and my current read—a Stephen King novel—tucked in the outside pocket. I added a question, my thumbs flying over the keys: *Favorite books . . . fiction or nonfiction?*

TB: *Nonfiction. Preference for hiking stories. You?*

Me: *I'm reading one of King's classic horror stories right now, but I usually lean toward true crime. Favorite movie?*

TB: *Hiking documentaries, or films based on true stories.* A Walk in the Woods *especially. You?*

Me: *Haven't seen it.*

TB: *Not yet anyway.*

I blushed with unexpected pleasure. What else did I want to know about him? And what else should I reveal about me?

MONDAY MORNING ROLLED AROUND FAR too soon, as was usually the case. Cathy was at her desk when I arrived, her blue blazer already covering the back of her chair. She looked like she'd been there for a while. I don't know why she gave me such a hard time for working too much; her ambition matched mine. She peered over the cubicle wall as I dropped my bag and sat in the chair in front of my computer.

"How was your weekend?" she asked.

I shrugged. I'd had quite the breakthrough, but didn't want her to get carried away.

She lifted an eyebrow. "Soooo, what happened?"

"We texted back and forth for hours."

"You and TB?" When I nodded, Cathy continued. "Sweet! A miracle!" She grinned.

"He's quite the catch," I smirked, as I brushed off a dog hair I'd missed removing from my dark pants that morning.

"TB, huh? What's his real name?"

"Tom. Tom Flynn."

"Let's check him out. Is he on social media?" I stood and leaned on the cubicle wall to watch her attack the keyboard in front of her.

"Go ahead. I already have. I couldn't find much under Tom Flynn, but he posted a lot of photos on Insta under his trail name. There are all kinds of shots of him on the AT."

"Can you imagine having a job that allows you to take that much time off? He must be good at what he does."

"His boss loves him. That's what he told me. And his job is flexible. He does some kind of tech work for *Outside Magazine*—their website and sales stuff—so he can work from anywhere. Sometimes he gets free gear to try out for his hikes. He said he's even pitched several story ideas to one of his writer friends."

"Impressive. What're you going to do?

"We connected." I grinned. "I gave him my number."

She squealed so loudly that Lenny, three cubicles over, popped up and scowled at her.

Holding my finger to my lips, I muttered, "Shhh. Jeeze." I waved at Lenny, but he'd already dropped out of sight.

She lowered her voice. "What happened?"

"We talked Saturday night. For over two hours. You were right. His stories were unbelievable. He said he grew up in Maine, spent his summers hiking Katahdin and the northern sections of the AT."

"Sounds promising."

"Mmmhmm. One time he came across another hiker in the Whites who'd collapsed on the trail. Gave the old guy mouth to mouth and chest compressions for an hour." At her furrowed brow, I added, "The Whites, the White Mountains up in New Hampshire."

"Ah." She leaned back in her chair and stretched her arms over her head. "So what happened?"

"Saved his life."

"No kidding," she chuckled. "You're blushing. Hang on, that isn't just from the phone call."

I grinned, so wide I showed her my teeth.

"No way!" Her eyes darted toward Lenny's desk, and she lowered her voice again. "You met up?" She held out her fist for a bump. "Where did you go?"

"A coffee shop. And not at a Starbucks, but a local place. He suggested it. Coffee House or something like that."

"How'd it go?"

"I don't know why I was so nervous. He was quite the charmer. Had me laughing within minutes. I think he's the one. Can't believe it. Cathy, after all this effort, I think he might actually be 'The One.'"

"Are you going out again?"

"Are you kidding? Of course. We've already made plans for dinner next Saturday night."

"Well, if he pays for dinner, I'd take that as a great sign." She clapped her hands. "We're on our way!"

AFTER A SATURDAY DINNER DATE at an upscale pizza place—where TB paid, Cathy would approve—TB invited me to join him on a hike up Mount Washington. Since I wanted to impress him, I couldn't say no, although it was ambitious for me. I liked to hike, but wasn't in the best shape after spending too much time in recent years at my desk.

The next morning, we met at the Pinkham Notch parking lot of the Appalachian Mountain Club. He'd said he didn't have a car, but he had gotten a ride from some Boston friends and was waiting for me on the porch of the visitor's center when I arrived.

I admired TB's well-worn North Face pack, and he told me that he'd carried it on his thru-hike, all the way to Katahdin from Georgia. His beat-up T-shirt and shorts looked like they must have been on the same trip, and perhaps back again. His boots were so scuffed they might have walked part of the way on their own. I appreciated that he wasn't a man with expensive new gear trying too hard to impress a woman.

I tightened my hiking boots and rechecked my extra gear, food, and water bottle, then threw on my yellow daypack. I knew that on the trails of the Presidential Range, it was important to be prepared. They don't refer to Mount Washington as 'Home of the World's Worst Weather' for no reason. I even had extra water and iodine tablets in case we ran out. I'd had the trots from giardia before and would never, ever, want to repeat that discomfort.

We started up the 4.1-mile Tuckerman Ravine Trail, walking in silence for the first quarter-mile or so, our boots on the trail and my breathing the only sounds filling my ears.

"Your friends don't mind that you're spending the day with me?" I asked, as we took our first break.

"Who? Oh, no, they're good." He smiled and waved a hand dismissively before perching his foot onto a rock to re-tie his bootlace. "I'll catch up with them later."

"What about your family? Are they still in Maine?" I drank from my plastic Nalgene bottle, the cool water quenching my thirst. My shirt was already damp with sweat.

"I'm an only child." He opened his pack, found his water bottle, and took a long drink. "I didn't want to say anything on our first date, but I lost both parents in a house fire when I was ten, and then lived with an aunt and uncle for a while." He wiped his mouth with the back of his hand and fiddled with the bottle cap. "When they retired to Florida, I moved in with my grandmother in Portland."

"That's tough." What a sad story. What to say? "How did you survive the fire?"

"I was at a friend's house." He wiped the sweat on his brow with a red bandana he'd pulled out of his pocket and sighed. "I . . . I recently returned from my Grammy's funeral. She died a few weeks ago." Tears filled his eyes. He swallowed and glanced at me.

I gently squeezed his arm and whispered, "I'm so very sorry for your loss."

TB blinked a few times and smiled sadly, saying a quiet, "Thank you."

I blew a puff of air. I shifted my day pack and tightened the waist strap. "Life is unfair, isn't it?" We had something else in common. I knew a little of what he was feeling. "My mother died when I was a teenager." After fighting for five years with everything she had, my mother died of breast cancer. All these years later, it still stings.

"It sure is." He shook his head. "Some are a lot luckier than others," he added before shooing away a fly buzzing around his ear.

We hiked mostly in silence until we reached the trail above the treeline, the place where the wind and weather made it too inhospitable for trees to grow. Now the views of the surrounding mountains opened up around us. We paused for a quick drink and gazed out across the adjacent peaks.

"The mountains are helping me to heal," he said, interrupting the silence.

"Mmmm. I can see how." Closing my eyes and lifting my head, I savored the warmth of the sun and the light breeze on my face. "There is much to gain from these hills."

The trail steepened, becoming even more rocky and difficult. I had to focus on every step. After a mile or so, during another break, I asked him more about himself.

"I'd like to hear more about your job. You must have just as many stories working for *Outside* as you do about the interesting characters you met while on the trail."

He only shifted his feet, laughed, and nodded.

"I love working in technology too." I dropped my pack on a rock and enjoyed a large sip of water from my plastic bottle. "My job enables me to meet people from all over the country, all from my desk chair. I love what I do, but in-person is better. I'm gunning for a promotion to work more closely with our clients."

"It's good to have goals," TB offered.

"It is, isn't it?" Everything was going so well. Maybe dating apps work after all. "In fact, I'm working on a project now, which should help. My bosses will be very pleased."

"That's exciting." He smiled warmly and drank from his own bottle. "What's the project?"

"I mentioned that my consulting firm analyzes data for other companies." He nodded. "Well, I recently landed a large client."

He raised his water bottle like a champagne glass, the plastic lid bouncing on its leash. "Congratulations."

"Thanks. I'm optimistic but you never know, especially since my firm is part of the old boys' club. It's harder to get ahead."

Finally, we reached the peak of Mount Washington and took refuge in the observatory. The building was a welcome sight, and my legs and feet needed a rest. Cathy was right: I had been sitting at my desk too much, working too hard.

I was glad I'd brought an extra jacket. Even though it was the middle of summer, the air was cold. As the highest point in the Northeast, there was not much to block the strong wind. We sat at a table in the sun, looking out a large window, captivated by the beauty of the view. I pulled out my gorp, and TB chuckled, as I carefully picked out the M&M's, my favorite, first.

I held the bag out to share with him. "Raisin?"

He swallowed a bite of PowerBar and laughed. "Gladly. They're the best part."

The day was going so well, I couldn't quite believe it. I was astonished at how compatible we were, like two sides of the same coin. He liked raisins *and* didn't steal my chocolate.

My legs felt like jelly on the way down the mountain. I needed to get in better physical shape if I wanted a promotion. TB hopped from rock to rock like a mountain goat. Apparently, he wasn't spending much time at his desk. I was envious.

"Do all your friends call you TB?" I asked, as we sat on the porch of the Hermit Lake caretaker cabin where we'd stopped near the bottom of Tuckerman Ravine to rest my legs. I was grateful that I didn't have blisters, but the steep rocky trail had taken its toll. My feet hurt.

"My hiking friends. Others call me Tom." He relaxed on the bench seat and took a swig of water. "Only my Grammy called me Flynn." He drank another large swallow. "Although I would be honored if you called me Flynn too. It would help me to remember her."

Wow. He said all the right things. I couldn't think of anything wrong with this man. Refreshed and thoughtful, I concentrated on my footing as we finished the last remaining miles back to the Pinkham Notch parking lot. He said his friends were waiting for him somewhere nearby, and he would join them later.

"What about next week? Want to try another hike?" he asked, as I packed up my car for the journey home. "I'm heading out to summit Monadnock."

"Unfortunately, I have plans next weekend." Everything was happening so fast. We were really connecting, but I didn't want to rush things; history and experience had taught me that much.

* * *

THE NEXT WEEK WAS A busy one at work. Flynn and I continued our phone conversations, and he texted me several photos of himself hiking. He forwarded a photo of his grandmother too. Grammy was standing in a kitchen, holding what looked like an apple pie. She was the picture of a sweet old lady, the kind of person anyone would want for a grandmother.

Over the weekend, Flynn texted me a few selfies from Monadnock with the distinctive open granite peak behind him. He looked at home and in his element, at one with the mountain. His wide smile, his five o'clock shadow, his slightly mussed hair from the wind—or maybe his fingers raking through it—all had me kicking myself for not having gone too.

The next week, we made plans to see each other again. I couldn't wait. This time, the parking area for Mount Moosilauke, a mountain in New Hampshire partially owned by Dartmouth College, was our meeting place.

He gave me a quick hug as a greeting. "I brought you something," he said and held out a small box.

I felt myself blush. "You did?"

"I bought this as a keepsake of our first hiking date." The box held a mug from the Pinkham Notch Visitor Center store. "I have one too. When you drink your tea in the morning, think of me."

I cleared my throat and returned the hug. "You remembered." I'd put 'avid tea drinker' in my online dating profile. "Thank you."

He grinned, enjoying my surprise. "I'm happy you could hike today. When I went to Dartmouth, I used to come here a lot with the Outing Club."

After gently placing the mug on the front seat of my car, I was ready for our second hike. Throwing on our daypacks, we began the walk up the dirt road past the Moosilauke Ravine Lodge on our way toward the Ridge Trail. *Dartmouth? He went to an Ivy League School? Could this guy be any more perfect?* He seemed too good to be true.

ONCE AGAIN, ANOTHER MONDAY MORNING, and I was back at my desk at work. Flynn had met me earlier to borrow my car, and I took a bus to the office.

I texted him at 11:00: *How'd the meeting go?*

By 2:00 in the afternoon, I still hadn't heard back from him and my concern was growing. I texted Flynn again: *Everything okay?*

I tried again five minutes later: *Where are you?*

No response. I tried again: *Where are you? You said you'd be back by now.*

He finally responded: *I'm at the bank. Waiting for the manager.*

I inhaled and let out a huge sigh, but then I remembered his meeting was at 9:00.

Cathy returned from the conference room and must have seen the puzzled look on my face as she entered her cubicle. I was staring at my phone, hoping he'd text again.

"Uh, oh. What happened?"

"TB—Flynn—borrowed Christine this morning."

"Your car?" When I nodded, she continued. "Did he say for what?"

"He said he had to drive to a bank in Portland for a meeting, something related to his grandmother's death. Apparently, she left him some money. This weekend we talked about some of the hiking equipment he wanted to buy with it. He was very excited."

Cathy avoided my gaze. "Do you believe him?"

"I want to. Most people would. Until I noticed—check this out." I grabbed the handle of my messenger bag to pick it up off the floor. I dug through the contents for the wallet. Flipping to the credit card slots, I held it open for her to see.

She groaned. "One is missing?"

"Yup," I said, roughly pushing the bangs away from my face, and sighed again. "I thought maybe he'd surprise me, that he was different. I should know better by now."

"You left your wallet out?"

"He must have taken it while I was in the bathroom, when I asked him to watch my bag."

"How long has it been since you've heard from him?"

"You don't think—"

"Brie, how long?"

"Except for one brief text . . ." I looked at my wristwatch. "Over seven hours."

"Why'd you wait so long? You should have reported it hours ago."

"I just wanted to see what he'd do."

"Do you think—" Cathy's lips began to twitch.

My phone chimed with an alert notification. I glanced at it and then showed her the screen. The company credit card displayed multiple charges totaling over $50,000, all in my name.

I looked at Cathy, and then I grinned.

"He took the bait." I scanned the charges. "My, he's a fast worker."

"Ha! Well done, Brie!" She pumped a fist into the air. "I knew you could do it. How many does that make?"

I checked the bulletin board hanging on the cubicle wall; there were ten photos tacked on it, each a different mugshot. "He's the eleventh."

Cathy pointed to the ceiling. "The brass upstairs will be pleased."

With the smile lingering on my lips, I texted Flynn again: *It's interesting that you said that you worked at* Outside Magazine. *Quite the coincidence.*

This cryptic message must have gotten his attention because he suddenly replied: *Gotta go, bank manager just arrived.*

Immediately, I added: *Because it was in* Outside *that I read an article about a man posing as a hiker who stole from other hikers. Female hikers. Like me.*

I pushed a button on my keyboard to wake my computer screen. I typed in a password code and a small dot appeared on a map on my screen. It was moving. I scanned out to see where the car was currently located. "Tsk, tsk, Flynn," I mumbled. "Where are you going?"

Christine was heading west, hours away and nowhere near Portland.

I pulled a steering wheel out from under my desk. The unattached wheel, or as I referred to her, Christine2, was a clone except that it was attached to a console. Some might think it looked odd outside a car, but I'd driven her almost as much as the original, so I didn't think twice about it anymore. I plugged the duplicate into my computer, and then added a gas pedal, or, in my case, since my car was electric, an accelerator, and placed it on the floor, followed by a second pedal, a brake.

"Cathy, could you tell me the closest State Police barracks on Route 2 near North Adams?"

"Yes, of course." I heard keys clicking as her fingers hit the keyboard.

"It's south of Adams, in the town of Cheshire, on Route 8. Shall I give them an update too?"

"Thank you." I typed in the coordinates and flipped a switch so that a display of moving images filled my screen, as if I were seated in the car itself.

"Are you ready already?" Cathy jumped up and entered my cubicle, nearly clapping her hands with glee. "Ooooh, can I watch?"

I grinned and flipped another switch. "Absolutely, you helped identify him. You deserve part of the credit. In fact, do you want to drive? You could use the practice anyway, and I have several more messages to send. One should NEVER text and drive."

Cathy snorted and sat in my chair, taking hold of the steering wheel, now resting in front of my computer monitor, and placed her foot over the accelerator.

I typed: *Do you know what she did after he was arrested?*

He texted in return: *On my way back.*

I still did not expect him to answer my questions. Not yet. He wouldn't have realized how bad things were. I almost felt sorry for him. The fun hadn't even started for me, though, and I shivered with delight.

I answered my own question and texted: *After he was arrested for stealing her car and robbing her, she found his password for his Facebook page. She posted photos of him in an orange jumpsuit. It was not his best look.*

His response: *I'll be back in a few hours.*

I'd stopped believing his messages long ago. Christine was still moving west, away from where I was currently standing. I thoroughly relished the fact that I no longer had to keep up the pretense. Flynn was good. I could give him that much. Better than most of the others. I could see why some women would fall for his charm. None of the stories he'd told me were true, not about his parents, or his AT hike. Even the photo of his Grammy was copied from the internet. It had only taken me thirty seconds to find the same image, and another thirty to discover who she was for real. She was someone's Grammy, but not his.

My thumbs pressed the next message: *Do you want to know what I think?*

I didn't give him a chance to respond, adding immediately: *She let him off far too easy.*

"Ready?" I asked, and Cathy nodded. I reached next to her and flicked one last switch on the computer console. "Just take care not to bang up my car. Christine is very sensitive."

Cathy jerked the wheel, swerving a little. "What about the A-hole in it?"

I shrugged and said, "Eh," when I realized she couldn't see me. My thumbs went to work again: *Do you want to know what I'm going to do to you?*

I didn't expect a response. The reality of the situation had to be sinking in for him. I smirked. God, I loved my job.

I added: *You'll see.* And tossed the phone on my desk. I sipped tea from my new mug. It was perfect. I'd already added honey.

"Christine is very responsive," Cathy chortled and turned the wheel a hard left. "I'm remembering now why you named her after one of King's characters."

"She may not be a 1958 Plymouth *Fury* like in the book, but to the person trying to drive her," I snickered and added, "he would believe she was possessed."

I pictured the panic on Flynn's face as he turned the wheel and realized he could not steer the car or control the speed. I opened my desk drawer and pulled out my gun and my badge. The computer screen provided a view of the moving cars, trees, and street signs as Christine passed them. Flynn was trapped, completely under our control now.

I patted Cathy on the shoulder. "Great driving."

Next time, I'm also installing a camera inside the car, so I can watch.

CAPONE'S CHAIR

WRONA GALL

NONA SMOOTHED THE RED-CHECKERED APRON over her ample hips. She was looking forward to moving into Labella Active Living, where her best friend now lived. Angie raved the home had Chicago's best dining service, offering three delicious meals, and morning and evening snacks every day. Nona would never have to wash another dish for the rest of her life.

For fifty-seven years now she'd made her home on Taylor Street, the best Italian neighborhood in the city from foods to friends to family, and her living room showed it. She'd have to get rid of a lot to fit into her room at Labella. She grabbed a box for her Rat Pack collection, then decided Frank, Dino, and Sammy could wait till she called Angie. Some guy bought her entire collection of family antiques, and Nona intended to call him too. Now she figured he could save her some trouble and pack up her stuff as well as paying for it. All she needed was his phone number.

Settling in with a cup of coffee and Nutella toast—Angie did like to talk—Nona asked about the guy.

"Guido Acari is his name." Angie rattled off his number, then kept talking as Nona wrote it down. "He's wonderful. When I realized Social Security wouldn't finance my online poker games and bi-weekly deliveries of Prosecco, I asked around. Maria Ciaglia—you know her, still does the same red dye job she used when she was a teenager with curls—told me about the guy who bought all her stuff when she moved in here. Just a second, my coffee's getting cold."

Slurping sounds came over the phone. "Anyway, he told me my mother's dining room set was positively beautiful. He said it's crazy that people think Victorian is old-fashioned now, and it's not worth what it used to be, but he'll store things until they get popular again. And he took everything. Swept the storage unit after, according to the manager. Check out his website. Cash for junk, all one word, dot com."

"Thank you, Angie. I don't think I care for him calling people's heirlooms junk, though."

"Anybody who gives me nine hundred bucks for all that old stuff can call it whatever they want."

"Maybe you're right."

The doorbell, followed by three knocks, interrupted their call. Her favorite and only grandson, Alfredo, had arrived.

"Gotta go, Angie." Nona opened the front door and grinned with delight. "You remembered."

"Of course, I remembered. You'd hit me upside the head if I forgot your creams."

"That'll be the day. I never even scolded you when you painted the living room with that Zombie mural."

"Hey, it'll bring big bucks one day."

"And for now, you get a kiss." She left a crimson smudge on his cheek, slipped a twenty-dollar bill into his pocket to pay for the candy, then accepted the box of Fannie Mae chocolates that he had balanced on a thick manila envelope.

Alfredo ran his hands through the luxurious black waves that haloed a face that could be printed on a Holy Card. Nona knew she'd be the envy of the home when he visited her. She winked at him. "I've decided everything goes. I'm going to buy all new stuff."

"No way. I thought you loved your furniture."

"I do, but I can always use the money. That's why I asked you to have the photos printed. I can make an album up and look at everything if I ever miss anything. And these things really won't go with the gray carpeting in my new apartment. I read HGTV when I get my hair done, and they say I need black and white furniture."

Alfredo's eyes widened. "Aren't you the slick city girl. I'd help, but I'm painting Louie Lucerna's living room for rent money this week. Who you gonna sell to?"

"Angie gave me the name of the man who just bought all her parents' furniture."

"Angie thinks anything male is wonderful. Let me ask around." He checked a text on his phone. "Gotta go. Louie's cat sat in my roller pan. Gotta get over there and get the turquoise out of his fur. The cat won't come out from under the bed. Really should have cleaned that up before I left. See you Monday for the big move."

"Here, I found some of my Holy Water for you. Blessed by Pope Francis himself."

"Nona, holding a bottle up in front of the TV when Francis says the Mass doesn't mean he blessed it."

"He made the sign of the Cross and that's good enough for me."

"No more selling on the internet. You could get arrested for fraud."

"Like anyone would believe a nice old lady like me ever scammed anyone in her whole life." She fluffed her white curls and flashed the smile people said reminded them of Mrs. Claus. She opened the shiny white box and inhaled the heavenly scent of milk chocolate creams. A quick scan convinced her the third candy in the top row had the largest swirl on top. She bit into the creamy lusciousness and savored every calorie.

"Would you like one before you leave?" She clutched the candy box an inch from her chest.

"No, all for you." Alfredo refused as always while she bit into a second cream. "I'll let myself out and check the lock before you remind me."

"You're a good boy. I'll see you Monday."

She lifted her cheek for another kiss, then sat down at her desk and typed *cashforjunk* into her computer. She wasn't going to wait for Alfredo to come up with another name, but he had a point about Angie. Better to do her own checking. Turned out Guido Acari was a member of the Antique Dealers Association of America Inc. and a member of the Better Business Bureau. He must be good. She dialed his number and made an appointment for three that afternoon. Then she ate another chocolate cream on her way to the kitchen to make lunch.

* * *

WHILE SHE WAITED FOR GUIDO to keep their appointment, Nona decided to look through some of his items for sale for a sneak preview of the money she could expect to make. There were five screens' worth of furniture. More reading than she wanted to do. She typed in antique dining room sets because that was her biggest item and was pleased only three photos appeared. She scrolled through the listings, then stopped and stared at a dark mahogany Victorian table with twelve chairs and a buffet with matching china cabinet.

Mary, mother of God. He was selling Angie's mother's pride and joy dining room set for an opening bid of $2,700. What happened to storing Angie's things until they got popular again? They seemed pretty popular to her with that opening bid. That bum Guido had stolen all Angie's furniture for a measly nine hundred.

She was dialing Angie's number when the front bell rang. She shut off her phone and computer, then slippered to the front door. Nona threw open her front door to see a Sumo-sized, bug-eyed cretin bulging out of a sharkskin suit. "I'm Guido Acari. You're Mrs. Ponticelli?"

With a huge effort, Nona pasted a welcoming grin on her face and invited him in.

GUIDO'S EYES SIZED UP EVERY stick of furniture. Cherry wood dining set. Four armchairs and six side chairs. Huge sideboard with enough Mikasa dinnerware to host a neighborhood party. The coffee and end tables were spotless, and the gold damask couch would be an easy sell. A rocker and chaise longue were jewels. Probably worth nine to ten retail, so he'd offer her fifteen hundred. Moving around the walls, he examined the photos. He lingered over one of a white-suited man sitting on a chair with carved lion heads and claw feet. The gentleman wore a white fedora, had dark hair and squinty eyes in a fleshy face, and held up a pocket watch that looked like it was encrusted with diamonds. "Is that the same chair over there?" Guido pointed across the room.

The old lady nodded. "That's it."

"Nice chair. How much do you want for it?"

"I'm selling everything for eleven thousand."

"You're dreaming." Just his luck, an old broad who knew her stuff. "I can do fifteen hundred tops. And that includes the pictures."

AFTER HEARING GUIDO'S OFFER, NONA hissed Italian words that would have made her grandson blush. "Ten thousand but no photos."

Guido rocked back and forth on his pointy black shoes. "I like that chair. Might even give it to my pop."

"What a nice son you are. I still want ten thousand." Nona gave him the look she lasered at the crows when they pecked her tomatoes.

"You may want ten, but I don't buy retail, and I don't have that much to spend. Will you give me a discount for cash?"

"I only take cash." She glanced at the clock. She had plans to watch Judge Judy over some warmed-up mostaccioli left over from lunch. Plus, this guy was starting to annoy her. "I'll take $9500 in cash if you pack everything and move it out now."

"Who carries that kind of money?"

"True. Today you're crazy to carry a hundred. You can Venmo. We learned about that at Bingo last week, so we don't get mugged."

"I can't Venmo that much."

"Then we drive over to the Taylor Street Branch of the Old Second National Bank. They know me there. They'll take care of everything."

Guido glowered. "That includes all the photos?"

"All the photographs. I'll drive with you to the bank. It's only four blocks away." Nona locked the front door, then made it into the cab of the truck with arm boosts from Guido. She stretched the seat belt to cover her red flowered dress.

On the way, Nona made a call. As they approached the Taylor Street branch, a young man was waving a silver Ford Bronco away from the curb a few spaces from the bank's front door. He grinned at Nona, then yelled, "Frankie said he didn't mind moving his truck for you."

Nona waved at her neighbor's son and sat until Guido figured out she was waiting for him to open her door. She lumbered out and led the way inside the bank where she got her favorite teller, Maria—her nephew's wife—to handle the money transfer. She then took a seat on a chair by the counter and waited until Maria confirmed the money transfer to Nona's account.

This time Guido led the way out of the bank, and they returned to Nona's house. She let them in, then pulled a gray folding chair in front of the TV and squirmed until she felt comfortable. "You can load now. Don't block the screen."

"I'll be right back." Guido jogged out to his truck and came back with furniture blankets, a dolly, and two guys that matched his physique. She welcomed them into her home. They kept their eyes focused on the floor and lifted three chairs each like they were made of cardboard. By the time Judge Judy ended, they had sweated through their polyester bowling shirts and emptied the rooms.

"Mrs. Ponticelli, we're all done. You got quite a deal."

Nona smiled her Mona Lisa smile as she bustled to the front door. "Of course, I did. Gray hair doesn't mean a feeble brain. I want to eat now. Goodbye."

GUIDO LAUGHED LIKE A HYENA while he drove east toward Halsted Street. The old broad thought she'd put one over on him. Little did she know that he and every dealer in Chicago had drooled over the Al Capone auction last November. Memorabilia brought thousands over their estimated value. Hell, that watch went for $84K. Having the photo of Big Al sitting in that lion-headed armchair was worth a fortune with establishing provenance. And if anyone questioned its authenticity, he'd sic them on the old lady. He had her address.

NONA GRINNED WHILE SHE LOCKED the door and returned to the living room. After warming up her pasta, she filled a glass of wine and called her grandson. "Alfredo, I forgot to thank you for the photos. They were just what I needed."

"Anything for you, Nona. I know why you wanted the copies, but why did you want me to Photoshop Big Al into grandpop's chair holding that knock-off watch?"

"It'll be a laugh at the home. The girls will love it." She didn't add that it got her triple what her furniture was worth. "I'll even have money to share with Angie."

"You owe Angie money?"

"No, it's a long story. I'll tell you about it one day."

PLAYING IT AGAIN

M. R. DIMOND

THERE'S NOTHING MORE GLORIOUS THAN waking to find a naked blonde in your bed.

I yawned as New Orleans' hazy morning light coaxed my eyes open to appreciate the sight. With her golden hair glinting across her face, she remained in the arms of Morpheus—also mine.

I'm not that kind of detective; she wasn't some random blonde bribed to my bed by liquor and worse, but my own beloved Heavenly, my second and (I hoped) last love. Today she'd board a train for California and leave me alone to wallow in the world's best wallowing city until I could join her.

I lay perfectly still, mentally caressing each feature, every pale freckle, while silently cursing the morning noises that might disturb her slumber. She slept through the clink of early morning milk bottles and the rumble of the bread van, but the whine and static from the Philco tabletop radio downstairs was too much.

As Nat King Cole crooned his latest, Heavenly's dainty lashes flickered open to reveal her tawny eyes full of dancing bronze flecks. Her lips curved as she realized where she was—maybe even with whom.

"Lou," she murmured, settling it.

The comedy of two women getting dressed in a closet-sized bedroom mixed with the tragedy of our upcoming separation was bittersweet and memorable. Heavenly asked me to hook her bra. I reached around to cup a breast in each hand and rested my head on her shoulder, inhaling the scents of Chanel, rose soap, and lovers' sweat. All that moved in the room were sheer curtains in the spring breeze and her nipples beneath my fingers.

After that timeless moment, the day blasted ahead like the trains at the L&N station. We clattered downstairs, and she dashed out the door while

Mam'selle Julie, the aging ballerina who was my landlady and employer, screeched, "You're almost late for class! Bad enough you're planning to leave me in the lurch. Now you can't be bothered to get out of bed on time? How can you leave New Orleans?"

It was a fair question, sufficiently answered by Heavenly's luscious form under her polka-dotted shirtwaist. As she glided across the street, I watched her through the lettering on the plate window: "*Les Trois Grâces Studio de Danse*" in florid script with "Lou Delacroix, Investigator" in sturdy serif letters, shoved into the lower corner as an afterthought.

As *Mam'selle* continued her contradictory criticism and aspiring tap dancers filtered in for my class, I flipped through my mail. An unexpected letter on thick, ivory letterhead caught my attention, and its delicate pink enclosure altered the course of my day.

As soon as my morning class ended, I changed out of tap shoes and dodged the lingering students. I made my way across town as fast as the streetcar system could whisk me through the tangled web of bars and Katz & Besthoff drugstores.

New Orleans was as familiar to me as the pockmarks on my face. Its post-war incarnation was a mix of new and old. A major port, New Orleans found prosperity during the recent war that it hadn't seen since the Great Crash. Now, gleaming new buildings were shooting · up amid the disapproving elegance of traditional brick and stucco. Artistic iron grillwork was giving way to metal and concrete. Piercing angles warred with decorative curlicues.

How would I get around Heavenly's city in California? Would I sit inside the house, immobilized by the lack of purple buildings and shared history? Or would I evolve into something new, like my new surroundings? For years, I thought that 1950 and my thirtieth birthday would be the dawn of important changes for me—maybe my final vows as a nun or head of my own nursing ward or clinic. Instead, that birthday would find me in Heavenly's arms on the West Coast, not something I imagined as I entered the 1940s and the convent, which had its own drastic changes for me.

Landrieux Law sat on the edge of town and combined the old and new of New Orleans. Originally a squat brick-and-stucco structure, it was now renewed in modern materials, slashing straight posts replacing the iron lace.

I stood for a moment admiring the building. The sun had burned away New Orleans' foggy morning hangover, and clusters of white gardenias released their candy-sweet scent in sensuous counterpoint to the fruity oleanders guarding the porch. Giant magnolias loomed nearby, their lemony fragrance just a promise of their next month's glory. Maybe they'd bloom before I left. I inhaled again before stepping into my past.

A RECEPTIONIST IN A PURPLE scarf greeted me as I opened the office door. The nameplate on her desk identified her as Vonnie Laviolette.

"I'm Detective Lou Delacroix. Mr. Landrieux sent for me." I held up the morning mail's ivory envelope, sans its contents, of course.

The receptionist frowned. Then she stood up and stuffed the day's mail into her shabby envelope bag. "We're closing now," she grumbled. "Saturday's a half day." She stepped away from her chair. "I'm going home," she called over her shoulder. "Your tea is ready and on my desk." She gave me a wide berth as she made for the door and left without another word.

A specimen of New Orleans manhood came out from the back office. He looked like he could have escaped from the silver screen. Seeing the envelope, he said, "Marie-Louise Delacroix?"

"So my parents said," I agreed. "Call me Lou."

"Thank you for coming in, Lou. I'm Gerard Landrieux." As he spoke, two other men appeared in their office doors. The taller man looked very like Gerard except where Gerard's expression was open and welcoming, the other man scowled and crossed his arms. The third man was fair and bore no family resemblance. His expression struck me as curious and . . . sad? Gerard gestured to each in turn. "This is my cousin Bernard Landry—" that explained the resemblance "—who started the practice with me, and Kent Blanchard, my old roommate, who joined us just this year." Gerard's smile held genuine warmth.

"And you know my wife, Gabrielle," said Gerard, stepping aside to reveal her presence behind him.

In the time it took my heart to resume beating, Bernard and Kent said something about a tee time and excused themselves from the office. As the door rattled shut behind me, I swallowed hard and managed to speak. "Yes."

Oh yes. I knew Gabrielle. The short story is that we entered the Ursuline Convent from separate directions, but with the mutual goal of becoming nurses. We became friends when we discovered a mutual love of dance; Gabrielle was a promising ballerina, having danced Clara in Nutcracker when she was sixteen. At the same age, I won the Miss Louisiana Tap crown. When our friendship evolved and we became lovers, the nuns kicked us out. My godfather hired me as an investigator in his law office, and *Mam'selle* Julie, queen of New Orleans lesbians, hired me to teach dance. Gabrielle did not rejoin the New Orleans Ballet, but returned to the thorny bosom of her family, who tried to cure her with the latest medical treatment, all the rage since 1941: shocking her poor brain with electricity. Last I'd heard, she'd married a nice young lawyer on his way to war. Gerard.

All that was long ago, and I didn't recognize the petite brunette with rich, shiny hair waving around her shoulders. Convents forbid hair, as well as the Tangee lipstick, Canal Street frock, and perfume Gabrielle wore today. I inhaled the scent. Its name escaped me.

Gerard was speaking. "With our business growing, we need a detective for regular work, mostly property research. Gabrielle saw your name among local detectives, and I like working with family and friends."

"Thanks," I said, relieved and sorry. "I'm not your best choice, though. I'm moving to California in June." It was a tough decision. On the one hand: steady income and seeing Gabrielle regularly. On the other: seeing Gabrielle regularly.

She made a sound as her husband said, "I'm sorry to hear it. Could you work with us that month while we look for someone else?"

I let out a breath. "I could."

Gabrielle placed a hand on her husband's arm. "Why don't you go play golf, *mon cousin?* Ken and Bernard can't be too far ahead of you. I'll go over our urgent cases with Lou."

Mother of God. Her voice. Flat as a crêpe, all the music burned out. And her eyes, hesitant, like she couldn't quite remember something important.

"Thank you, *ma cousine.*" Gerard said, patting her hand. "We're cousins," he said to me.

"Second cousins. We share great-grandparents," Gabrielle answered in a practiced patter.

Moving away from his wife, he said, "Gabrielle used to spend summers with my family to study ballet." With a fond smile, he left the office.

"Would you like something to drink?" Gabrielle asked, gathering files.

"Your receptionist said something about tea."

She made a face. "No, her tea is terrible. How about coffee or a soft drink?"

I accepted a Nehi and followed her into an office. Time to be professional. "Your hair grew back nicely." I could have done better.

She touched a victory roll. "You didn't let yours grow much."

"Easier to take care of. I never could get the smallest curl to hold. I decided not to fight my nature. . . . You prefer secretarial work to nursing?"

She shuddered. "I wanted to take care of children, but they cried so, never understanding that we were trying to heal them. After the hospital released me—yes, I do. And you?"

"During the war, I volunteered—still do at a Ninth Ward clinic—but I needed a better paying job, with my mother sick."

What we weren't saying was that hospital nursing had too many memories.

Gabrielle handed me a list. "I wasn't sure I'd remember . . . I just folded bandages during the war. I went to secretarial school to help Gerard."

"Do you dance?" I asked as I took her list—straightforward property research.

"No. Do you?"

"I teach at *Les Trois Grâces.* Keeps me from missing it. Helps pay the bills . . ." I let my voice trail off as I scanned the list. "Anything special about this research?"

She clutched the folders so hard that the bare half-moons on her nails turned as red as the polish. "There's something I couldn't tell anybody else."

And that's why I was there. Because in the envelope with Gerard's request for an appointment, she'd included a pink onionskin note that read: *help me.*

She moved to sit behind her desk. "Have a seat," she said, as she emptied the bottom folder on the desk between us. She turned away while I examined the contents, but not before I noticed her cheeks flaming under her rouge.

As a precaution, I used the mechanical pencil from her fancy pen set to poke the letters and envelopes apart. I'd bet my lunch the ink on the envelope was Washable Violet Quink, faded by the city's eternal rain to Katz & Besthoff's lurid purple. No return address, letters printed in block capitals.

Like the envelopes, the paper was cheap and rough. It conveyed its message by cut-up newsprint in the tradition of all anonymous correspondents.

How can you *go* to **church** YOU miserable SIN*n*ER? God *Will* judge

does you*r* HUSBAND *know* what A nasty Dyke YOU *are*? what **Would** YOU **pay** *to* keep HIM *from* finding OUT?

I cleared my throat. "My advice to blackmail victims is always: tell. Take away the blackmailer's weapon."

"I couldn't!" She shrank back in her chair and covered her face. "I've never told anybody."

"I'll do it for you. You were innocent—didn't understand. Get your story in first, before this person injects his poison."

"I can't hurt Gerard like that. He gave me another chance." Pressing against her desk, she leaned forward and said with more life than I'd heard in her voice today. "He saw how Mother—how unhappy I was and asked me to marry him. But he wanted to make it easier to get a church divorce, if I felt differently later, so . . . we waited. After the war, we tried so hard—we both want children—but I lost the baby in March. I was so sick! He's never said a word of blame—not even about the money . . . so . . . please find this man and make him stop, Lou. I can pay you out of my own money."

Money was involved? Money changed everything, and not for the better. My hair would be curling, if it could. I said, "Tell me about the money."

"My grandfather set up a mill in Bogalusa and changed his name to Landry. According to his will, his children and their children get an allowance. His great-grandchildren inherit the principal."

"He didn't like any of them, did he?" I asked.

Gabrielle nodded. "My allowance would increase with each child, to provide for and educate them. When the great-grandchildren reach age thirty, they'll inherit a lump sum."

Hmm. The fewer great-grandchildren, the larger their inheritance. It's a wonder Grandfather still had more than one descendant. "Does your allowance increase as the previous and current generations die?"

"Yes."

"That's why somebody thinks you can afford to buy silence." *Anyone in the family might have it out for her, but anyone who knows about the inheritance might be blackmailing her. Except, the blackmailer clearly knew about her history in the convent. Interesting.* I opened my bag and pulled out a blank contract. "Fill out and sign this and give me some change. You—just you—are hiring me for this service."

She hesitated on the last page. "You want to search the office and the house?"

"To eliminate a few of the thousands of New Orleans residents. Go get us some lunch, and I'll start searching."

As the front door creaked shut, I scolded myself. "Marie-Louise, you are close enough to thirty to stick your tongue in its ear. You will not dive into Gabrielle's office to caress her possessions."

I started with Cousin Bernard. As a family member on the Landry side, he knew Gabrielle had money, and he might have heard rumors of her past. Then I did Gabrielle's office to finish before she returned. Right.

To summarize:

- The only ink in the place was Parker's Permanent Black, the most suitable for lawyers.
- The financial records of Bernard Landry's real estate wheels and deals made as much sense as a Bourbon Street drunk. Some of his associates made me queasy. I took photos.
- Gabrielle's ornate silver desk frame displayed people so ugly they had to be ancestors. Behind that photo were two fuzzy snapshots

from her time in the convent: the first of Gabrielle in arabesque with me supporting her, and the second of both of us tapping. I had copies of the same photos in my dancing scrapbook, wedged behind my official portrait as Miss Louisiana Tap 1937.

- Gerard's roommate-turned-coworker Kent had an envelope with photos of a recent vacation, all groups of men. Innocent enough, but I recognized the lighthouse in the background. Fire Island in New York—a haven for men who . . . vacation with men.

- Gerard's desk sported a photo of Gabrielle, age sixteen, as Clara in the New Orleans Ballet *Nutcracker*, the most exciting thing in his office, I swear.

- Vonnie Laviolette read romance magazines and had one amethyst earring in her desk. I found the other under the beverage station in the file room.

- I took samples of Vonnie's tea herbs—vile smelling things, definitely not from Helen Lawton Coffee and Tea.

- The wastebasket, which smelled better than the tea, contained shreds of handwritten paper. I collected them to assemble later.

When Gabrielle returned, I asked for a copy of her grandfather's will, a family tree, and case notes on disgruntled clients. As I left, I wondered if I was taking on too much for someone leaving in a month.

I paused on the porch to gaze at the surrounding flowers. Would I find them in California? The lemony-woody scent of the magnolia tree goosed my memory: Gabrielle's perfume was My Sin.

I WANTED TO GO UPSTAIRS and breathe in Heavenly's perfume, but *Mam'selle* was in the studio sewing recital costumes with past girlfriends and mothers of current students. When she collects people, she does it for good, or at least for permanence.

Waving her arms, she shrieked, "Marie-Louise, you must not leave New Orleans. And even if you do, you could at least sew costumes."

"Busy-busy! Any phone calls?" I called, frozen in the doorway. That was stupid: Heavenly's train just left.

Mam'selle shook her head, and I closed the door on her admonishments. Outside again, I turned to the one place I knew I could count on both a welcome and being ignored.

Café du Monde backed up to the Mississippi River. Its open front gazed over Jackson Square, New Orleans' center of religion, government, and retail. It was only polite to order mud-thick coffee and sugar-drenched beignets as I studied the will and Gabrielle's family tree. Three remaining children (including Gabrielle's father) and eleven grandchildren (including Gabrielle and Bernard) were receiving allowances, and so far, three great-grandchildren were in line to inherit. The far edge of the page was smeared and cramped as the writer ran out of room. I could make out that Gabrielle's aunt, Alyce Landry, married Jean La—— and had Jean-Paul and Y—— as issue. There might be one more child on that branch drawing a grandchild's allowance. It being in everyone's interest to keep their numbers down, they must have been disappointed when Gabrielle left the convent and married.

Gerard Landrieux wasn't on the tree at all, being related to Gabrielle through their great-grandfather, but he certainly knew about her grumpy grandfather Landry's will. Gabrielle and any of her first cousins would score high on the marriage market, bringing to the union a lifetime allowance and a potential inheritance for any children. Bernard would have his pick of the debs when he decided to settle down.

I left the café and sauntered to a less savory part of town. As I walked, I wondered if Gabrielle and I would have ever spoken if not for the convent's holy deprivation. Our bond came from being the only girls who danced, but her people had money to pay for the best. My father usually had a job, but tap classes were expensive. I wore everybody's cast-offs and ate free lettuce-and-tomato sandwiches from the Martin Brothers' Coffee Stand to afford my lessons. Now Gabrielle shopped on Canal Street and I at the parish thrift store. She wrote with a Cross pencil set; I rescued nubs that other people threw away.

Far away from Gabrielle's world, I went looking for an old voodoo woman who sometimes came to my clinic. I brought a bag of beignets as an offering. Mother did, despite other evidence, raise me right.

Jeanne-Mère's shack remained standing, mostly out of habit. She herself always looked older than the dirt in God's garden, but now she seemed frail. Her warm mahogany skin had turned muddy. Panic seized me as I contemplated New Orleans without Jeanne-Mère.

I handed her the samples of tea from the Landrieux office. She sniffed them and made a face. I've no idea how she could smell anything in the welter of biological odors and river rot.

"What for you need this, child?" she asked, frowning.

"It's not mine. I've no idea what it's for," I said.

"Queen Anne's Lace, for your courses. They stop, you drink, you bleed again."

Spontaneous abortion. Gabrielle lost her baby. I felt sick.

Jeanne-Mère shook the one labeled 'Special Blend' and squinted at the components. They looked like prairie clippings to me.

She drew back. "Oleander! You trying to kill me? Or didn't your fancy nurse school teach you what everybody know?" With a small stick, she poked at some beige peas.

"Would it kill a person if you brewed it in a tea?" I asked.

"No matter what, it would," she said. "You still got the *gris-gris* I made you? It protect you, if you not be stupid."

I held up a little bag. I always carried her *gris-gris* with my rosary, figuring it's best to cover all bases.

I said goodbye and hurried back across town. I had to get to Gabrielle. When I was back on the streetcar, I reviewed my findings. It made sense that Cousin Bernard might want Gabrielle out of the picture. Perhaps lovelorn Kent had his sights set on his former roommate and was making mischief in his marriage. But why would Vonnie want Gabrielle to miscarry, and why would she keep dangerous poison with her tea? Did Vonnie want someone dead? Who? And why? Was Vonnie working with Kent? Bernard?

EVEN TRAVELING BY STREETCAR, I was sweating when I arrived in Gabrielle's neighborhood—whether from the heat or from fear, I wasn't certain.

To my relief, Gabrielle answered the door of their lovely historical house. "Lou, what's wrong?"

"Do you have any of Vonnie's teas?" I gasped.

Gabrielle shook her head. "She gave me some at Christmas, but I threw the box away."

"Thank God! Literally! And his Blessed Mother and the saints! Also Jesus."

Gabrielle pulled me into the house, past rooms full of heavy dark wood and burgundy furnishings into a room so light and airy that I blinked. I sank down on a puffy white couch covered in the same floppy pink roses that adorned the drapes, the walls, and (God help us) the rug. In one corner, a square table held a partially finished jigsaw puzzle, a fancy hand-cut one.

I wrung my hands while we observed the formalities of Southern hospitality. Gabrielle brought me a glass of Delaware Punch with ice and a straw, and I clutched the damp glass in both hands, terrified of the purple liquid staining the white couch. I felt like I was sitting in a dollhouse. Not the kind of dollhouse I had—cardboard boxes glued together with sewing-spool furniture—but the kind that delights passersby in the Maison Blanche windows. The kind Santa never brought me.

Gabrielle sank into the pink armchair beside the sofa. "Why'd you come all this way to ask about Vonnie's teas?"

I sipped my drink, calming myself with the familiar flavor of grapes and berries. "They're poisons," I said. Unable to meet Gabrielle's eyes, I studied the ice floating in my glass. "One is Queen Anne's Lace, which causes abortion. The other is an oleander blend. Oleander kills you."

I looked up. Gabrielle sat unmoving in her chair. Her back was as rigid as the steel girders throughout the city.

There was a light rap from the doorway, and I turned to see Gerard, who said, "I don't want to interrupt. Just wanted to say hi to Lou—Gabrielle, what's wrong?"

"Vonnie gave her poisonous teas," I explained. "I've no idea why."

Gabrielle shot into her husband's arms. "She killed our baby," she sobbed. "She said that horrible tea would help the nausea."

Gerard blanched. He pressed his lips to her head and murmured into

113

her perfect hair. "She killed—no! I'm sure it was a mistake, but—" he looked up at me. "Are you sure?"

I snorted. "How sure do you want to be? I'm sure she has poisons in her office tea supply, and Gabrielle has drunk tea from that supply. She could have made it herself. I'm sure the men never made their own tea."

He returned his attention to his wife. "I'm so sorry, *chérie*. Such a terrible mistake. You never have to see her again." He frowned. "I'll give her a month's severance. That and her Landry allowance should be enough until she finds work."

Wait a minute. "She's part of the Landry crew? Another first cousin?" I fished the family tree out of my bag while Gerard settled Gabrielle back into her chair. "She's not on here." I offered Gerard the paper.

He took it and pointed to the paper's edge. "It's hard to read. Gabrielle's Aunt Alyce married Jean Laviolette. Their children are Jean-Paul and Yvonne. She goes by Vonnie."

"Why did she kill our baby?" asked Gabrielle, her voice deader than usual, clogged with unshed tears.

Gerard frowned. "It was a mistake . . . wasn't it? Am I missing something?"

"We all are," I said, touching Gabrielle's hand. A tear dripped down her cheek, so I reached into my bag for a handkerchief. My fingers brushed the pieces of torn-up paper from Vonnie's wastebasket. When I looked down, two pieces came close enough together to make sense. I handed the pieces to Gabrielle. It wasn't a new wood-cut puzzle, but its text might help us. "Here, put this together while I talk to Gerard."

I emptied the bag onto the frilly coffee table in front of the sofa and Gabrielle's chair. Her hands automatically reached for border pieces.

Gerard led me into a burgundy-mahogany library where hulking bookcases held portentous tomes.

After we settled into facing wing-back chairs, I handed him the blackmail letters.

"She wanted me to find the author of these. I told her to tell you about them, but she didn't think you knew why she left the convent, so she refused."

Gerard waved an impatient hand and answered in a voice singed with sarcasm, "The whole family knows. Gabrielle's mother does not keep her sufferings to herself."

"But you still married Gabrielle," I observed.

He half-smiled in a French way. "Her mother does lie. And young girls often form such attachments and later make happy marriages."

I didn't believe that, and I'm sure it showed.

"I've always thought physical love overrated," Gerard said with enough earnestness to convince a jury.

Thinking of Kent, I asked, "Really? You don't prefer your own sex?"

Angry, he waved his hand. "New Orleans and wartime Europe gave me opportunities to discover any preference I might have. I wanted to be a priest, but I'm my father's only son."

I stared. "Lord have mercy, you didn't marry her despite her Sapphic love, but because of it. The apostle Paul talked about the gift of celibacy, but most people wouldn't have it as a gift, not even with double Green Stamps."

"I've loved Gabrielle all her life. And I was happy that I wouldn't be depriving her. We want children, but we can manage."

I started to say how they could manage in a doctor's office without the icky bits, but Gabrielle banged the door open.

"I've solved it," she said. "Even without all the pieces together, I can see she wrote my name over and over. Is this voodoo?" She held out her work, the scraps taped together so we could read "Mrs. Gerard Landrieux."

I asked, "You never wrote boys' names in your school notebooks?"

She blinked, surprised. "No."

"Me either. But other girls did. She's writing *her* name, she hopes."

Gabrielle dropped to her knees beside my chair, her skirt flaring out into a circle. "I wrote *your* name over and over," she whispered. "When I went into the hospital, they told me I'd forget you, and I couldn't let that happen." She glanced sideways at Gerard. "You know now?"

He reached over to squeeze her hand. "I always knew."

I kept to the topic. "Now it makes sense. I think this is what happened. Instead of—or in addition to—a bigger slice of Granddaddy's pie, Vonnie wanted Gerard for herself. She gave you a box of her handmade teas for Christmas. We don't know what was in that box, but it wouldn't have done Gabrielle any good. Vonnie knew something went wrong when Gabrielle was still alive and pregnant in the new year, so she gave Gabrielle a cure for nausea." Seeing Gabrielle's head droop to hide sparkling wet eyes, I skipped ahead. "Vonnie had to act fast, especially with Gabrielle turning down drinks. She wrote the anonymous letters—you can't tell me anybody but Vonnie Laviolette uses purple ink. Instead of recovering her health, Gabrielle grew more fragile and distressed. Who would be surprised if she died, maybe from oleander berries in her coffee and strewn over her desk? There could be a short note whose handwriting no one would question in their haste to hush the scandal. Of course, all Vonnie's teas would disappear."

Gerard's face grew taut and grim. "I'll call the police. I don't know if they can make charges stick, but they can get her away from us."

"You might warn your other office mates," I advised. "Cousin Bernard's accounts look like *Through the Looking Glass*, and he deals with people who make cops nervous."

Gerard grimaced. "I've been uncomfortable about his deals. I'll tell him he needs to find another place. What about Kent?"

I looked into his eyes. He knew, and he knew I knew. "Kent might want to remove some personal items, but he's not a thief or an embezzler."

His warm smile took in both of us. He pressed Gabrielle's hand to his cheek. "I'll bring in the police on Monday. Why don't you spend some time with your friend, since she's moving soon? I want you to be happy, *ma cousine*, whatever that means for you."

She turned agonized eyes from him to me and back again. "But I don't know! I try to be happy when someone tells me I should be, but inside I'm a heap of rubble."

"My poor girl. If only I'd married you from the convent door." His eyes glistened.

I echoed that emotion silently, but she chose respectability, and I—joy swelled my heart as I knew for sure—I'd chosen Heavenly, chosen to leave the life that was crumbling around me and start the new decade in a new land.

Gabrielle looked at the carpet and chewed her lip. She snapped her head up and said to her husband, "I miss dancing. We could go to one of those schools where they draw the steps on the floor."

I choked back laughter at his expression, horrified at being trapped into ballroom dancing. I took pity on him. "Gabrielle, on Monday we'll go see *Mam'selle* Julie of *Les Trois Grâces*. She needs a new dance teacher."

THE GRIFT OF THE MAGI

MARY DUTTA

JUDGING FROM THE WOMEN CLUSTERED around Oliver, the divorce rumors were heating up. Marlene's soon-to-be ex was holding court before *The Adoration of the Magi*, and the Three Wise Men weren't the only ones offering gifts. The museum director, Jasper Stevens, practically knelt at Oliver's feet. Only instead of frankincense and myrrh, Jasper had given Oliver a seat on the board and a fawning profile on the museum website.

Marlene knew Oliver saw himself as the savior in this scenario. Without his donation of this painting, Jasper would have been out of a job. The story even boasted a manger of sorts, given that the picture had been discovered in a barn after disappearing in World War II.

Marlene was as sick of the story as she was sick of everything else about Oliver. Still, she knew the dramatic tale added value to the painting. She had a very precise idea of how much it was worth on the open market, especially since Oliver would have to buy out her half of the rest of their art collection. Marlene had been calculating the value of all their other marital assets for months. She could have hosted an estate sale at a moment's notice with the mental price stickers she had put on everything.

What she could not put a price on was the value this painting held for Oliver. He had incrementally bought his social entrée at gallery openings and auction sales, acquiring enough canvases and bibelots to donate them to local museums and gain even more social capital. His gift of *The Adoration* to the museum would forever cement his position in the art patron firmament.

Oliver's female fans departed one by one, each with an air kiss. The last to go trailed her hand down his arm as she left. As the director left his side to make a beeline for the bar, Marlene headed toward her husband. She

119

slowed her pace as a man in a velvet jacket and designer stubble came to stand next to him.

The man leaned close enough to the canvas to make Oliver flinch. "Nice work," Marlene heard him say.

"It's a Tiepolo," Oliver said. "His only painting of the Adoration."

The man stepped back and tilted his head to appraise the picture. "Is it?"

"I should know, I own it," Oliver said, and gestured at the accompanying label.

"Promised gift of Oliver and Marlene Sanders," the man read aloud. "Do you always keep your promises?"

Marlene could have answered that one.

"Do I know you?" Oliver asked, summoning his most condescending tone.

"You can call me Raphael."

"Like the Ninja Turtle?" Oliver chuckled, amused as always by his own wit.

"Like the artistic genius," the man said. "You know, Oliver, technology's come a long way. X-rays. Micro-spectroscopy. It's a lot harder now to get away with art fraud."

Oliver bristled, his face flushing in a way Marlene could have warned the man about.

"And provenance," Raphael continued in the same conversational tone, seemingly unaffected by Oliver's increasing agitation. "Digitized records have made it much easier to verify authenticity."

Oliver stepped closer to the other man, who didn't step back. Just then, Oliver noticed Marlene standing nearby and turned even redder.

"I'll be in touch," Raphael said and walked away.

"Who was that?" Marlene asked. "What did he want?"

Before Oliver could answer, Jasper rushed up with two glasses of champagne. He handed one to Oliver, then sipped from the other one rather than offering it to Marlene. Jasper had spent a six-month fellowship in London that had left him with a permanent British accent and a fondness for waistcoats. He did not seem to have acquired any manners to go with them.

* * *

TWO WEEKS LATER, THE HOLLOW tinkle of socialite laughter rose above the crowd assembled for the official announcement of the painting's donation. Partygoers clutched prints of *The Adoration* in one hand and drinks in the other. Jasper Stevens circulated, compulsively patting a binder that matched his waistcoat. Marlene knew it contained the final gift agreement. Oliver had arranged the whole event to stage the signing and celebrate his own apotheosis.

Marlene circulated through the crowd, passing from one tedious conversation to another. She spotted Raphael. He had trimmed his stubble into a goatee, but wore the same velvet jacket.

"Oliver," he called, heading straight for where her husband stood talking to an elderly man in a faded dinner jacket and ascot. "You didn't respond to my email." Oliver blanched and extricated himself from the conversation so quickly that his companion was left open-mouthed. He hustled past Raphael and into a side gallery. Marlene trailed the two men and found a spot to eavesdrop hidden by a statue of *The Penitent Thief.*

"It's a simple proposition," Raphael was saying. "If you donate the painting, I'll expose it as a fake. You'll get nothing but a ruined reputation. But if you sell it and give me half of your proceeds, I'll take my cut and keep quiet."

"The museum did its own due diligence when I offered the gift."

Raphael laughed. "And I bet they found exactly what they wanted to find. Come on, Oliver. What's more likely? A random art dealer stumbles across a long-lost Old Master in a barn? Or he hires someone to forge an Old Master and sell it for a fortune?"

"The dealer's dead now," Oliver said, hope fighting with desperation in his voice.

"Yes, but I've got letters between him and the forger. And evidence that the original painting was destroyed. I sent you plenty of proof.

"It's not just your reputation that's at stake," Raphael continued. "It's the value of your entire collection. If you own one fake, who's to say that all your other art isn't fake as well? At least if you sell *The Adoration,* you'll get some money and protect the rest of your investment."

Oliver stood silent for a long moment. "I'll have to talk to my wife."

"I have a feeling she'll agree," Raphael said. He grinned and strolled out of the gallery.

Marlene waited until he had rejoined the crowd before slipping out from her hiding place and approaching her husband.

"Who was that? He looked familiar."

Oliver took a deep breath. "No one," he said. "Listen—"

"Yoo hoo, Oliver, are you in here?" One of Oliver's fans stuck her head into the gallery. "Have I got you alone at last?" She stepped closer but hesitated when she saw Marlene.

Oliver gave her a smile that was more of a grimace. He pulled out a handkerchief to pat the sweat off his forehead. "Not yet, but I'll be back to the party in just a minute. Excuse us."

He grabbed Marlene's arm and hurried her past the woman and into the museum lobby. He looked around wildly, then dragged her into the coat room and shut the door.

"What the hell is going on?" Marlene asked, pressed against a row of furs.

"I've changed my mind," Oliver said. "I don't want to do it."

"The divorce?"

"No, the donation. I don't want to give *The Adoration* to the museum."

She opened her eyes wide, hoping she wasn't overplaying her feigned confusion. "It was your idea to donate the painting in the first place."

"I know, but now I want to sell it. Believe me, your share of the profits will be a lot of money."

"But I want to donate it," Marlene said. "This makes no sense. What aren't you telling me?"

Oliver backed up as far as the crowded space allowed. "Nothing. I just changed my mind, that's all."

"Well, let me talk to my lawyer and see what he thinks."

"NO!" Oliver shouted. "No lawyers. Let's just work this out ourselves. Come on, Marly."

He had to be really desperate if he was pulling out the nickname.

"All right, Oliver. I'll agree to sell as long as you give me half your proceeds from the sale on top of the fifty percent I'm already entitled to."

Oliver's face flushed its familiar red. "You don't know what you're asking."

But Marlene did know. She knew that giving half of his proceeds to her, and half to Raphael, would leave Oliver with exactly nothing. A small price to pay to preserve the value of the collection that meant more to him than she did. That art would be all he had left when his social circle shunned him over his disappearing donation.

"Half your proceeds on top of my fifty percent," she said, "or I don't agree to sell. And *you* have to tell Jasper Stevens."

Oliver nodded wordlessly and opened the coat room door. He gestured for Marlene to go ahead of him, then followed her back to the reception with a heavy sigh.

The museum director waved them over from his position in front of *The Adoration*. "There you are," he said. "We need to get the signing started."

Marlene raised an eyebrow at Oliver. "Jasper," he said, "we need to talk. In your office."

Jasper gave Oliver a far-from-adoring look when he learned they were reneging on their promised gift.

"Y'all can't do this," he said, his British accent slipping in his agitation. "We've built our whole yearly exhibition schedule around that painting. We're in talks to lend it to other museums."

"I'm sorry, but circumstances change."

Jasper slapped both hands on his desk. "We'll sue."

"We haven't signed all the paperwork," Oliver said. "And you don't want to alienate other donors. People may hesitate to work with the museum if they're worried about you coming after them if things don't work out with a donation."

"You'll pay for this," Jasper hissed.

Oliver sighed again. "I don't think so. We're simply no longer in a position to donate, and that has to be the end of it." He pushed back his chair and left the director's office. Marlene followed a moment later, casting a look back at Jasper, who sat speechless, staring at his hands on the desk.

The director caught up with her near the coat room.

"Marlene," he said, "I need that painting. I'm going to lose my job over this. I can't offer you anything like the value of the painting, but there are things in the collection that aren't on display, lots of things that no one would ever know were gone."

He swiped feverishly through pictures on his phone. "Here, look. Here's an Egyptian figurine. You could sell that. Or how about this ring? It's unique, but you could reset the stones, and no one would ever guess where they came from."

Marlene looked at the picture, then back at Jasper. "This was Oliver's decision," she said. "Terribly bad manners, I know." She walked out with a smile.

SHE WAS STILL SMILING THE next month when *The Adoration of the Magi* appeared on the auction catalog cover. The Wise Men had a star to guide them, but Marlene had found her way all on her own. Hatching a plan. Concocting evidence of supposed art fraud. Hiring Raphael to blackmail Oliver. Hitting her husband where it hurt by undercutting the art world status he so desperately wanted, and then making him give up all his profits on his prized possession. Setting up an account in Raphael's name that actually belonged to her. Now Raphael had disappeared with his fee. All that was left for Marlene to do was enjoy the auction and spend the proceeds.

She flipped through the catalog as she reached for her ringing phone. Maybe she could start a collection of her own with some of the profits from the sale.

"There's been a development," the auction house manager said. "A woman has come forward claiming ownership of your painting."

MARLENE WATCHED THE NEWS CONFERENCE in disbelief. The claimant wore a corduroy jumper over a turtleneck sweater. Her blonde hair looked like she had dyed it in her sink, and she had a prominent mole under one eye. She looked like she had emerged from the same barn where *The Adoration* had been found.

The woman stood with folded hands and answered reporters' questions. "There were always family stories about my great-great uncle in the old country and his love of art. I'm glad his precious painting has made its way home to us," she said. "But we're simple people. We don't need the money we could get by selling the painting. The Magi brought gifts to the Christ child and in that spirit, we'd like to pass this gift along to the museum. I know how much Mr. Stevens cares about the painting and I think my great-great-uncle would have wanted it to go to people who would appreciate its real value."

Marlene was on the way to her lawyer's office before the local reporter had tossed it back to the studio anchor. "Isn't it just a little suspicious how these people suddenly came out of the woodwork with a claim on the painting?" she said after blowing past his assistant.

"The cancelled donation did get a lot of publicity," he said in a maddeningly calm tone. "That might have gotten their attention."

"What proof of ownership do they have? Provenance can be faked, you know." Marlene knew Raphael had made that very clear to Oliver. She had written the script herself.

"They say they have some kind of receipt and old correspondence. It's a credible enough claim that the challenge over ownership could drag on for years," the lawyer said. "This is going to involve European courts. And the whole situation is a little . . . delicate."

"Meaning?"

"Given the painting's problematic whereabouts during World War II, and the controversies over looted art, some very unpleasant associations could come to light that would not help your case."

Marlene could think of another unpleasant association a lawsuit would bring: Oliver's inevitable involvement.

"Your best option might be to take the high road and concede ownership of *The Adoration*," her lawyer continued, "rather than rack up untold legal fees fighting to keep it. And letting the painting go to the museum will build your reputation as a patron of the arts."

As if she cared. Marlene sagged in her chair, waiting for an epiphany that never came about how to salvage her ruined plans. If they didn't sell the painting, she couldn't take Oliver's share of the proceeds. And if they agreed not to contest the museum donation, he would gain back some of the art world status she had worked so hard to strip from him.

"Let's just get this over with," she said.

THE TAXI DROPPED MARLENE AT the departures curb. She needed some time away after her artistic and legal debacles. And at long last, she had a finalized divorce to celebrate.

A car slid into the space vacated by her taxi. Jasper Stevens hopped out, straightened his waistcoat, and walked around to open the passenger door. Marlene had not seen or spoken to him since their conversation by the coat room.

The museum director seemed in good spirits. Why wouldn't he be? Once the donation came back to the museum, his job was secure. The museum was capitalizing on the painting in all its fundraising and exhibit planning, and with its even more dramatic new backstory *The Adoration*'s value had climbed to new heights.

A dark-haired woman in black leggings and a fitted jacket got out of the passenger seat. Jasper handed her a bag and they shook hands. The woman sashayed toward Marlene in her high-heeled boots, an ornate jeweled ring weighing down the hand pulling her suitcase. The ring looked familiar. As did the woman, whom Marlene couldn't place until the woman saw her and winked. Marlene would have recognized the mole under her eye anywhere.

OCCUPIED WITH DEATH

KIM KEELINE

"NILDA SANTOS: DEATH DOULA" IS not a great icebreaker at parties. Obituaries, wills, and funerals—death's my business. I help the dying and their families prepare. It's rewarding because you're a part of their lives— or at least, a part of their deaths.

Today, I didn't want to advertise my position. The whole point was to blend in, mingle, and help everything run smoothly.

I took a quick glance around the chapel. Everything was set. Hector stood stiffly in a new dark suit, looking at the oversized photo of his uncle Eduardo I'd placed near the guest book. Hector was a quiet young man who had clearly been devoted to his "*tio* Eddie."

I crossed to stand beside him and placed a hand on his shoulder. "How are you holding up?"

"Well as can be expected, I guess." Hector smiled wanly. "I miss him, Ms. Santos."

"Call me Nilda, please," I said. "He was *so* proud of you."

Eduardo told me his 19-year-old nephew was the first in his family to go to college and was already a computer whiz. "He's going to own a computer business someday," Eduardo had said repeatedly.

Car doors slammed outside. I patted Hector's arm. "Come on, let's greet the others."

Heading out the side door of the Little Chapel of the Roses, I nervously brushed lint off my gray-and-black-striped skirt. Hector trailed behind me.

The chapel looked like something out of Victorian England, but the Santa Ana winds blowing hot air off the desert reminded me we were in southern San Diego, not many miles from the Mexican border. Marble tombstones lined the park around the chapel in symmetrical rows. Like all aspects of life, death is always around us.

The parking lot was filling up. Hector and I greeted the mourners who approached the chapel.

THE NEXT HOUR WENT BY quickly. A touching ceremony was followed by a brief reception in the hall nearby.

After Hector and I ushered Eduardo's friends into the hall, I circulated, putting people at ease by asking questions that would elicit stories of the deceased. Standard playbook for a funeral in my profession. Everyone has something interesting to say, if you are willing to listen.

I felt myself start to relax when the reception began to wind down. My job was almost complete.

Then a shrill voice cut through the conversations around me. "You might not like it, but that doesn't change the truth."

Hector was making shushing motions to a young woman in a black dress near the hall's entrance. I couldn't hear his reply, but he looked a bit panicked.

I headed in their direction.

"I have plenty of proof," the young woman said. She pulled a large manila envelope out of her oversized purse and waved it around.

I stepped in next to Hector. "Is something wrong?"

"She says she's Eduardo's daughter." Hector frowned. "But he never had a daughter."

"Oh, he had a daughter." She flourished the envelope again. "He just didn't know about me for a long time. Once he found out, he rewrote his will—which he sent me a few weeks ago."

She was drawing stares.

"Why don't we go into the next room?" I herded them out even as the woman made small noises of protest.

My mind was reeling. I wrote Eduardo's obituary under his direction. We discussed every aspect of his funeral and burial during the last weeks. I hadn't seen his will, but he had assured me he'd made one.

"My nephew will be surprised." Eduardo had laughed. "I almost think I should tell him just to see his face, but I think it's best this way. Don't like people hanging over me, showering me with gratitude." His laugh had quickly turned into a cough, so I'd fetched him a glass of water.

The purpose of a death doula is to ease the burden on survivors and make sure the deceased's wishes are carried out. If there was going to be an issue like this, you'd think he'd have mentioned it. I closed the door. "He—he never said he had a daughter."

The woman grinned and tossed herself down on a nearby sofa. "Here." She threw the envelope on the table next to her. "Copies of the will, a letter written to my mother before I was born, and a photo of him from when he was dating her."

I picked up the envelope and handed it to Hector, who stood in stunned silence just inside the door.

He opened it and pulled out several sheets of paper. "It looks like his handwriting on this letter."

"Of course," the woman said. "Since we're cousins, I should introduce myself. I'm Leticia Darrel. The letter is made out to my mother, Cynthia." She brushed her long black hair out of her face with a graceful flick of her wrist.

Leticia appeared to be in her mid-twenties. She was very pretty, glamorous even, but more like a praying mantis than a butterfly. I couldn't shake the feeling that there was something off about her. Almost like she was familiar to me. Was it a resemblance to Eduardo? I couldn't place it.

Hector looked at her for a few seconds and then at me. "Thank you, Ms. Santos—Nilda. I'll handle this from here." He crossed to sit next to Leticia on the sofa. "I thought *tio* Eddie was the only close family I had left. So, it's nice to meet you." He stuck out his hand and she shook it, smiling sweetly.

I hesitated at the door. Leticia's eyes narrowed at me. I retreated to the other room where the last of the guests were trickling out the door.

As I began cleaning up, my mind kept going in circles. A long-lost daughter? A new will? Was this what Eduardo meant when he said his nephew would be surprised?

* * *

"I JUST WANTED TO MAKE sure you were okay." I'd forced myself to wait several days before calling Hector, but I was dying to know about his new cousin.

There was a pause. "That's very kind of you. I'm fine." Hector sounded a bit distant. I couldn't tell if his grief was still so raw that he was in a state of shock, or if he was simply giving a rote reply, as people often do when they don't want to discuss their emotions.

"Good." I tried to think how to ask about Leticia.

He must have read my mind. "You're probably wondering about my cousin."

"I *was* surprised."

"My *tio* never mentioned anything to you?"

I'd been wracking my brain for any hints. "No. You'd think he would, since it should have been reflected in the obituary, the announcements of the funeral, and, of course, his will."

"The will Leticia showed me is dated two months after the one he left in his lockbox. If the lawyers decide it's valid, she'll inherit pretty much everything." His tone was neutral, like it didn't really matter to him. I had had the impression that he'd really been counting on that inheritance to pay for college costs, so maybe it was just shock.

"I'm sorry."

"Don't be. I loved my *tio* Eddie and wasn't there for his money. He was my only family. Though I guess I have Leticia now." He paused and then blurted out, "Apparently, he had a lot more money saved than I ever knew."

"I see." Eduardo had lived frugally, but his assisted living place wasn't cheap, so it made some sense. "Bit of a shock, then."

"Not for Leticia." Hector's tone had a bitter edge. "Why didn't he tell me about her? Why did she wait all this time to show up, will in hand? I don't understand any of this."

"Is there anything I can do to help?"

He seemed to recall himself. "There's nothing anyone can do. I'll be mailing a small tip to add to the fee my *tio* paid. Your help to him—to me, during the planning of his funeral—was invaluable." He hung up.

My job was done. So why did I feel so unsatisfied? The niggling feeling that something was wrong just wouldn't leave me.

A FEW DAYS LATER, I entered the lobby of Eduardo's assisted living home. I was meeting a new client but had an hour to kill before my appointment. I couldn't stop thinking about Leticia.

I signed in at the front desk. A gaggle of workers was gathered behind the counter, chatting during their break. I waved to Rita, whom I'd gotten to know the past few months.

She worked physical therapy for the independent living residents. A chatty middle-aged woman, Rita's tightly pinned black hair and way of carrying herself radiated a sense of business-like responsibility and practicality, belied by her bubbly personality and the tattoo of a bird sitting on a rose vine encircling her wrist. I liked to imagine the roses spoke to some romantic past where she'd been wilder. She was fun to talk to because she always saw the humor in her work and had the best gossip from around town.

She joined me on the other side of the counter, and I leaned forward, lowering my voice. "Did you know Eduardo Calvera?"

She tilted her head quizzically. "A little. He was well known in the community—well liked. He lived in the assisted living wing, though, and wasn't my patient. A bunch of residents attended his service, you know."

I nodded. "Could I talk to anyone close to him? His nephew needs some info about Eduardo's past, and one of his friends might be able to help."

Rita sucked her lower lip. "My next appointment is one of his friends, but I don't know . . ."

"It's important."

"Don't you have a client to meet or something?" She looked like she was going to refuse, her eyebrows drawn together.

"Not yet." I tried my most winning smile on her. "Please?"

* * *

131

IN A CHAIR OUTSIDE RITA'S office sat a thin, pale, balding man. He was hunched slightly over a cane and peering at me through wire-rimmed glasses. Dave was just like dozens of old men you'd see in a retirement home, with bushy eyebrows and hair sprouting out of his ears, but his small smile and twinkly eyes spoke of a quiet humor. Still, even toward the end, Eduardo had been a bigger, more vibrant personality than this wispy gentleman.

I sat down next to Dave and asked him about his friend.

He nodded sadly, the hand on his cane shaking slightly. "Eduardo will be missed. Used to visit him after dinner once he was stuck in his bed."

"Did you ever meet his nephew?"

"Eduardo talked about him all the time," he said slowly. "Had a couple photos around."

That fit with my memory but didn't help much. "What about other relatives? Did he ever talk about past relationships? A girlfriend? Or a daughter?"

Dave laughed. "He certainly had his pick of the ladies around here."

Rita leaned on the wall next to her office door. "More women than men in a place like this. He's not the only man with his choice of dance partners." She chuckled. "And bed partners. The doctors prescribe meds for STDs more often than you might think."

"I haven't done too badly myself." Dave grinned. "Although you'd not think so, looking at me now."

"We need to start your exercises if you're going to remain spry enough to woo the ladies," Rita said, opening her office door. She gave me a warning look, but I had to push one more time.

"A woman claims to be Eduardo's daughter from some relationship he had 20-something years ago. Do you know anything about this?"

Dave slowly pulled himself up with his cane. "He mentioned someone he was serious about a long time ago, but it ended. He told me his nephew was the closest family he had." Dave patted my hand as he went past.

I thanked him as he entered Rita's office. With a worried glance, Rita closed the door in my face.

I wasn't sure what to do next. Or even what I hoped to accomplish.

* * *

BEFORE EDUARDO'S FINAL ILLNESS, HE had lived in a one-bedroom apartment in the independent living wing. He ate meals in the main dining room and participated in poker tournaments and bean bag tossing with the other seniors.

When residents become unable to care for themselves, they're moved into the assistance wing. On-call nurses, hospital beds, and visiting doctors take residents to the end of their lives. That's the wing where Eduardo had lived when he hired me and where I headed now.

Hoping to find staff who'd spent time with him, I rambled down the hall. Some nurse I didn't recognize nodded to me as I passed by.

Toward the end of the hall, the door to Eduardo's room was cracked open.

I paused. The room should have been locked until Hector, or now perhaps Leticia, came to claim his belongings.

I considered calling out to the nurse. But maybe there was evidence to disprove Leticia's claims. Or maybe to prove them and put my mind at ease. Either way, I needed answers. Eduardo wouldn't cut his nephew out of his will like this, even if he did have a secret daughter. I wouldn't believe it until I had an explanation that made sense.

The room was empty when I peered in the gap of the door, so I quickly entered and pulled the door behind me almost closed. The space was much as I remembered it, except the bed was completely stripped.

The small rolltop desk seemed a good place to start, so I opened the top. There wasn't much. In a left-side cubby, I found a bank ledger. Turning to the last page, I found record of a very large bank balance. Hector wasn't kidding about Eduardo having more money than he had let on. But that didn't explain Leticia.

I moved to the drawers. The first two contained normal office supplies and not much else. The bottom drawer, however, appeared to be a sort of keepsake area with letters, small photo albums, and loose photos. I rifled through it quickly, trying to keep an ear out for footsteps in the hall. I needed to hurry.

Several pictures of a young boy who was almost certainly Hector were

133

among the stack, but also a lot of older photos of a young Eduardo and his family. In one, he posed with a slightly older girl labelled as Isabelle, Eduardo's sister—Hector's deceased mother.

I thumbed through a small stack of letters and found two that were marked *return to sender* and addressed to a Cynthia Darrel. So that proved, at least, that Leticia's story might be real.

Still, these letters were returned to Eduardo, so what had happened? With the postmarks smudged, it was impossible to know when they were written without opening them. I hesitated. It would be best to tell Hector and have the lawyers examine them. Opening the letters myself could cause legal problems for me—and hurt Hector's case.

I put the letters back and closed the drawer, giving a quick glance around the room. Beyond a few chairs, which I knew from experience weren't very comfortable, there wasn't too much furniture. Just the desk, hospital bed, and a side table. I moved to the side table and opened the top drawer.

A cough came from behind me. I started guiltily and faced a young nurse's assistant in purple scrubs standing in the doorway with her hands on her hips.

"What are you doing here?"

I struggled to think of an excuse. I had seen her give Eduardo his medication and check his blood pressure when I stayed late to go over his obituary and funeral details. "Monica?"

The woman nodded but looked confused.

I tried to look like I had every right to be there. "Don't you work the night shift?"

"Usually." She glanced around. "Nobody's supposed to be in here."

The drawer behind me was still slightly ajar. I blushed and tried to push it closed with my hip. Monica raised an eyebrow suspiciously.

"I misplaced a pen. It was a special gift, gold and engraved with my name. Have you seen it?"

"I doubt it would be here."

"I last used it when I was helping Eduardo. Mind if I check?"

She shifted feet. "I need to lock up."

I put on a cheery voice. "It won't take but a minute, especially if you help me." Not waiting for an answer, I turned toward the side table again, closing the drawer the rest of the way. "You look over there, will you?" I opened the bottom drawer, but nothing looked interesting, just some paperback books.

Monica gave a perfunctory glance at the floor by the foot of the bed while keeping an eye on me. "I don't see any pens." She gestured to the door. "I'll tell the rest of the staff you are looking, in case someone turns it in."

"Don't bother. I'll tell them myself." I gave up and headed into the hall.

Monica followed me out of the room and locked the door behind her.

I thanked her and retreated to the other wing. Why had the door been unlocked? Was Monica there before me, or had someone else been searching?

AFTER MEETING WITH MY NEW client, I headed behind the main building. I had parked near the back of the visitor's lot. It's one of my few nods to the need for exercise.

Suddenly, I felt eyes on me. Pulling my bag closer, I slid the keys on my key ring between my fingers.

I was probably being paranoid. What sort of danger could there be in broad daylight in the parking lot of a respectable assisted living home? Still, I picked up my pace toward my car.

A rustling in the oleander bushes near my little Honda startled me.

"Is someone there?" I didn't like the quaver in my voice and tried for a more assertive tone as I tightened my hold on my keys. "Come out of there."

More rustling. Then what sounded like footsteps running away. I darted forward but couldn't see a soul. But there was glass all over the driver's seat. Someone had smashed my side window.

I sighed. There wasn't much to steal, but it was still an awful inconvenience. The lot was empty and there was no sign of whoever had been in the bushes—if anyone had even been there.

I pulled out my phone to take pictures of the damage in case insurance covered it. That's when I noticed the flat front tire. Had someone slashed it? What was going on?

* * *

HECTOR RELUCTANTLY AGREED TO AN appointment the next afternoon. That gave me time to get a new tire. The window would have to wait.

He lived in Eastlake, in one of the many cookie-cutter communities that had sprung up on the east side of Chula Vista. It was just a short drive from my home in San Ysidro, but my air conditioning was ineffective against the hot Santa Ana winds blasting me from the broken window. I rehearsed what I was going to say.

I was still trying to convince myself that the car vandalism yesterday had nothing to do with my suspicions about Leticia. I just couldn't shake the idea that Eduardo would have mentioned her, if only to make sure she was notified about the funeral plans.

Hector's condo was half of a Spanish style duplex with beige stucco exterior and red tile roof. Smoothing down my wind-blown hair, I waited a good minute before Hector answered my knock and stood there blocking the doorway. I asked if I could come in to talk, and he finally stepped back to let me enter.

I was surprised to see Leticia, in a skimpy blue sun dress, sprawled across one corner of a tan leather sofa in the living room.

A stack of papers lay on the coffee table in front of her. She raised a glass of iced tea in a salute when she saw me. Hector crossed and sat next to her, so I sat in the overstuffed chair across from them.

Hector picked up his own glass of iced tea. He didn't offer me any. Probably not planning on letting me stay that long.

"So, what can I do for you, Ms. Santos?" Hector took a sip of his tea and exchanged glances with Leticia, whose smile widened.

Everything I'd rehearsed flew out the window. I could hardly tell him about the letters I'd found or any of my suspicions. Not with the woman sitting right there.

"I—I wanted to see how you were doing." That sounded weak even to me. I tried again. "Make sure you didn't need my help with your uncle's estate."

"We're actually going over the final documents right now," he said. "The lawyer is working to get it all get straightened out."

Leticia's smile was charming—but cold and didn't reach her calculating eyes.

I didn't feel reassured.

"We won't be needing your help anymore." Leticia's treacly voice set my teeth on edge.

Hector leaned forward. "I said I'd mail you a tip, but let me take care of it now."

"Darling Hector, let me." Leticia practically purred. "It's the least I can do as executor of the estate."

She reached for her bag at her feet.

I held up my hands to protest. "I didn't come here for a tip."

"But you'll get one." Leticia opened her wallet and began counting out twenties. "Hector told me how much help you were." She fanned out $120 on the table in front of me.

The money *would* help after yesterday's vandalism. My wallet contained more proverbial moths and dust than dollars. I stood up. "I appreciate it but can't accept." Not with my suspicions.

Hector followed me to the door. I lowered my voice. "Do you trust her?"

He looked surprised and paused, his hand halfway to the front door's handle.

Before he could answer, Leticia came up behind him, the twenties in her hand. "Take it, Ms. Santos. God sees everyone, even the sparrow. We have to take care of each other." She shoved the money toward me. On her right wrist was a small tattoo of a sparrow sitting on a small red rose.

Something clicked. "A nice sentiment." I took the money, looking closer at the tattoo as I did.

As I walked back to the car, I tucked the money carefully into my bag. Now I knew what had seemed familiar about Leticia that first day. The sparrow on her hand looked very much like Rita's tattoo.

Her hair and eyes were a bit like the physical therapist's, as well.

Maybe it was a coincidence, but something told me it wasn't.

* * *

137

I FOUND DAVE IN THE library room, playing solitaire on a small tray. I told him I suspected someone was trying to cheat Eduardo's nephew out of his inheritance.

"Eduardo made some good investments a few years back," Dave said. "He'd joke—'Hector's in for a big surprise if healthcare doesn't eat up all my money.'"

"His nephew only inherits if the other will is proven fake."

"And you think it is?"

"Did you ever talk about Eduardo to Rita during your appointments?"

Dave frowned. "We talk about a lot of things. She's real nice. But Eduardo was her patient too, before he got so weak and moved into the assisted wing. You don't think she's involved, do you?"

"Does she have a daughter?"

His bushy eyebrows raised. "I've never met her, but she's mentioned her once or twice. Don't think she lives nearby."

"I think Eduardo's fake daughter may actually be Rita's."

"It can't be."

"Leticia Darrel claims her mother Cynthia had a relationship with Eduardo. There are letters to Cynthia in Eduardo's desk. Rita might have taken one."

Dave straightened up in his chair. "One night we were talking with Rita after one of my appointments. Eduardo joked that Rita's last name was the same as someone he once loved. She laughed and said she wished it had been her. She's always been kinda flirty." He scowled. "I can't believe she'd do this."

"That's probably what got her thinking," I said. "If her daughter is the right age, they wouldn't have to fake as much."

"You're just guessing. I don't even know her daughter's name."

"Both women's social media is locked down, but there has to be a way to get enough evidence to start an official investigation."

"There's the patient emergency contact files," Dave said thoughtfully. "Even the staff are listed in case of a problem."

"Can you get access?" *This might be the proof I needed.*

"Only staff can access it."

"Then I've got an idea."

* * *

DAVE VOLUNTEERED TO STAY IN the lobby and watch for Rita while I went down the hall of the assisted living wing to track Monica down at the nurse's station.

She looked up as I approached. "We haven't found your pen."

I decided I had no choice but to confide in her. "Someone's claiming to be Eduardo's long-lost daughter and cheat his nephew out of his inheritance."

Monica's eyes widened. "What do you mean?"

"I think a staff member is using info she obtained from Eduardo's room to commit fraud."

"Impossible."

"I can prove it—with your help. I just need you to look in one little file." Monica started to interrupt, but I cut her off. "Just get me the emergency contact person. I think the staff member's daughter is the one posing as Eduardo's heir."

IT TOOK SOME CONVINCING, BUT a few minutes later I propped myself outside an office, pretending to be engrossed in my phone like it was the most interesting thing I'd seen all day.

The door cracked open, and Monica slid out looking guilty.

"Did you find it?"

She held up her phone. Within seconds, I had the information. Bingo. Emergency contact for Rita was Leticia Darrel.

I thanked Monica and was about to go tell Dave when I froze. Rita came out of a room a few feet in front of us. She was talking quietly with an older woman with purple highlights in her hair.

I put on my best fake smile and prepared to bluff my way out of the situation.

Monica unfortunately had different thoughts. "There she is!" She pointed like an accuser in an old-fashioned mystery.

Rita whirled around. Her eyes darted about, and then she turned and hurried down the hall toward the lobby.

I swore and took off after her, shouting, "Stop!"

She was steps from reaching the lobby. If she got outside, she might flee and never face justice.

Suddenly, Dave appeared at the end of the hall, his arms and cane stretched to block the way. Rita slowed. Grateful she didn't knock the sweet man down, I drew level with her. "We know what you and your daughter did."

"You're crazy," Rita said loudly. "I knew you were trouble. You wouldn't even back off after I sent you a warning."

"You mean by vandalizing my car?" How could someone who had seemed so nice be so manipulative? Several residents and staff were heading toward us. Dave looked crestfallen, and Monica hovered nearby, watching intently. "Monica, call the police."

Rita's shoulders slumped. Dave finally lowered his spread arms and leaned shakily on his cane once again.

AFTER THE POLICE ARRIVED AND interviewed us, I sat in the lobby with Monica and Dave.

Monica shook her head sadly. "I don't understand how Rita thought they'd get away with it."

"Using that letter and an old photo from his desk made the claim seem real. All they had to fake was the will."

"She probably regrets all the physical therapy sessions with me." Dave laughed and patted his cane. "If she hadn't helped me regain my balance, I never could've blocked her way. How did you figure this all out?"

I smiled. "A little bird told me."

RESEARCH

SHANNON TAFT

I'M A CONSCIENTIOUS FRAUD. WHEN a woman seems worried about her husband cheating, how do you know what answer to give? If you're serious about your work, you drive past his office building when he's supposedly working late and see if his light is on. How do you know which window is his? That's even more effort, but if I'm going to con people into thinking I'm a genuine psychic, then I'm damn well going to invade their privacy to get the right answers.

I didn't go to school for this. My original goal was to become a psychologist, but that proved far too expensive. My "four-year degree" in psychology took six years and $120,000 to complete, so when I graduated, getting deeper in debt seemed like financial suicide.

Instead, I took my roommate, Jane, up on her offer to move with her to Northern Virginia. She was going for a master's degree and needed a roommate.

"There's nothing for you here, Becca," she said. "But, in Fairfax, everything's so expensive—"

"And that's a selling point?" I'd demanded.

"It means employers have to pay people more. You'll be able to pay off your student loans a lot faster than here in East-Nowheresville."

Being a debt-ridden orphan with no better prospects, I agreed. As it turned out, Jane was right about the cost of living, but wrong about the job market for psychology majors with just a bachelor's degree.

Fortunately, I had one skill set capable of generating enough cash to cover my loan payments. In undergrad, I'd worked part-time in a psychic's shop to afford my books. While there I'd studied my employer's act and how her customers had reacted to it. In the end, it was a more valuable education in human psychology than the one that had gotten me eyeballs-deep in debt. So, I rented a large storage room from my Fairfax landlady and offered to throw in an extra fifty bucks if she wouldn't complain about me running a business out of it. She agreed—for a hundred—and that's how I came to be a tarot-card reading, aura-sensing, tea-leaf-analyzing psychic. It may sound like an easy scam, but it's hard work if you want to do it right. That's what I mean when I say I'm a conscientious fraud.

After six months, and only moderately unethical snooping, I was building a healthy client list based on referrals. That's when I met Michelle Satterlee.

She'd booked her appointment online, taking a Monday morning slot with just a few hours' notice. It meant my research was lacking, but I started my analysis the second she walked in. Michelle had a balayage hair treatment, which is a fancy way to say she paid a hairdresser to paint it with lots of different shades of blond and brown. It's time intensive, which means pricey, so I knew I had a client willing to shell out money. The Bottega Veneta purse was another clue, as was the large diamond ring she wore, which sparkled in my artificial lights in a way that told me the cut and clarity were good. The rest of her outfit was normal jeans with a pink knit shirt—not much different from what I had in my closet—so I adjusted my assessment. This woman was willing to spend big bucks, but only when she saw something she really wanted. I just needed to make my services something she'd want badly and often.

I was already seated at the wood table I'd snagged at a yard sale and gestured to the nicer of my two chairs, which I'd left empty for Michelle. Except for a small cabinet, there was no other furniture in the room.

Since she hadn't indicated on the intake form which services she wanted, I had my tarot cards ready, as well as the tea service with steam coming from the pot, in the hopes that having the stuff on the table might make her feel obligated to do both. My Bichon Frise, Nostradamus, was waiting on his dog bed in the corner and eyed the newcomer hopefully. I find many clients feel better when holding a dog, which leads to return customers for me and lots of fur-stroking for Damus.

Michelle sat. I saw her glance at the business card I had waiting right in front of her, but she didn't pick it up. Her hands were busy clutching the yellow purse on her lap so tightly that her knuckles whitened. She finally blurted, "Cynda Hobbs referred me to you."

That's the sort of thing I wished Michelle had put on the form. There was a spot for it and everything, but she'd left that blank.

I scoured my memory, not that it took long. Cynda's husband had been a cheater, which I'd discovered the old-fashioned way—spying on him with binoculars. But instead of saying that outright, I'd told Cynda to bring me an article of his clothing. When she came to our next meeting with a tie, I'd held it for a moment before claiming that a 'psychic vision' had given me the necessary details about her husband's activities—like that his mistress had a pierced nose, and I was suddenly smelling eucalyptus.

"My husband's yoga instructor has a pierced nose! He comes home smelling of eucalyptus oil!"

I'd put one hand to my chest and worn a suitably shocked expression at how accurate my vision had been. Then I'd given Cynda a business card for a private investigator that I'd made friends with. It always helps sell the legitimacy of your psychic visions when someone else can hand over the pictures you've already taken of the yoga mistress giving naked hubby a rubdown with the bottle of eucalyptus oil. Within two weeks, I'd gotten my cut from the PI and—nice surprise—an extra bonus from the grateful wife.

If Michelle was referred by Cynda and looked this upset, it wasn't hard to figure out why she'd come. But it's best not to be too obvious about such things.

Michelle waited silently, and I began my routine. "I sense . . . disloyalty." That was a safe bet. If Michelle did have a cheater in her life, disloyalty applied. If it later turned out that she was wrong, then the disloyalty would be Michelle having unfairly suspected the person. And if she hadn't come to see me about a cheater after all, well, who doesn't have at least one friend who has said something unkind at one point or another? Disloyalty was a common theme in my work.

Michelle nodded, her brown eyes looking vulnerable and worried. "I think my husband cheats on me when he goes out of town. His new job has him traveling a lot on business."

I wanted to curse but suppressed it. How was I supposed to show off my brilliant psychic powers if she gave me all the details up front? I lowered my eyelids to just a slit, then intoned sagely, "Yes, I sense traveling. Distance. It may be emotional distance. Possibly just physical." That last part was crucial. No one wants to pay hundreds of bucks to be told right up front that they already had all the answers before walking in my door. Plus, I needed some cover in case she was wrong about the cheating.

"He might not be cheating?" Michelle asked, sounding surprised.

I watched her put her purse on the table, and as she tucked my business card inside, I foresaw a profitable future with this client. "The tarot cards may be able to tell us more," I said with a meaningful look at the deck.

Damus knew exactly what it meant when I said 'tarot.' I'd used enough chicken breast to train him. He perked up and headed right for our new client, giving her the soft-eyes treatment, with a pleading whine added for good measure.

An hour later, Damus had gotten lots of absent-minded strokes, and Michelle had paid me for both a tarot and a tea-leaf reading. The answer to whether her husband was cheating was still regrettably unclear. It had to be, of course, because I hadn't gotten the chance to do proper research and there's no way I'll ever claim a thing like that until I know for sure that I'm right. I prefer not to burn in hell, thank you very much.

"It would help if I could see his luggage," I told Michelle. "If it was present when he betrayed you, there may be an aura around it that I can read."

She squinted at me in confusion. "You want me to bring you his suitcase?"

I paused, as if considering it, before saying, "It might be best if I could be near the clothes and everything else that he takes with him too. Auras can seep, and you never know which object will hold the most negative energy."

Basically, I needed to check his out-of-town toiletries for condoms and other clues.

Michelle swallowed, then stammered, "I . . . I'm not sure about . . . If Justin sees me taking the suitcase out of the house, or comes home and it isn't there . . . and he doesn't always use the same one or pack the same clothes . . ."

I nodded wisely. This was what I'd been hoping for. "Would you prefer I make a house call?"

There were two big advantages to this approach. First, I could charge more for a home visit. Second, there'd be more stuff to search. All I had to do was tell her I needed to be alone because her aura was interfering with the reading, and then I'd rummage through the pockets of the guy's clothes and his dresser drawers.

Michelle paused, looking almost like she was holding her breath, before she said, "Can you come to my house at ten tomorrow morning?"

I SPENT THE NIGHT REVIEWING Justin Satterlee's social media and found surprisingly little. It could be that he valued privacy, or it might be that he knew better than to post pictures of places where he was hooking up with women. When I discussed it with Jane—interrupting her research on adolescent bullying—she rolled her eyes at me. "Your work is making you a pessimist about human nature," she said. "If more people stayed off social media, the teenage suicide rate would drop."

Since she had a point, I put aside the laptop—after ordering a pizza. Damus and I then had a nice time streaming a BBC mystery on TV, while Jane went back to earning her degree in social work.

The next morning, I was on my way to the Satterlees' house when my phone received a text. Being a responsible driver, I waited until I'd stopped at a red light before checking the message, which read:

I'm making something in my kitchen.
Left the front door open for you.

I wondered whether that meant Michelle was planning to feed me like a real guest and, if so, whether I'd be getting a treat or something I'd have to pretend to like.

Fifteen minutes later, I pulled into the driveway of the Satterlees' McMansion. When I got to the porch, I found the front door open just a sliver. Some sort of classical music was coming from inside. I pushed the door open wider, then called out, "Michelle?"

She didn't reply, so I stepped inside. The smell—and most houses have one—was of vanilla. Not real vanilla, but the overpriced scented candle kind. It didn't bode well for whatever was happening in the kitchen.

I didn't see any security cameras and was tempted to take a quick peek around, but accepted it wasn't worth the risk of getting caught. Instead, I followed the sound of the orchestral music. As I worked my way through a dining room with chairs for ten, I again called out, "Michelle?"

Hearing no reply, I pushed open a folding door that seemed likely to lead to the kitchen, even though I still couldn't smell any food. A cast-iron pan sitting on the otherwise empty countertop caught my eye first, followed by the sight of my client, sprawled face-down on the pale bamboo floor. There was a small pool of blood by her head, and both of her bare hands were spread wide open, like she'd tried—and failed—to push herself up.

I crept closer to check for a pulse, but found none. "Why did you leave your door open?" I whimpered.

There was no reply from the dead woman, proving what I already knew—I'm not really a psychic.

I pulled out my phone and dialed 911.

The operator asked me to go outside to wait for the police, and I promised I would.

I was barely out the front door when I heard sirens coming. A patrol car arrived first. It was soon followed by an ambulance, then another patrol car. Eventually, a middle-aged detective named Jennifer Rodriguez arrived on the scene.

She asked me to show her some identification, so I handed her my driver's license. Then, she wanted to know why I'd been at the Satterlees' house. I explained my brief history with Michelle. To prove that I'd been invited, I showed her the text message on my phone.

That turned out to be unwise. She wanted to confiscate the phone.

I declined to hand it over. Not because I had anything criminal on the device, but because I needed it for my business. And it was a freaking expensive phone. "I can't afford to replace it," I said as pathetically as I could.

"Would you like me to get a warrant?" Detective Rodriguez asked with cool disregard for my strained finances.

I clicked the button on the side to shut down the screen and said, "If you'll let me keep the phone, I'll let you snap a photo of the text message about the open front door."

She stiffened, and I knew I'd made a mistake. She wanted to be top dog, and any negotiating by me denied her that role. I'd never been a murder suspect before but thought that antagonizing the investigator might not be a good strategy, especially if she could get a warrant to seize the phone as evidence anyway. I meekly handed it over.

"The passcode?" she asked.

I considered my options, pondering how little goodwill my cooperation with her thus far had bought me. "Maybe I should call a lawyer." I held my hand out for the return of my phone in what I hoped was a very unsubtle way.

I thought I saw a small glimmer of respect in her eyes, but she didn't give me back my property. "You can go home now, but stay available."

"That would be a lot easier with my phone," I muttered as she walked away.

As I drove home, I replayed the events over and over in my mind. Michelle's hands had been bare against the wood floor of the kitchen. Could this be a simple robbery? Had someone killed her for that huge diamond ring she'd been wearing when we met?

Then it hit me. The front door was supposedly open because she was cooking in the kitchen, but I hadn't smelled anything but the fake-vanilla candles. And the countertop had been empty, except for the iron pan. No food.

Something wasn't right.

I pulled into my apartment building's parking lot, took the slot next to my landlady's SUV, headed inside, and wearily trod the stairs to my third-floor apartment. I drew my keys from my pocket, but when I grabbed the doorknob, I found it unlocked.

I entered the apartment, calling out, "Jane?"

The only response was Damus running from my bedroom to greet me.

"Hey, Buddy. Where's Jane?"

Damus blinked up at me, waiting for something. Most likely, he expected to be picked up and petted.

The silence was unnerving. Jane was probably in class, not that I had her schedule memorized, but the unlocked door was freaking me out. Had someone picked the lock?

"Jane?" I called louder, hearing the panic in my voice.

I scurried around the apartment, focusing on the floors to make sure there wasn't another corpse anywhere. Damus followed loyally at my heels. I found nothing unusual, then realized I'd just reenacted every bad horror flick where the stupid person goes to check things out instead of getting far away.

"I'm an idiot, Nostradamus. That doesn't bode well for your future—having an idiot for an owner."

He yipped a reply I chose to interpret as: "I love you anyway, as long as the chicken keeps coming."

I went to the fridge and pulled out the container that had his chicken chopped into tiny cubes. He started dancing in place, knowing exactly what was coming. Sometimes, I instruct him to do an easy trick before handing out treats, just to reinforce his training, but I was so relieved that the apartment was fine that I gave him three pieces for free.

As soon as I returned the container and shut the door, Damus trotted away from the kitchen. I sighed as his perky tail rounded the corner and disappeared from view. So much for loyalty.

When I heard a yip from my bedroom, I ignored it, going to the living room instead and plopping down on the sofa with my laptop. I had research to do.

Damus barked again. And again.

After less than a minute of that, he came out of my bedroom, marched far enough down the hall to meet my eyes, gave a single impatient yap, then went back to the bedroom.

I sighed and went to see what he wanted.

My bedroom is almost as sparse as my office downstairs. I've got two Ikea chests of drawers, plus a mattress and box-spring on a cheap frame with no headboard. The bed has a dust-ruffle, not because I waste money on things like that, but because the sheets I'd bought on sale included one in the package. Damus was pawing at a corner where it met the bed.

He looked at me and issued a demanding bark.

Just to convince myself that nothing was wrong, I heaved up the edge of the mattress. That's when I saw the side of a plastic baggie. With a feeling of foreboding, I reached out to tug on it.

It was a zip-lock sandwich bag with Michelle's diamond ring and a matching pendant inside it. I suddenly had a lot of questions, like whether someone had dog-bribing food residue stuck to their gloves while planting the baggie, since that would explain Damus's interest. But one question soon took precedence: How soon would the police get an anonymous tip that I had a dead woman's jewelry under my bed?

I shoved the baggie back where I'd found it and raced downstairs to my car. I rushed to the rear passenger tire-well, silently begging for help from whatever angels watch out for frauds and fools.

It took five seconds of fumbling to find what I sought, but they were some of the longest seconds of my life. I seized the magnetic key box for hiding emergency fobs. Nearly the size of a cigarette pack, I got it when my parents died because I'd felt alone, like there was no one I could count on to come help me if I locked myself out of my car or home.

I hurried back inside and upstairs to my kitchen. Panting, I emptied the key box, dropped it in a bowl, then reached under the sink and pulled out the bleach. I didn't know how long it took to destroy DNA, but I wasn't going to risk sending a question like that over the internet.

I filled the bowl and wasted at least a minute staring at it. Then I retrieved the baggie with the diamonds, put plastic grocery bags over each of my hands, thoroughly rinsed the key box, wiped it down, put the diamonds inside it, and sealed it back up.

I pulled a bag off one hand and grabbed the key box with the hand that was still covered. The question was how to go outside the apartment with a plastic grocery bag on my hand without looking suspicious. The answer was a dog. Beautiful, wonderful Nostradamus.

We headed down to the strip of grass between the sidewalk and parking lot, whereupon I begged him to "go potty." While he did that, I knelt by my landlady's SUV on the side furthest from my own car. Two minutes later, the diamonds were safely attached to someone else's property, and I held a plastic bag of dog poop—one of the most ubiquitous sights in Northern Virginia.

We went back to the apartment, and I gave Damus several more pieces of chicken as a reward for being so helpful, before resuming my research. I used my laptop's contact files to look up the number for Cynda Hobbs, and gave her a call on the landline.

I needed her to be gossipy, not horrified, so I made my voice nonchalant in case Cynda hadn't learned about Michelle. "A friend of yours, Michelle Satterlee, requested my services."

"Really?" Cynda drew out the word, sounding more confused than intrigued.

"Apparently, her husband travels a lot on business?"

"Oh." Now Cynda sounded guilty. "I'm sorry about that."

Cynda explained that Justin had worked for her husband, who'd sold his business as part of their divorce proceedings because he couldn't afford to pay her the court-ordered alimony any other way. "Justin was superfluous for the company that bought us out. They already had a guy doing what he does, but for a lot less, so he was laid off in the first week."

"Ouch."

"Yeah. Someone told me he got a job over at Yeardley-Huston, but I doubt they're going to pay him nearly as much. And I heard a rumor that his gambling problem is getting worse."

The gambling was interesting, but if it was such common knowledge, it felt odd that Michelle hadn't mentioned it. "Why did you seem surprised that Michelle had hired me?"

"I'm afraid Michelle doesn't believe in psychics," Cynda said apologetically. "She told me you were probably making it all up. I showed her the photos of Mike with his yoga instructor to prove to her that you'd been right, but Michelle said you'd likely taken them yourself and that's how you'd known what to tell me."

Michelle was cleverer than I'd given her credit for. I was worried that her killer might be too.

I thanked Cynda for her time, then ended the call so that I could focus on reassessing the situation.

Michelle did not believe in psychics and could've easily searched Justin's luggage herself. So, what had she really wanted from me, and why have me come to her house?

She couldn't have been planning to frame me for her murder, but if the Satterlees were having money troubles, what about a theft? She could claim something had gone missing from her bedroom—like her diamond jewelry—and place the blame on the con-artist psychic who'd been stupidly planning to find an opportunity to be alone there. Michelle could then collect from her insurance company, all while keeping the items or selling them herself.

Had someone known about her plan and changed it to a murder?

My musings were interrupted by a knock on the door. I answered it to find Detective Rodriguez standing there with a search warrant for my apartment, car, and office.

"According to the victim's husband, we should've found a diamond ring and pendant on the body," she told me as four other officers made their way into my home. "And Justin Satterlee says his wife doesn't believe in psychics. He suggested we call her family to confirm it."

"I have the credit card charge to prove that she paid me for a tarot and tea reading session," I said with some relief.

"That only means you could've gotten her card number. It wouldn't be the first time someone's credit card got stolen."

I didn't even bother to remind the detective that Michelle likely had my business card too. I could've easily planted that while in her house. "There's still the text message I got from her this morning."

The detective arched an eyebrow. "Was it from her? We're getting the records from her provider to see, since you refused to give us the passcode to your own phone."

I was suddenly quite confident the number would prove to be from a burner phone, since her killer would want the message to look like I could've faked it. That meant planning, getting the burner in advance. And the sender had to be someone she'd told about me coming to the house. Someone who already knew quite a bit about me in order to plant the diamonds so quickly. It seemed I wasn't the only one who could do research.

The police search of my bedroom and the apartment common spaces went on for ages, since jewelry is rather small, and thus can be hidden nearly anywhere. When Jane came home, the cops asked to be allowed to search her room too. I felt it was safe, since I knew where the diamonds were, so I gave Jane a nod to say that we were better off letting the cops feel they'd looked in every possible place. She gave her consent, added a glare at me—likely for causing the police to even be there—then left for the university's library so she could get some studying done in peace.

I looked out the window to watch her go and saw the cops towing my car away.

"We're taking it to our garage," Rodriguez said as she came to stand beside me. "We've got experts on drug smuggling who know how to rip it apart."

"Great," I replied dully, wondering how well the car would operate after that.

The downstairs office didn't take long to search, but it was nearly midnight before they were finished with my apartment. Detective Rodriguez was the last to head out. I let her get as far as the apartment's front door, then asked, "Did Michelle's husband have life insurance on her?"

She turned around and gave me a smile. "Yeah. He admitted it since we were bound to find out anyway. A five-million-dollar policy taken out quite recently."

I assessed her through narrowing eyes, wondering at her willingness to be so candid with me.

She leaned with seeming nonchalance against the doorjamb. "He insisted that we needed to search your apartment for the missing jewelry. Not your office. Not your car. Not your house, condo, or townhome, but your apartment." She arched her eyebrows. "Funny how he knew you lived in one."

"Funny," I repeated with absolutely no humor.

"I'd love to know where he hid the jewelry," she told me.

I suspected she meant where in my apartment he'd hidden it, but I wasn't willing to risk saying a word.

She straightened but still didn't turn to go.

Our eyes met, then she said, "The prosecutor is going to have to explain to a jury what happened to the diamonds. If you had to guess, where do you think I could find them?"

I blinked as innocently as I could. "How should I know?"

The detective pursed her lips and paused before taking a deep breath, followed by a long exhale. She looked down the empty hallway, then told me, "The Satterlee house is still a crime scene, so he's staying at a hotel on the corner of Chain Bridge Road and Route 50."

"I can't imagine why I'd care." It was true. Only an idiot would go near his hotel given the inevitability of security cameras in the parking lot, elevators, and hallways. "But I hear that patience is a virtue."

Her lips curved up for a second before she turned and left.

I waited two days before I took an early bus to Merrifield. Dawn was breaking as I walked the half-mile to the coffee-shop opposite the Yeardley-Huston building. I ordered a latte, paid cash, and slowly nursed my drink in a seat by the window.

Justin Satterlee arrived for work promptly at nine. I waited another half-hour to make sure no one was watching before planting the jewelry in the wheel-well of his SUV. Then I strolled away, merrily humming off-tune.

Eight hours later, it made the news that the police had searched his car and arrested him for the murder of his wife. I wondered how Detective Rodriguez had known to do it that very day, and how she'd found the stones so fast. Had she been following me or watching him?

Either way, it seemed she was good at research too. That, or it was time to start believing in psychics.

THE ASS-IN

MERRILEE ROBSON

I BLAME THE DOG.

I mean, if there was a Good Neighbor award in the building, Irene would win it every time. She's the kind of neighbor who'll water your plants and keep an eye on your place when you're away. The kind who'll give you a key so you can do the same for her.

But the dog, man, she'll bark all day if Irene leaves her alone.

I guess that's why Irene named her Dorothy Barker, but I don't know why Irene and my grandmother think it's such a funny name. They're always laughing about it.

The building manager doesn't think it's funny, that's for sure. She complained to Irene about the noise, saying she'd have to evict her if she couldn't keep the dog quiet.

So, Irene always takes Dorothy with her if she goes away. She doesn't want to lose her home.

It's a good building. The building manager can be a bit of a pain, but she keeps the place looking real nice, even though the rents are low. It's the kind of building where people live for years.

Like Irene. She's lived across the hall from my grandmother for must be twenty years or more.

So, it's only neighborly, now that she's away on holiday, to take the key with the little blue plastic tag and pop in to check that everything's okay. And I'm sure Irene wouldn't begrudge me a little something for my help.

Nonna's always trying to fatten me up, saying, "Have some of this cake I made, Wally. You're too skinny."

155

Maybe my grandmother's right. Because when I'm suddenly knocked flat on my ass, I sure could use some extra padding. She says the fir floors in the building are softwood, but the floor doesn't feel soft to me.

Not that I have time to think about that because something is on top of me, baring sharp teeth and barking so loud I think my eardrums are going to burst, if I don't get eaten first.

Irene *always* takes the dog with her when she goes away. So why is Dorothy here, making so much noise the building manager is sure to be banging on the door any minute?

I race to the kitchen, with the dog barking at my heels. I know where Irene keeps the dog food.

But the bag of food isn't on the counter where Irene always keeps it.

Dorothy barks even louder.

And then she growls.

And, man, those teeth look big.

I pull open the fridge door, thinking I could at least get it between me and the dog. And, miracle of miracles, there's a package of hamburger right there on the shelf.

I pull open a corner of the plastic wrap and toss a hunk of hamburger to the dog.

And just like that, she stops barking.

I know she's just going to start up again.

I toss her another bit of hamburger, and she wags her tail, giving me time to look around the apartment.

And, what the hell! There's a duffel bag dumped against the wall by the front door. Cripes, what if Irene hasn't left yet?

I edge toward the door, tossing hunks of hamburger to the dog.

But that duffel bag stops me. It isn't really Irene's style. I've helped her carry her luggage down the stairs a few times, trying to be helpful. She's mainly pink, hard-sided matching suitcases, not duffel bags.

I'd better check.

And, sure enough, the bag is filled with jeans and a few T-shirts, not Irene's style at all. I throw some more hamburger to the dog and slide my hand into a side pocket.

And then I hear a key in the lock.

The duffel bag is zipped up again and I'm standing with one hand in my pocket when the door opens.

I'm trying to think of a good excuse for being in Irene's apartment when I see her niece, Keira.

"What are you doing here?"

We say it at the same time, but she manages to look more outraged than I can. I do try to sound surprised.

"Oh, hi, Keira," I say.

"What are you doing here?" she repeats.

"Um, your Aunt Irene gave me a spare key so I could water the plants while she's away."

She narrows her eyes. "Why would she do that? I'm staying here. I can water the plants as well as look after the dog. And besides, you're not watering anything. What are you doing with that ground beef?"

Damn, I'd forgotten about the hamburger. I'm still clutching it in one hand. Drops of red would have been staining the carpet except that Dorothy is licking them up as fast as they fall, wagging her tail and grinning.

"Um . . . well, I heard Dorothy barking, and I thought she must be hungry. You know the building manager gets mad when she barks. Just trying to help."

I hold the hamburger out to her but she frowns.

"Give me the key."

"No. I told you, your aunt gave it to me for when she goes away."

"She can give it back to you if she wants." She puts her hand out and holds it there. "I mean it, Wally. Do I need to call the police?"

I pull the key out of my pocket, being careful not to dislodge what I stuffed in there, and scuttle out the door.

Much later, I'm glad for the money I found in the duffel bag. It isn't much, but I'll worry about that later.

Right now, I just want to sit on Nonna's balcony and enjoy a quiet smoke. The weather is finally warm enough to sit outside in the evening and the mosquitos aren't too bad yet. Or maybe the smoke is keeping the bugs away. Another of marijuana's benefits.

Keira's voice is low, but I can still hear her.

"Mom, have you met Aunt Irene's neighbor?" There is a pause, so she must be on the phone.

"No, not Mrs. Alfano. She's lived across from Aunt Irene for years. I mean Wally, her grandson. Do you know him?"

"Yes, that beard is terrible, isn't it?" she adds after another pause. "Yes, I know Aunt Irene thinks he's helpful."

And I am helpful. I do the shopping for my Nonna, especially when her bad hip makes it hard for her to get around. And I've done things for Irene from time to time: changing lightbulbs and moving furniture around.

Hell, I should probably get a Good Neighbor award.

"Yes," I hear Keira say. "I suppose you could say he has pretty eyes . . ."

This is starting to get interesting, but then Keira's voice is drowned out by the woman upstairs.

"Hey, you. You can't smoke here!"

The old lady is on the balcony above me. She's even older than my Nonna, but she's leaning over the railing and screaming at me.

My voice sounds friendly, slow, and mellow. "Yeah, yeah, I can. They changed the law. It's not illegal anymore."

"But you can't smoke here! This is a non-smoking building. We all agreed."

"I'm outside," I reply. My words seem to float up to her with the smoke. "I can smoke outdoors."

"You're not supposed to be here at all," she yells. "You don't live here. What are you doing here all the time? And where is your grandmother?"

I start to tell her about Nonna's hip, and the operation, and how I'm keeping an eye on things, but she drowns me out. "If you don't stop, I'm calling the police."

I sit up. Pot is legal here, but the stuff I have isn't exactly from one of those stores they have all over the city.

I hear the faint sound of a siren.

I grab one of the cushions from Nonna's patio furniture and wave it around to blow the smoke away. I hear Keira coughing as if she is trying to make a point and the old woman upstairs is yelling again.

The sirens are closer. Shit!

I run indoors, grab the packages, lean out over the railing, and throw one over the edge.

I hear a splash.

Shit, it's right in the middle of that pond the building manager is always fussing with. The package floats for a moment, like one of those waterlilies she planted in there, and then sinks slowly.

I stop for a moment, thinking about the goldfish in that pond. How goldfish would behave if they were stoned. Would they start looking around that pond for more fish food when they got the munchies?

I start to laugh, but then the siren sounds closer.

"Shit."

The second package lands on the bench in front of the building, but the next one joins the first in the pond.

There are more sirens now.

And then I hear heavy steps on the stairs and a pounding on the door.

I climb over the railing and get ready to jump.

But it's just the old woman from upstairs yelling through the door. As the sirens continue past the building without stopping.

I start to climb back over the railing.

But my foot slips.

I start to fall.

I grab the railing at the last minute.

But now I'm dangling by one hand.

It's only a one-story drop, but I don't like the look of the rock garden underneath me.

"Keira?"

I hope she can hear me over the sound of the old woman still hammering on the door and yelling about smoking.

"Keira, are you there? Can you help me?"

I look over at Irene's balcony and see Keira leaning over toward me.

"There's no way I can reach you, Wally."

"Irene has a key. My grandmother gave her one. She keeps it in the blue vase in the living room. Can you come over and help me up?"

She disappears into Irene's apartment.

But my hand starts to sweat.

I try to reach up with the other one, but that was a bad idea.

As I fall, I have time to wonder if my scream sounds too girly.

Then I hit the rock garden.

The rocks I land on are even harder than the floor in Irene's apartment.

I lie there for a moment, wondering how many bruises I'm going to have.

I'm happy to find I can move my legs and I try to stand up. But my foot hits one of the planters on the patio below the rock garden, and it topples over with a crash that seems to shake the building.

The dog is barking. I don't want Irene to lose her home.

But the crash of the falling pot sounded louder even than the dog, and I really don't want Nonna to be evicted.

And then I remember the packages in the lily pond.

I need to get them!

Man, those water lilies look pretty, but up close they're all slimy and slippery. And the water is cold and kind of smelly.

I reach around in the water, trying to find the packages. I'm thinking about those stoned fish and how they probably really have the munchies by now.

Would they think my fingers look like a snack?

That's when I slip and fall face down in the water.

And it tastes as bad as it smells.

Good thing I landed right on the packages.

I scoop them both up, pick up the one on the bench and head to the door, hoping to get inside Nonna's apartment before the building manager sees me.

If I move fast, she won't find out that it was me that caused the damage.

I mean, the people who live here are mostly in their eighties, but who says they're too old to cause trouble?

It's all going good. The old lady from upstairs has probably stopped pounding on my door, and there's no one to see me slip back into the apartment building.

Except I don't have my keys.

I pull hopefully on the front door, but of course it's locked.

I look up at the balcony of Irene's apartment.

"Keira? Keira, are you still there? Can you let me in? I don't have my keys."

She looks kind of grumpy when she comes downstairs and opens the door. And she seems even more grumpy when I remind her that I need the key to Nonna's apartment that Irene has.

I mean, duh, what did she think?

But I try to be a gentleman like Nonna taught me and thank her very much.

"This is great," I say. "There's no need for anyone else to find out that it was me that messed up the garden and the pond."

Keira has a funny look on her face, and she is staring at the wet footsteps on the stair carpet.

I mean sure, there were some water drops leading straight to my door. But they'd dry pretty soon.

And the mud . . . well, the carpet was kind of beige anyway, it will probably blend in when it is dry. It's all good.

Until the next day.

That's when Keira starts banging on my door *waayy* too early, yelling that I stole her money.

"Don't try to play innocent, Wally. I left my tips from the restaurant in my bag and know they were there before I left for work."

She's shouting and banging on the door, and I think between Dorothy Barker and the noise Keira is making, Irene is going to be evicted for sure.

I'm trying to tell her that when I open the door, but she just barges in and keeps yelling.

"It was money I was saving for my mom's birthday present and now it's all gone. And you were in the apartment yesterday, so don't try to deny it was you."

I've met Keira's mom and she's as nice as Irene. And I remember what she'd said about my eyes being pretty.

"Well, Keira, sure I had the key—but the building manager must have one too . . ."

"I didn't find the building manager in my aunt's living room yesterday. It was you and now my money's gone. You may be an idiot. I am not! Are you going to give it back, or do I have to call the police?"

"I'm not saying I did it and I don't have any money right now," I say. "But I will later. How much was it? Maybe I can help you out. You were good enough to let me back in last night."

She just glares at me, but it's nice and quiet now that she stopped yelling. Except for Dorothy, who is still barking.

"You better get back to her," I tell Keira. "You know what she's like and your aunt—"

"*You* have until this afternoon to give *my* money back, or I'm calling the police."

Keira's not nearly as nice as her aunt. But, no worries, I have a plan to get more money.

See, when I bought the weed, I didn't have quite enough money. But Roy, the guy I got it from, said I could have it for that price if I just helped him out a bit. I just have to sell it, give Roy his money, and I'll get to keep some of the money for myself. Then I can pay Keira back.

No problem. I know a few guys who will be happy to take the stuff off my hands.

Except that was before the events of last night.

One bag is fine. No problem there.

But the two that went into the pond . . .

I probably should have tried to dry them out last night. Those packages are covered in mud and algae. And they stink.

But worst of all, the water got inside the plastic wrap. Everything is soaking wet.

That's when Roy calls.

I start to complain that the bags were supposed to be waterproof.

But he just starts telling me what he'll do if he doesn't get his money. And it is way scarier than Keira's threats to call the police.

"It's not my fault," I say. I complain again about the bags not being waterproof.

But he interrupts me.

"Yeah," I say finally. "I was the one who dropped them in the pond."

Then he says a bunch of other stuff.

"Okay," I say. "Yeah, okay, I'll do it."

I get the gun Roy gave me when I first started to deal for him. I've never had to shoot it, but it works well to keep people in line.

The guy I have to go after is probably some law-abiding wimp who will give me what I'm after when he sees the gun.

I limp down to the parking lot—I must have hurt my ankle worse than I thought when I fell—but I finally make it and start the car.

I scream when I try to press my foot on the gas. Probably not as loud as when I fell, but there is no way I can drive with my foot like this.

I think of what Roy said and tears start to form in my eyes.

I'm not crying. It's probably just the pain in my ankle. But what Roy said . . .

And then I think of Keira.

She wants the money as much as I do.

Well, maybe not as much as I do because Roy . . .

But still, she does want to get a present for her mom and her mom's so nice, so . . .

I limp back up the stairs. You'd think, with so many old people in the building, they'd get an elevator, wouldn't you?

I knock on her door. "Keira, I need your help. I got hurt when I fell last night and I can't drive. I can get your money right away, but could you drive me?"

Her jaw drops. "You've got to be kidding!"

Then she looks at where I'm hiding Roy's gun under my jacket.

"You hurt your arm?"

"My ankle . . . yeah, and my arm. Could you drive, Keira? I just have to see a guy and I'll give you your money. You'll be able to get your mom's present today."

That does the trick. Or maybe she feels sorry for me. But soon she is driving Nonna's aging Corolla as I direct her to the shopping strip Roy told me about.

"Stop here," I say, as we get to a row of single-story shops. "Just wait here and then pull up when I come out. I'll have your money in a jiffy."

She frowns. "Wally . . ."

I hop out and limp a few doors down to the pot shop. I should be able to get enough dope to replace the stuff that fell in the pond, and maybe more. I've made fun of the gummies those stores sell, but I actually want to try them. I mean, marijuana and a snack, all together. What more could you ask for? And he'll probably have some cash in the till. I can pay Keira back right away.

163

I pull the gun out from under my jacket as I get to the door of the store.

The guy looks clean cut, dressed in a nice shirt. This is going to be a piece of cake.

Until he pulls out an even bigger gun.

"Drop it," he says.

So I do.

Then I turn and run out the door.

Or try to.

I'd forgotten about my sore ankle.

The guy must have had an alarm in the store because I can hear it screaming as I limp down the sidewalk as fast as I can, signaling to Keira to pull the car up.

That's when my ankle gives way and I crash to the sidewalk.

The guy from the store catches up with me and points the gun at my head.

And then I hear the sound of sirens.

The guy from the store is telling the cops that the security cameras would have caught the whole thing.

Roy should have known about those cameras.

I start to relax because, if I go to jail, Roy won't be able to get to me to do what he threatened.

At least I hope that's true.

I hear Keira saying she'd just been doing a favor for an injured neighbor.

Like she's trying to win that Good Neighbor award the building doesn't have.

The cops tell her to leave the car where it is and she can leave.

I see her turn and start to head toward the bus stop.

"Keira!"

She keeps walking.

"Keira! Can you help me?"

She stops.

"Were you really planning on shooting that guy, Wally?"

"What? No! It was just to scare him. I'm not a murderer."

She frowns.

"You know, Wally, I recall something about the word assassin. Isn't there something about the term being derived from murderers who used hashish before their killing sprees?"

"I told you, I'm not an assassin."

"No, Wally, you're just an ass."

"That's mean, Keira. Why can't you be nice like your Aunt Irene? Will you do me a favor and call me a lawyer?"

Her eyes widen.

"I can't, Wally. Remember, I don't have any money."

So you see, none of this is my fault.

I suppose I could say I blame Keira.

But, really, it all started with that stupid dog.

CATCH AND RELEASE

LISA ANNE ROTHSTEIN

THE PLANE BANKED SHARPLY AND dropped out of the sky onto the postage-stamp runway. My body tensed as the pilot decelerated. The nose of the plane stopped uncomfortably close to the seawall and the cerulean water beyond.

"Do you think you could let go of my hand now, Ma'am?"

"I'm sorry," I said, releasing my grip on the flight attendant seated beside me. "I hate small planes." She didn't need to know that I'd cheated Death eight months ago—that I was living on borrowed time. I could feel Death hovering in the space behind me, waiting patiently for his next opportunity. Death has infinite patience.

The doctors told me I'd recovered after eight months of intensive, painful rehab, so I took the R&R—a week in paradise on the island of Sainte Hilare—before I returned to tempting Death on a daily basis.

I stepped off the plane. Heat radiated off the tarmac and up through the thin soles of my flip-flops. Kat had given me hell about my flimsy footwear when she dropped me off at O'Hare. I had pretended that the blare of a cab horn drowned out her worried question. I hadn't needed her asking me again if I was okay. She'd have known I was lying if I'd said yes. I don't like to lie to my sister.

I stilled for a moment, taking in the deep turquoise blue of the Caribbean. I felt the warm breeze flow over my arms, bare since I'd chucked my sweater. My muscles relaxed. I felt the vacuity that I normally got from alcohol. I didn't even hear Death breathing behind me.

The sound of steel drums filled the open-air arrivals room where I cleared customs. I couldn't help bouncing with the music as I headed toward the resort shuttle. *Kat was right. I did need this. It might even help.*

I spent the afternoon lounging by the pool, empty deck chairs all around. The attentive staff plied me with piña coladas. A half-read paperback lay on my lap as I watched waves roll into the sheltered cove. The clear water called to me, but I couldn't overcome my desire to be idle.

As sunset turned the sky an orangey red, I made my way to the beachfront restaurant and slid onto a stool at the bar. *I could do this for a week, easy—mimosas on my balcony at breakfast, piña coladas by the pool in the afternoon, whiskey at the beach bar in the evening.*

The bartender dropped a napkin in front of me. "What can I get you?"

The woman looked like she belonged here—at a beach bar in paradise—her skin wrinkled from the sun, her hair falling in beautiful, gray dreadlocks, and her expression serene. Even the name stitched into her shirt, Delia, radiated calm.

"You got Lagavulin?"

Her lips formed the obsequious smile resort staff reserved for guests who tested their patience. "We do, but there's an upcharge for that."

"Not surprising." I tapped the napkin. "Lay it on me. My first night here, I can splurge."

Delia poured the liquid amber cleanly—not a splash of wasted whiskey.

"Enjoy." She slid the drink over. I closed my eyes, lifted the glass to my lips, and felt the familiar burn as the whiskey flowed down my throat.

"How long you here for?" she asked.

I opened my eyes to see her observing me, one eyebrow slightly raised as she wiped down the spotless bar. I wanted not to engage. I wanted to stay in this comfortable, solitary head space. Something about her brought the words from my throat anyway, words I wouldn't normally have given anyone I barely knew.

"A week. Name's Amanda Wallingford. From Chicago."

Her hands stopped moving, her cocoa eyes focused on me with an intensity that made me squirm. I'm usually better at covering my reactions. I tilted back, my body poised to go. The whiskey, though, was too good to slug down and walk away, so I counted to ten like the therapist told me. I picked up the glass and waited for her to speak.

"I heard about you," she said, leaning into my space. "You're that FBI agent who got blown up."

So much for escaping to someplace where nobody would know. I tilted the glass, letting the smoky warmth of the Lagavulin caress my tongue.

"Where'd you hear that?" I asked, trying to buy some time.

"With all the deaths, tourists are staying away. So, I spend time on the Internet. There's a lot of talk about that explosion, and the problem you Americans have with your homegrown terrorists."

Her eyes shifted to my right, where another guest had seated himself, only two stools away. Even off duty in a tropical paradise, even with the alcohol, I sensed that. Did I always need to be hyper-alert? Could I not have a break?

"You could go down some rabbit holes that way, that's for sure. The—" I stopped as she raised a finger.

I looked down at my drink, contemplating the way ripples formed with the slightest movement. The reflected blue-green of the neon palm tree above the bar made the liquid shimmer like an oil slick. She had some kind of power, this woman, making me talk like that. Making me *stop* talking on command.

The man moved next to me, the scent of coconut sunscreen rising from his body, his hair the shimmering gold of a surfer. I kept my eyes on my drink, fighting the pull of his presence. No men. That had been my one promise to myself. I could wallow all I wanted, but no men. Except—I *wanted* him.

"Hi," I said, turning my body toward his. "I'm Amanda."

His white teeth flashed with the kind of mischievous smile that populates cheesy romance novels—like the half-read one stuffed in my beach bag. Except . . . except. Something dark hid back there behind the light. It was the darkness that drew me. I leaned a little closer.

Delia made a low "tsk" sound as she walked away to serve a couple down at the end of the bar. She saw too much.

"Kieran. Kieran Bonhomme," he said, extending his hand to mine.

I slipped my hand into his, then yanked it back as the name penetrated my fogged brain. "Seriously? Can't you come up with a better fake name?"

He closed the space between us, his leg brushing mine. "It's real. It's a corruption of Bonny." I heard the subtle lilt of an Irish accent, and found myself resting my hand on his leg, almost without thought. "One of my ancestors was Anne Bonny, the pirate," he whispered in my ear, raising goosebumps on my flesh.

I moved my hand up his thigh. "Is there buried treasure?"

"Can I get you all anything?"

I jumped. Delia stood behind the bar, but I felt a physical presence between me and Kieran. Like a warning. I stared her down. Nobody tells me what to do. Even when what I'm doing is stupid.

"Caipirinha for me." Kieran smiled, his lazy grin suffused with something I couldn't place.

Delia broke her gaze away, but not before I felt a push of energy from her. I shook my head. I did not believe in this woo-woo stuff. Even if I could hear Death regularly.

I turned back to Kieran and asked him about his day. We talked, dancing around the conversation, waiting for the right "let's get out of here" moment. He wasn't a local, but a resident of one of the resort's condo units. He got work as a dive instructor when he could and explored the reefs for shipwrecks when he couldn't. I suppose that's why I told him about my injuries, about the FBI, because his life sounded so much more like the life I'd rather have.

"Don't you think it's so cool, though?" he asked, finishing up a story about the pirates who had roamed the seas around the island centuries ago. He was so cute when he talked about the pirates, dimples forming as his face lit up with excitement. I liked being distracted, disengaged, without thought. He made it easy.

"I guess." Unable to resist the urge to touch him, I ran my hand down his stomach, fiddling absently with his belt. His eyes widened as his brain registered my meaning. I got him to ask first.

"Should we get out of here, babe?"

I WOKE SCREAMING. A DISEMBODIED arm pressed on my chest, suffocating me. I needed to dislodge it. I thrashed. The arm moved. Did I cause that, or could a severed arm still move—like a decapitated chicken?

Shhhh. Gas hissed from the broken mains. I had to find my team. If I was alive, some of them were too. I tried to lever myself up but sank into the soft ground instead. Was the tightness in my chest external or was it my heart? Something pushed against my shoulders. My body shook.

"Mandy! Hush. Wake up. It's a dream. Mandy!"

Mandy? None of my agents called me that.

"Shhhh." I jerked as something brushed my face. The downward pressure abated. I could move a little, open my eyes. I saw ice-blue eyes looking into my own. Alive eyes. A concerned face. Kieran. Only Kieran.

I took a deep breath. I smelled the coconut from his sunscreen. Late afternoon light filtered into the room through the gaps in the shutters. I remembered that we'd come back to his condo after our morning snorkel, worn ourselves out finding new ways to arouse each other. The man was inventive, I'll say that. I hadn't had a bomb dream in the two nights since I'd met him, longer than I'd gone without one yet.

His muscles tensed; his embrace felt like a vise. Darkness encroached on my vision as my claustrophobia kicked in. I didn't want him close like that, didn't want him restraining me. I rolled out of his arms.

He rose up, his face creased with concern. "What's—"

I waved my hand, shoving away his words. "I'm leaving. I promised myself I wouldn't do this."

He lay there, resting on one arm, the sheet draped over his body like a loin cloth, a wry smile transforming his face. "What are you afraid of? That you'll heal?"

I tugged my bikini on and threw the cover-up over my head. "You have no idea." I collected my key card and phone from the side table. "And nobody calls me Mandy. Nobody." I walked away, letting the door slam behind me.

I SETTLED ONTO THE BAR stool as darkness fell. I'd spent the last few hours walking the gardens—pacing really. Trying to get my head together, to pull myself up out of the place that wanted only oblivion.

"Trouble in paradise?" Delia asked, gazing pointedly at Kieran at the far end of the otherwise empty bar.

"Better that I tend to myself," I said, avoiding her eyes, focusing on the sound of the waves breaking behind the bar.

She set a glass in front of me, filled with a deep caramel liquid. "Laphroaig. On me."

"Not sure why I deserve that, but I'm not going to refuse." I took a sip and savored the velvety heat. "Unless you're going to ask me what happened."

"Your business," she said, leaning back and crossing her arms, her gaze hard.

I laughed. "Uh huh. You know I'm trained to read body language."

That got a brief smile.

I rolled my glass on the bar. The whiskey rose up the sides as it rocked. "Not going to kiss and tell. But I do want to know why this place is so empty. You said something about deaths."

She leaned closer, lowering her voice. "Tourists have been dying. The police say it's natural causes, from heavy drinking, or hard partying, or out-of-shape Americans doing water sports their bodies aren't used to. I don't buy it."

"What about toxicology?" I asked. "Or the—" She shook her head, silencing me before I could ask the second question.

"The blood samples had to go to the U.S. for sophisticated toxicology tests. Who knows how they could've been tampered with?"

I felt a waterfall of questions forming. I wanted it to stop. "Sometimes a rose really is a rose, though."

She huffed. "Could be. I guess you're not ready to be who you are, huh?"

"Who I am?" My voice rose. "You don't know anything about me."

I threw back the rest of my drink and stalked off, feeling ridiculous as I sensed the weight of Delia's and Kieran's gazes follow me out.

I listened to the sound of the tree frogs and the waves while I enjoyed a room-service burger and a beer on my balcony. I relaxed, but not enough to shut the agent brain down. Or Death. He came with the agent brain.

He wouldn't go away that night. Not without Kieran. I wouldn't sleep without Kieran either. It's disturbing how quickly dependency can creep up. I grabbed another beer and booted up my laptop, settling in for an extended research session.

A rooster crowed and I looked up from my screen. The sky had turned peachy pink. The ocean reflected the light of the rising sun. I could count another night without the dreams, even without Kieran. That was something, although not sleeping wasn't a long-term solution. Anyway, Death sat with me as I researched. He sat quietly, but I knew he was there.

After the bomb—once I had recovered my ability to talk—the therapist and I had discussed the inner conflict that occurs when you want two things equally that can't exist in the same space. I wanted my job—my calling— and I wanted Death to leave me alone. I still wanted both of those things. What good is a therapist if they don't tell you how to fix your problem?

After my research, I had even more questions for Delia. I'd have to wait until evening when her shift started. For the first time since I'd arrived, I was up early enough to catch the resort shuttle into town. I craved something more than passing the day in an alcoholic haze, so I showered, grabbed some breakfast, and set off to explore the tourist haunts.

I plopped onto an unoccupied bench on the shuttle, content to watch the lizards in the trees while I waited for the stragglers. Someone moved in next to me, encroaching on my personal space. I twisted around. My irritated words fizzled as I met Kieran's ice-blue eyes.

"Hi, Sugar."

Damn it. His voice held the same promise of heat, the same pull as whiskey. Why is it always the way? I turned back to the lizards. Maybe if I didn't answer, he'd disappear.

He put his arm around me, leaning in. "Want to come with me to the pirate museum?"

I sighed. He hadn't vanished. Truth was, I didn't actually want him gone. What I wanted was the intensity of being with him, the emotion strong enough to obliterate everything else. I gave up on the lizards. "A pirate museum?"

"It is a tourist trap, but there's nothing more fascinating than pirates. You know why this place is called Pirate's Cove? Because of the cove where we snorkeled." The animation I saw in his eyes hovered in the gray area between excitement and insanity. Every time he talked about pirates, he seemed like a different man. Normally, I'd be wary, but I could feel my need for distraction winning, shouting down the voice telling me to leave.

I nestled into the crook of his arm. "Pirates in the Caribbean isn't an unusual thing, I don't think."

He pulled me in closer as the shuttle accelerated toward the road to town. "True, and stories of buried treasure aren't either. But this one's real."

"Uh huh."

He brushed his lips against my hair. "You'll see."

We returned to the resort mid-afternoon. Kieran took off for a snorkeling session in a part of the cove that he had raved about, filled with unusual fish and even a resident octopus. I told him I didn't want to expend that much energy, but really, I wanted to talk to Delia. Questions had been clanging around in my head all day, distracting me from being in the moment. I needed to talk to Delia to make that stop.

I claimed my usual spot. Delia walked over.

"You're early." Her smile appeared genuine this time. "Should we start with the Irish whiskey today? Or maybe a Japanese one?"

"I'll just have a ginger beer and a club sandwich."

"Did I miss the world turning off its axis or something?" The intensity of her gaze didn't match the jokey tenor of her question.

I wanted some kind of barrier I could raise to protect my psyche. What was it about her that made me feel so vulnerable? I trusted my instincts, but maybe they'd been over-taxed lately and were misfiring.

The silence lasted a little too long for social nicety. I blinked and dove in. "I've been researching."

Her right eyebrow rose.

"The deaths. I wanted to ask you some questions."

Delia patiently answered my myriad questions, confirming my research, but not adding much. Five American tourists had died in six months, their deaths attributed to heart failure or an underlying health condition. I could understand why the authorities put the deaths down to coincidence, given the tiny percentage of the total tourist population that represented. Although in the way of Leroy Jethro Gibbs, I didn't believe in coincidences.

The running theory had been that the tourists consumed counterfeit booze tainted with methanol, which could produce similar looking deaths. None of the autopsies had been able to pinpoint anything, just a constellation of things that pointed toward natural causes. Improbable five times over, but not impossible. Sometimes when you hear hoof beats, it *is* a zebra.

Delia set the can of ginger beer in front of me, popping the top with a satisfying hiss. "You're looking far too serious."

"Sorry. I guess I'm processing." I poured the ginger beer over the ice in my glass and watched the bubbles rise to the top, each bubble producing a microburst of liquid spray as it popped. Solving crimes was like that, looking at minutiae, tracing connections, watching individual clues to see where they led.

I looked up at Delia, who smiled encouragingly. Almost like she'd been leading me to examine the case. I grinned. I'd thought of it as a "case."

"Are you doing that on purpose?" I asked her. What incentive she'd have to rehabilitate an FBI agent was beyond me, and yet I couldn't shake the feeling that she was trying.

She brought a dish of nuts over. "Doing what?"

I thought I saw just the barest glint of amusement in her eyes. More than likely, I was projecting. The state of detachment I'd been in since the bomb went off had been like a drug, the recovery an excuse I'd given myself to not be responsible. The blankness held me under, made me want to stay like that forever. Except I didn't actually want to.

I contemplated the melting ice in my ginger beer, the salt on the bar from the nuts. I felt an unexpected calm. The thought came unbidden: *I'm rehabilitating myself.* Maybe Kat was right, telling me to come here, to get away, to heal.

Still, there was something . . . I couldn't yet identify what, but Delia was telling me something.

A couple at a table waved her over for refills. It struck me that I hadn't sensed Death the whole time I'd been quizzing Delia. A frisson of excitement ran through me. Maybe there was hope I could be an agent again without Death hovering.

Hope died as I felt a presence behind me. A hand settled on my shoulder.

"Hi, Sweetheart." Not Death. Only Kieran. "Whatcha drinking?"

He vibrated with energy. I pulled back. Something *was* going on with me if I was recoiling from bad choices.

"What?" Kieran asked, a flash of irritation crossing his face, immediately replaced by a seductive smile. "I know. You missed me." He lifted my hair off my neck and kissed me softly there.

My brain resisted for only a millisecond, my body even less. I leaned into him. That's the thing with bad choices. The pull is strong.

He waved Delia over. "Bring us a bottle of Hibiki 17. The whole thing." She looked like she might object but turned to the shelf for the bottle.

"Whoa. Kieran. What's the deal?" I asked.

"I'm celebrating. I got some amazing underwater shots by the rocks on the south end of the cove." He brushed the hair off my face. "I want to go out to the beach with you and watch the sunset. Get very drunk."

Delia slid glasses our way, plunked the bottle in front of Kieran.

His voice dropped so low I could barely hear him. "And then, I intend to spend the night making you whimper."

He poured me a generous slosh of whiskey. I drained the glass. He poured me more.

"You best be careful out in that section of the cove," Delia said, a hardness to her voice I hadn't heard before. "Hunterfish live in those rocks near the far edge, out by where the reef ends."

"Those fish are spectacular. Not dangerous," Kieran said.

"Don't you know about them, then?" Delia asked. "They're an invasive species from off the coast of Thailand. Their main defense is venom. There's a gland near their mouths. They can shoot the stuff right into the eyes of their attackers." She paused, casting her gaze from Kieran over to me. "Or their prey."

Kieran laughed. I shook off Delia's gaze. Whatever Delia's problem was, I didn't need it. I lifted my glass and found it empty. Kieran filled it, leaving the bottle almost half gone.

"Anyway, I'm not going to get close to the fish," Kieran continued. "There's a cave there behind the rocks. I've looked everywhere else."

"For what?" Delia asked.

"Never you mind," Kieran said, a tremor of manic excitement in his voice. I tamped down the flutter of concern in my stomach. I wanted to have fun. Manic usually meant fun.

He jumped off the stool and took my hand, pulling me toward him. I stumbled, more affected by the drink than I thought. He wrapped his arm around my waist, leading me away.

"C'mon, Babe. Let's go watch the sunset."

Something pulled at me from behind. I turned to see Delia looking concerned. *Maybe I should stay here.* I shook the thought off.

"No worries, I'll see you at breakfast," I told her.

Kieran kissed my cheek. "Babygirl. We'll miss the sunset. Let's go." He took my chin, turning my eyes to his. "You know you want to." I did want to. I took his hand, guided it back where it belonged and turned toward the beach.

I CAME TO SLOWLY. THE gray light of dawn cast strange shadows. Kieran's face formed out of the darkness, his eyes animated as he watched me wake, a small smile on his lips. Damn. That had not been the plan. I didn't remember coming back to my room with him, didn't remember anything, really, after we'd emptied the whiskey bottle.

I tried to roll toward him. My body didn't move. Was I wrapped up in the sheets? I reached down to extricate myself. My arm didn't respond. Why could I not move? I screamed, but only muffled sounds came from my throat. Kieran's smile widened. He ran his palm over my hair.

"Hush. Don't panic. You aren't going to be able to move. I put the Hunterfish venom in your whiskey. You were easy to distract." He leaned in so close that I could see sweat beading on his forehead. "It has a progressive paralytic effect. Right now, it's just your big muscles, but soon your heart will slow until the blood stops moving to your brain." He caressed my face, his eyes wide with wonder. "You'll die. It won't be painful; you'll be at peace."

Why is he doing this?

"I know you were sent here to stop me; you gave yourself away with all the questions. Your government is after the treasure. It's not going to work."

He was talking nonsense. *I could talk him down. I'm trained for that.* I tried to reason with him, forcing a muffled whimper from my throat where words should be.

I tried to scream again as his hand traced the scar on my chest. I couldn't move. I could feel my heart racing, though. Was that a good thing, a sign of my body fighting the venom?

If I concentrate on moving just my arm, or just my hand, can I do it? Nothing. I couldn't even blink. I felt a tear roll down my face.

He sat cross-legged on the bed, looking down at me. "I've almost found it. The treasure." He shook his head. "I keep having to deal with interference. Before, it was just people getting too close, posing as tourists but really trying to take my treasure. Easy to get rid of them with the venom. No test for it. Looks like a heart attack."

He sighed, caressed my arm. "But you? You are exceptionally good at what you do. Pretending to be wounded, to need to heal. Worming your way into my bed. Even worse, making me *want* to be with you. You even got me to tell you about the treasure. I see why those guys tried to blow you up."

Maybe why I hadn't sensed Death was because he wasn't watching anymore. He wasn't waiting for his opportunity. He'd found it. Kind of fitting, really, that I wouldn't go doing my job, that I'd succumb instead to my vices.

The room lock snicked. A beam of light shone through the slit as the door opened.

"Housekeeping."

I tried to scream again. Even the whimper was gone. The venom must have reached the smaller muscles of my vocal cords. I didn't have much time.

Kieran draped himself over me, fitting into my curves like he belonged there. I could feel metal against my neck, his dive knife probably. He turned my head to the side and lifted my arm so it draped over his shoulders, tugging the sheets down to reveal the tableau of two lovers entwined. No one would be able to see the knife.

"Housekeeping," the voice said again.

"Come back later," Kieran said, uncoiling himself from me as the door opened wide. He kept the point of the knife pressed into the side of my neck.

Delia stood in the doorway. "Amanda, I got worried when you didn't come for breakfast." Hope flickered until I felt the knife break skin, the familiar wetness of blood.

Kieran knelt next to me, making a dismissive wave at Delia with his free hand. "Oh, it's just you. You're in on it too. Don't interfere, or I'll kill her." A laugh bubbled out of his throat. "Or, well, I'll kill her instantly. She's dead already anyway."

He twisted my head around to face him. "It's close now. I want to see the light go out of your eyes."

How could I have let myself be seduced by such a disturbed man? Why did I ignore the red flags?

His eyes shifted between me and Delia.

"Don't move." He chuckled. "I mean you, Delia. Of course, Amanda can't."

Kieran's eyes found mine, his chest moving as his breathing grew more rapid. His pupils dilated. A slight flush crept up his cheeks. I recognized the signs of pleasure.

I was going to die. I needed to scream, to fight. Nothing came out. My heart wasn't racing. My breath wasn't coming in rapid gasps. That was a bad sign. What would happen now? Would I just slip away, or would I know I was going?

I focused on the rise and fall of Kieran's ribs. The rhythm calmed me, a measure of peace as my life drained away. As I watched, his torso jerked and a bright crimson flower bloomed at his sternum, the stem golden and shimmering. *Was that a knife?* The pressure on my neck disappeared. Kieran's body catapulted over itself, hitting the floor with a thud hard enough to vibrate the bed.

A skull loomed up in front of me . . . or no, it was Delia. She glanced sideways, apparently satisfied Kieran was no longer a threat. She lifted me into a sitting position.

Something pricked my shoulder. "It's the antivenin. If I'm not too late, this should work. Look at me." She gripped my chin. "Look at me Amanda Wallingford."

Her eyes were deep, black pools. Something seemed wrong about that. The skin on her face flickered, grew transparent. I could see her skull, see it cleaned of flesh. *Maybe this is what happens when you die.* Which meant

179

she was too late. That would be okay. I'd get peace. I wouldn't have to feel Death behind me anymore.

"Look at me."

I blinked.

She smiled. A great rictus, the bleached bones of her skull visible before shimmering back into her weathered face like a mirage.

"Good. The antivenin is working. It isn't your time yet. There's more for you to do."

I tried to speak, to rebut her platitude, but the words wouldn't come.

Delia sighed, a long-suffering kind of a sigh. "Don't try to talk. I can wait. My patience is infinite."

DEAR LATHEA

KM ROCKWOOD

THE RECEPTIONIST STOPPED ME. "MR. Jennings prefers to see his clients alone."

Dear Lathea leaned heavily on her walker. I knew the pain from her arthritic knees must have been agonizing.

I kept my hand under her arm. "I believe Mrs. Markowitz *prefers* me to accompany her. For support."

The attorney's voice emanated from the inner office. "Nonetheless, I will see Mrs. Markowitz alone. You may wait out there for her."

"Sometimes she can get a bit confused . . ." I started to say.

"My understanding is that Mrs. Markowitz is here to draft a new will. Either she is competent, or she is not. If she is, she is quite capable of handling it without your support. If she is not, the will cannot be changed now."

Knowing when to acquiesce is an important skill in my chosen field. "Of course. Just sometimes she gets a bit dizzy. Heart palpitations. Nothing to do with her cognitive functioning."

"I'm glad we're clear on that," Mr. Jennings said. "I will be videotaping this session."

Maybe just as well if I weren't present. The less concrete evidence of my presence, the better.

I turned to Dear Lathea. "Would you like help to reach a chair?"

"Thank you, Roderick. I'm fine." She struggled forward.

"Do you need your inhaler? I can get it."

"No, Roderick."

Slowly, painfully, she inched across the office.

Her doctor said she needed a knee replacement.

The recovery from that procedure would be difficult. Under the best of circumstances, it would take weeks of agony, followed by months of painful physical therapy before she was reasonably functional and pain free again.

I am not entirely coldhearted. I often become quite fond of my ladies. I wouldn't want Dear Lathea's final days to be spent in such distress.

"I'll be right here waiting for you, Dear Lathea," I assured her.

The receptionist closed the door firmly behind her.

I sat down to wait. I am a patient man.

She was always "Dear Lathea" to me, even in my own mind. Especially in my own mind. Early on, I had spent months grooming a wealthy widow, only to inadvertently voice the term "Suzie the Sucker," which was how I mentally referred to her. She overheard, and despite my best efforts to turn it into a joke, the damage had been irreparable. A total waste of time and effort.

So, I always referred to subsequent ladies only in endearing terms.

We were here for Dear Lathea to update her will. In my favor.

She had no close relatives, making it hugely unlikely that any will would be contested.

Presently, the major recipient of Dear Lathea's postmortem largess was a cat sanctuary. I could put it to much better use.

She had a beloved cat, Ginger. I had to feign affection for him and pretend to be charmed by his antics, even when he relentlessly clawed at me. I suspected that, unlike his mistress, he was not deceived by my attentions and was taking his revenge. And he made me sneeze.

I had tried to get some idea of how large the estate would be, but Dear Lathea was either completely uninformed or far coyer than I would have anticipated. I suspected the former.

It had to be substantial, though. The house in which she lived was worth several million, and she wore jewelry that, to my semi-expert eye, ran into the hundreds of thousands. Each month, she sat down and unquestioningly wrote checks for all bills, even the ones I presented. Regardless of how outrageous they might be. At this point, though, I was careful not to go overboard.

I could only hope that a substantial portion of her wealth was not tied up in restricted trusts of some sort.

The original plan had been for me to marry Dear Lathea. That would automatically entitle me to a portion of her estate. But she explained that if she remarried, she would lose the quite substantial payment she received every month from her late husband's pension. We could, if I wished, have a formal "commitment ceremony," performed at her church and blessed by the pastor.

That would have no legal advantages for me, and somehow had never materialized.

Dear Lathea maintained that, since we were not married or "committed," it would not do for us to actually cohabitate. I had commandeered the most luxurious of her guest bedrooms and spent many nights there.

I kept my own condo across town, currently occupied by Janine, my girlfriend.

Janine knew exactly what I did for a living. Aside from providing welcome companionship, she had access to questionably acquired jewelry that I purchased when I saw the need for an impressive gift, and various pharmaceutical products, legal and otherwise, which often came in handy.

One facet of courting elderly ladies in somewhat fragile health required special diplomacy. They were seldom interested in the physical aspects of a relationship. Which was just as well. I could massage shoulders, pat hands, and kiss cheeks, but the whole idea of caressing flabby old bodies covered in dry sagging skin did not appeal to me.

Despite Dear Lathea's monthly pension that kept both of us living in style, it was time for me to cash out and move on.

I had identified a new lady, one with even more money and less sense than Dear Lathea. She appeared ripe for the picking. I needed to proceed with that project before someone else moved in. I had agreed to escort her to the opening of an art show this coming Saturday.

Here and now, though, the door to the inner sanctum remained closed for an inordinate amount of time. Perhaps setting up the video recording took a while.

Finally, another employee appeared from behind a closed door. He and the receptionist went into the office.

To witness the final will, I hoped.

I waited.

When they finally left, they left the door ajar.

Dear Lathea struggled to her feet. "Thank you so much, Mr. Jennings. I appreciate your explanations. I'm not sure I would have thought of everything without your suggestions."

What suggestions? And why was she so effusive with her thanks? The guy was just doing his job.

I rushed over to help Dear Lathea navigate the distance to the door. "You look so pale! Are you all right?"

"Oh, yes." She wasn't carrying a manila envelope or a folder.

Had she left it behind? I desperately wanted to check the wording, although I knew I would have to wait until we were at least out of the office. "Where's your copy of the will? Shall I carry it for you?"

Dear Lathea smiled. "I didn't get one. Mr. Jennings will keep it here in the office for when it's needed."

"Oh, no, my Dear Lathea. You must have it yourself." I turned to the receptionist. "Could you please run off a copy of the new will for Mrs. Markowitz?"

The receptionist frowned. "I'm afraid we've had trouble with the copier today. A service person will come in the morning to fix it. If Mrs. Markowitz would like, I will make her a copy then and mail it."

"That would be quite acceptable, thank you," Dear Lathea said.

"I can stop by tomorrow and pick it up," I offered.

Dear Lathea gave a short laugh. "Do you mistrust Mr. Jennings or his staff?"

The receptionist turned and gave me a hard look.

I took a deep breath. "Not at all. You would be more comfortable knowing that the task is completed."

"It is completed," Dear Lathea said. "I know what it says. I'll just file the copy away anyhow."

I wasn't happy with the delay, but I did not want to raise any suspicions with the attorney or his staff. "If you wish."

"I wish," Dear Lathea said.

With Dear Lathea leaning on her walker and my hand on her arm, I glanced back at the receptionist. She had her back turned, shuffling some paperwork on the credenza behind the desk.

I leaned sharply into Dear Lathea's shoulder and stuck my foot between the legs of the walker.

She stumbled.

I grabbed her to keep her from falling. "Dear Lathea! Are you all right?" I steered her to a nearby chair.

The receptionist whirled around.

"Sit here," I soothed. "Rest for a few minutes. Are you dizzy?"

"A bit." Dear Lathea put her hand to her forehead. "I don't know what happened. All of a sudden, I felt like I was falling."

I put my hand on the side of her neck. "Your heart is racing! I think we should get you to the doctor."

"No, no. It was just a brief spell." Dear Lathea closed her eyes.

"We should have you checked out. Suppose it's something serious?"

"I said no." Her voice had a hard edge to it.

"At least put a nitroglycerin tablet under your tongue." I fished the container out of my pocket and gave her one.

Mr. Jennings came out of his office. "Perhaps we should call for an ambulance."

That was the last thing I needed.

While it was important that they see Dear Lathea having her "spell," I certainly did not want a competent medical evaluation at this point. Definitely not at the hospital.

Fortunately, Dear Lathea rallied. "That won't be necessary, Mr. Jennings. I feel much better already. A few more minutes and I will be fine."

He cleared his throat. "If you're sure, Mrs. Markowitz."

"I'm sure." She leaned on her walker and winced as she lurched to her feet.

I hurried to steady her. "I'll call the doctor as soon as I get her home," I assured Mr. Jennings.

"And what doctor would that be?" he asked.

Dear Lathea said, "Dr. Remonin. He's been my doctor for years." She coughed.

Mr. Jennings nodded.

I steered her out the door. Dr. Remonin may have been her doctor for years, but I'd made an appointment and taken her to Dr. Solomen, who ran a somewhat shady pain management clinic. For her arthritis, I'd told her.

She'd gone, had the evaluation, come away with prescriptions for oxycodone and fentanyl patches. She had, however, insisted on remaining under Dr. Remonin's care.

Despite her obvious continuing pain, she only took a few of the oxys and didn't even try the fentanyl.

Much like Mr. Jennings, Dr. Remonin insisted upon seeing his patient alone.

What was with these people? Dear Lathea was an adult. She ought to be able to decide who she wanted to accompany her to appointments. That would be me.

When we got to the car—Dear Lathea had a classic old Bentley with a manual transmission which she could no longer drive—I broached the idea of supper out.

"We could go to that little Italian place. The one with the red checkered tablecloths and the delicious pasta."

Over the years, I'd learned to invite the ladies to cozy little restaurants, picnics by the lake at sunset or breakfast in picturesque retro diners. Much less expensive than the fancy restaurants they habitually patronized, and I could present it as "an adventure."

Supper at the Italian restaurant would inevitably include a bottle of red wine.

Dear Lathea often countered with proposals for high-end places. She would hasten to add, "My treat, of course."

Tonight, however, she demurred. "I'm tired. We can order in Chinese."

Not my first choice. We would drink tea with Chinese food. I really wanted her to have some alcohol in her system. The more, the better.

There was, however, the advantage that delivered Chinese food would go on her credit card.

We ate in the dining room. Ginger the cat climbed onto a vacant chair, stood with his front feet on the table, and watched every forkful of food.

When we were done, he clawed at my trousers and mewed. Almost as if he knew I was up to something.

After dinner, Dear Lathea went into the living room. I turned on the cozy gas fireplace and wrapped an afghan around her.

Then I cleaned up and started the dishwasher before I joined her.

I took Dear Lathea's hand and smiled. "Could I get you a little brandy? To relax? It's been a busy day. It will make you feel better."

Dear Lathea looked thoughtful. "How about Irish coffee?"

That would do. The strong taste of the coffee would go a long way toward masking anything else.

And I could serve Irish coffee with a stiff component of whiskey.

"Sounds good. Shall I bring some of that shortbread to have with it?" I asked, as I headed back to the kitchen.

"No, thank you. Just the coffee."

While the coffee brewed, I crept up to "my" room and retrieved a half-filled glass from the linen closet in the bathroom.

It was half-filled with water. Three of Dear Lathea's fentanyl patches had been soaking in there since yesterday morning. I took them out and flushed them, one at a time.

Back in the kitchen, I took the biggest mugs I could find. I wondered if I would be able to persuade Dear Lathea to have a second Irish coffee. I decided I'd better not count on it.

I put a jigger of whiskey into one mug, then a hefty pour into the other. I added as much of the fentanyl water to that cup as I dared. I would finish up with a fentanyl patch anyhow, so it probably didn't matter if the concoction wasn't quite strong enough.

Then I topped both off with strong coffee. A quick squirt of refrigerated whipped cream from an aerosol can, and they were ready.

Ginger sat in the doorway, his tail swishing in annoyance.

Too many frustrations today. My nerves were a bit frayed. The whiskey would be welcome.

I opened the dishwasher, stopping it and letting out a cloud of steam, and placed the glass from the bathroom in it. I didn't restart it—I would need to add the mugs later.

Paying careful attention to which mug was which, I carried them into

187

the living room where Dear Lathea sat. She was leaning back against a cushion with her eyes closed.

Ginger leapt up onto the end table next to her. I put the mug with the doctored coffee by her hand.

The blasted cat leaned over and flicked his tongue at the whipped cream topping.

Could the fentanyl wick up into the topping? I doubted it but wasn't willing to take the chance. A dead cat might raise questions I would not care to have asked.

I shooed him away from the drink.

"You know," she said without opening her eyes. "I think I would like to have a few of those shortbread cookies after all."

I suppressed a sigh. "Certainly."

What about the cat?

After putting my mug on the mantel, I looked around for him.

He'd have to come with me so he couldn't get to the cream.

I looked under the table.

There he sat, washing his paws and studiously ignoring me.

I reached for him.

He scooted away.

I dashed around the couch and grabbed him.

He let out a piteous mewing.

Dear Lathea didn't move or open her eyes, but she did say, "What does Ginger want?"

I thought wildly. "Whipped cream!" It was even the truth. "I'm going to take him out to the kitchen and give him a little squirt of it in a dish."

Her eyes still closed, she smiled. "You do spoil that cat! I like that in a man."

Ginger clawed my hands all the way into the kitchen.

Once there, I got out the can of whipped cream and half-filled a saucer with it. He sniffed at it, eyed me, and settled down to take delicate licks of the white mound.

The shortbread cookies weren't in the cupboard as I thought they would be, so I had to rummage around for them. Then the package hadn't been opened, so I struggled with that. The plate I normally used for cookies was in the dishwasher and was wet, so I had to dredge up another one.

When I got back into the living room, Dear Lathea was still leaning back with her eyes closed. The cat had come back and was curled up in her lap, sleeping. They looked peaceful.

Not time to sleep yet. She needed to drink the coffee.

Then I could help her to bed. Put one of the fentanyl patches on her back, the way Dr. Solomen instructed. Maybe two. Or three.

In the morning, I would call him and tell him Dear Lathea had passed away in her sleep. Probably her heart. Why, she'd just had heart palpitations but refused to go to the doctor. The staff at Mr. Jennings' office could attest to that.

Anxious to avoid any scrutiny of his narcotic-prescribing habits, he'd certify death from a heart condition.

She'd die quietly. And no more pain.

Even if that somehow went wrong and Dr. Remonin became involved, the death would be an overdose from the prescribed opioids.

What with alcohol in her system and the pain from her arthritic knees, it would be quite understandable that she became confused and used too much fentanyl.

I put the plate with the cookies next to the mug. "Dear Lathea? Here are your cookies. And your Irish coffee."

Her eyelids fluttered. "Thank you. But you know, I'm just so tired. I shouldn't have put you to all that trouble."

No! She couldn't go to sleep without drinking at least some.

I took my mug off the mantel and sat next to her. "Come on, Dear Lathea. Let's have a toast!"

She opened her eyes. "A toast? To what?"

"To us!"

At that, she did pick up her mug and brought it toward mine. We clinked rims. I smiled at her and took a big swallow.

She did the same.

"Another toast!" I said. "To our future!"

Once again, we clinked rims and took big swallows.

After that, she nibbled on the shortbread and took a few small sips. I noticed that whenever I took a drink, she did the same, so I kept on until my mug was empty.

She finally sat up. Ginger jumped off her lap. "You're right. That did make me feel better. I think I will sleep very well tonight."

"Good." Somehow I was having trouble forming the words. My limbs felt heavy. "I'm pretty tired too."

Ginger climbed up and settled in my lap. I didn't quite have the energy to shoo him away.

I sneezed.

"You know," Dear Lathea said. "I really didn't want to believe what Dr. Remonin tried to tell me. But then when Mr. Jennings said the same thing . . ."

I closed my eyes to rest them. I tried to say, "What did they tell you?" but my tongue refused to function properly.

"They said you were a con man. Taking advantage of a lonely old lady. A *rich,* lonely old lady. When I told Dr. Remonin about the fentanyl patches, he said you were probably a drug addict too."

Me? A drug addict? Never.

"Mr. Jennings said I needed to be careful. We set up a trust so that the cat sanctuary will get everything. And they will care for Ginger after I pass."

My head was too heavy to hold up. My lips were slack, and I felt saliva dribble down my chin.

"But I don't think either one of them thought you might try to kill me," Dear Lathea went on. "I came to that conclusion on my own."

I heard her get up. I managed to turn my head so I could see her.

"Don't worry," she said. "I'll get a few of those fentanyl patches and put them on you. You'll be very comfortable. Let me just clean up here. Then I'll go up to bed. I'm sure I will sleep well."

Mugs in hand, she headed toward the kitchen.

Ginger followed along, his tail swishing.

WISE ENOUGH TO PLAY THE FOOL

FRANCES STRATFORD

28 July 1540
Tower of London
Thomas Cromwell, former Chancellor of the Exchequer

I WOKE BEFORE DAWN, A condemned prisoner, and watched the summer sun rise over the Bloody Tower. The church bells rang from St. Peter-in-Chains. *Loud enough to wake the Boleyn witch from her sleep of death beneath those stones.*

My prison was the Queen's apartments in the Tower. The linenfold paneling was dark, a comfort in the summer, the bedcoverings precisely embroidered. *I could almost like it here.* When the Tower warden brought my letters, he confessed he fears the Boleyn ghost. *I hope she sees me sleeping soundly in her bed,* I wanted to say. But, as the soul of discretion, I bit my tongue.

My spiteful joy at her death—at the death of all but one of Henry's queens—did not sufficiently distract me from my circumstances. It was the day of my execution. Or so the world thought.

But the king, Henry VIII, had promised to hear one last letter from me. I planned to use it to set things to right.

I rose from my bed, put on my silk dressing gown. The silk was cool, and I walked to the door in anticipation of my breakfast of fresh bread, ale, and an egg pottage with butter, sugar, and currants. A good meal would help me answer the question that had plagued me since I was publicly

191

stripped of my office: who was the man in the black cloak who visited the king and persuaded him to sign my execution order?

Most did not know how gullible Old Harry was. That man would do anything his prick told him to. *Someone else who will benefit from his Majesty's questing pork sword is behind the signed execution order. That man is my murderer.*

I sat at the windowsill and caught the cool morning air. I took it as no small point of pride that there were many, many suspects. One does not rise in the swarming, feuding, grifting Tudor court without sufficient immoral behavior.

Was I a liar, an extortionist, a man bearing false witness?

Yes.

Was I, the blacksmith's son, the bastard from Putney, smarter than all the men at the Tudor court?

Yes to that too.

Still, it would be best to apply that intellect to the problem at hand. My friend, Christopher Hales, could provide me only what the gatekeeper's bribe had been able to extort—a tall man in a dark cloak visited the king two nights ago. He stayed for an hour. He left only when my execution order was signed.

Well, I had worked more damage with less intelligence.

A knock at the door let me know my breakfast had arrived. A timid cook's boy labored under a large tray. He was likely afraid I would toss the food at him, as I had the previous morning when my eggs had been far too runny. I lifted the cover to the dish. Red currants dotted the golden crust on the eggs.

"Very well," I waved him off. "Leave me." The door shut behind him. There was much work to do.

The clock outside struck five. Hales would be here by seven to take my letter. My execution was scheduled for noon.

I tucked into my eggs. They were good, maybe a little too much sage. I mopped up the butter with the warm bread. I vowed to complain at lunch that the ale was flat.

There would be no more lifeless ale once I was released. His gracious majesty was a tool of a foreign government or an ambitious subject and when I exposed that truth, he would certainly spare my life. Henry VIII, for all his blustering, was a paranoid man. I had exploited that paranoia for over a decade. I was a master at it.

But to manipulate the king, to unmask the motivations of the man in the black cloak, I had to name him correctly in the letter.

Ever the precise bureaucrat, I rose from my breakfast to light a candle—I do not always work in the dark despite my enemies' gossip—and sat down at the desk. It was not every desperate petitioner who could get to the king's privy apartments at night with none but the gatekeeper to see. The man had to be someone of power and influence.

I dipped the pen in the inkwell and pulled out a crisp sheet of parchment.

In no time at all, I had a list of over fifty men.

I've had a good career if I could move so many to murder.

The sun had risen, and the church bell rang six times. I could glory in the long list another day. I drank a last sip of the flat ale and began to pare down the list based on three criteria: access to the king, height, and level of incentive.

Was it some conservative in the church? Someone like Edward Lee, the Archbishop of York? I made enemies when I dissolved the monasteries. *Corruption, greed, blasphemy*, I whispered until the king brought all the mighty religious houses down. I circled Lee's name on the list.

Or was it some freethinker of the Boleyn faction? Marillac, the French ambassador? The French King Francis had found a great ally in Queen Anne. I made international enemies when I manufactured evidence so that Queen Anne lost her head. *Whore, traitor, witch*, I hissed until the king believed her death to be his own master stroke. Less likely to be Marillac, but he stayed on the list.

My pride in the list turned to anxiety. *What if I cannot identify the man in the dark cloak?*

There was a clanking noise in the courtyard. I looked down and saw men wearing the coat of arms of the house of Cleves.

It was someone who appealed to the king's codpiece, of course. I had encouraged the king's marriage to his fourth wife, Anne of Cleves, known in court gossip as the Flanders Mare. Yet when the king told me he could not consummate his marriage, I was the first to lay on oily assurances, *fat, ugly, unworthy.* Beauty was a commodity in the Tudor court, and she brought nothing to market.

Whatever failings Henry VIII's other wives had—and they were enough—none of them were as naïve and as easily led as the Cleves woman. When I negotiated the divorce, she simply nodded—likely not understanding a word of English—and agreed to everything.

I took pride in my ability to rid the king of extra wives. Katherine of Aragon to exile, and that Boleyn witch to the headsman. Likely I would have had to send his third wife, the Seymour girl, to her early end if she had not brought herself there without any need to bestir myself.

Yet with the Flanders Mare, I exceeded even my own brilliance. There was no finer lawyer in England for ending a royal marriage than me.

The king was effusively grateful. Why not? He had already fallen for another, Katherine Howard, the Duke of Norfolk's niece. His codpiece appeased, and his ugly wife demoted to royal sister, I had solidified my place.

No. It was not Old Harry's idea to end my life.

Through the open window, I heard the Cleves herald speaking German. I looked and saw Johann von Kleve. They were all named Johann von Kleve. They all spoke a language of phlegm and wrath. I vowed to rid England of all of them once I was released. If they would not take their Anne back to Cleves, I would make other arrangements for her in England.

The air was getting warmer, the sun was up. A trickle of sweat rolled down my back.

Think, I ordered myself.

I reviewed the list in the growing summer light. There was one man: a religious conservative who hated me for the Cleves marriage, who had regular access to the king, who was tall, and highly incentivized to have the king's divorce lawyer dead: Thomas Howard, Duke of Norfolk.

Today, the Duke of Norfolk's niece marries the king. Old Norfolk does not want me to be able to extricate the king from his new marriage. He wants his blood sitting on the throne of England when Henry is gone.

Taking another clean sheet of parchment from the pile, I set a candle under the sealing wax to melt it, and arranged the Cromwell stamp of ravens surrounding a Tudor rose next to the inkwell. My breakfast was settling well. All was in order, so I sat down to write.

My Most Gracious Sovereign . . . treason, murder, civil war . . . my venom painted the page.

Once the letter was done, I leaned back in the chair, finger crooked over my lips.

What if I am wrong? What if the man in the dark cloak was someone else? What if . . . no. I had applied my reason to the problem.

A loud knock interrupted my musings. A herald announced my last friend at court, Christopher Hales.

"Well met, Kit," I said rising.

Hales, smelling of his hard ride and sweat, embraced me. I pushed him away and handed him the letter. He had work to do.

His face held a funereal sadness. "How fare you? Should I send for your confessor?"

"Just take this letter to the king. The king's fool, Will Somers, will keep the wedding party in a merry mood until you arrive. If all goes well, we will meet again outside these walls."

The king will know Norfolk is trying to trap him into a marriage with his niece. It will be a marriage he cannot get out of without me. He would be a fool to think otherwise.

28 July 1540
Greenwich Palace Banquet Room
Will Somers, Henry VIII's fool

"THE KING IS A FOOL!" I began my entertainment of the wedding party as the breakfast wound down.

Henry VIII laughed from deep in his belly, spitting wine as he did. "Indeed, I am, Will! I am a fool for love." He eyed his pretty new wife, who was sitting beside him.

The French ambassador Marillac looked shocked at my words. Sir Kissbreech—for so I called him—gave me a cold appraisal up and down. Kissbreech thinks of me what most puffed up courtiers think. *Why is Will*

Somers, that lean, stooped, hollow-eyed jester allowed to burst the bladder of court hypocrisy with honesty?

The king's old tutor Erasmus called it "Fool's license."

Old Harry loves Erasmus and me.

With the Fool's license, I tell the truth nimbler and more lustily than a king would otherwise ever know.

Not the Pope, the Archbishop of Canterbury, not even his luscious sweetmeat of a wife could tell old Harry the truth as I could.

I would be a fool to abuse that privilege.

But I needed to use my sharp tongue to save Cromwell's life.

Old Harry had determined to pardon Cromwell. Not even a week earlier, he had declared, "He's my most faithful servant, Will. He will not meet the headsman."

Then, a man in a black cloak had visited him two nights past. After that visit, Harry signed the execution order.

Well, I had worked far more damage with less intelligence.

"Play some music, fool!" the king commanded, kissing the new queen's tiny hand.

I played one of his own compositions: *Alas, What Shall I do For Love?*

As I piped the familiar notes, I saw the king expand like a bullfrog. Good, he was easy to manipulate when happy. My eyes surveyed the room, searching for the murderer.

Most would think it was Norfolk who pressed for Cromwell's execution. The old duke wished the chancellor dead since Martin Luther picked up the hammer in Wittenberg. After all, why would that old bull's pizzle want the king's best divorce lawyer alive?

But I knew it was Kissbreech who visited the king. His nose firmly up the royal arse—first to sniff out what the body politic would purge.

As I danced around the room, I blew the spit out of the recorder toward the preening Frenchman.

A fool lives near the king—to be on call like a physician. With Old Harry, the worst sickness was boredom.

That's how I saw Marillac's dark figure on the back stairs. I did not see his face, but I saw the European cut of the cloak, heard the high tenor voice. *I will say the betrothal to the French Duke of Lorraine was not valid—that the Cleves marriage is true. You will not be able to marry the Howard girl unless you rid the kingdom of this wicked and unhappy instrument . . .*

I flourished the last note as I took a bow.

Guests mopped the last sauces from the wedding breakfast dishes. Servants placed a growing pile of wedding gifts in the center of the hall. I saw the king's new wife exclaim with delight. I had less than an hour to speak the truth and to expose Kissbreech and his master the French king.

"And ye, Sir Kissbreech," I sang to Marillac. "Your master the French king has an empty codpiece compared to our Great Harry!"

Kissbreech sputtered with rage as I scampered away from him to hide behind the king. The newly minted queen touched my arm and laughed too.

"Your majesty, you allow your fool to speak thus?" Marillac tried unsuccessfully to keep his girl's voice from cracking.

"Would ye have him cut off my head?" I mimicked his lady-voice. "Like you would have him do to that knave Cromwell?"

A look passed over the king's face. Then just as quickly, it was gone.

"What care do you have, fool, for the minister?" Marillac snapped.

What indeed? Cromwell was a liar, cheat, extortionist, and murderer. He had often hit my pate and called me "knave!"

Oh, I cared little for the blacksmith's bastard from Putney.

No, it was not Cromwell I would save, but rather my master's place in history.

My Harry was far more than a foolish mass of striving codpiece. My Harry made a once fractious England a secure nation. Now, parliament made laws, whereas before the poor—like my father—died for want of government. Under Henry VIII's rule, the courts heard petitions of scullions and dukes alike. Painters, musicians, actors, sculptors—even fools—were valued for their arts. Our Harry took a dark realm—a kingdom where the powerful worked a thousand mischiefs on their poor subjects, a half-island that tore at itself with civil war—and made it a nation to be reckoned with.

But unless Cromwell lived to work a divorce, the world would know Old Harry only as Sir Pump Breech, his jolly member taking maidens' heads as it swung.

"Well," Kissbreech insisted. "What care do you have for the minister?"

Rather than answering, I made to kiss Marillac's hand. Instead, I pulled rings off his finger and began to juggle them, allowing each to drop in my mouth, sliming them with my breakfast, and blowing them out again.

Old Harry laughed himself pink.

"In all the court there are none more beloved than my fool." The king cuffed the back of my head with a greasy hand, perhaps harder than he needed to. "At least until today." He turned his bulk toward his tiny wife, the seventeen-year-old Catherine Howard. Henry nodded to the waiting servants, who then brought the gifts to the side table. The queen and her household rose to cluster around the pile and began to exclaim at the treasures.

"Today I have married my rose without a thorn," the king yelled as he raised his glass.

The table roared their approval.

Old Harry turned his smile from his wife tearing into her gifts like a child at Twelfth Night to Kissbreech. "Come, Marillac, let us play a game of piquet." The king flashed a beringed finger, and a page brought him a deck of cards. He gave the deck to Marillac to cut.

"These are beautiful cards, your majesty." The ambassador waved off his right to cut the cards.

"They came from Cleves with my—" the king stopped himself before he could say . . . what? My wife? My Flanders Mare? Who knew Anne of Cleves' position in this world? Or how long she would live to hold it?

Finally, the king said, "With my Lady of Cleves."

Marillac dealt the cards. "Beauty is a valuable commodity."

He was right—Anne of Cleves brought nothing to *that* market stall.

I pulled a card out from behind the king's ear. I knew never to touch his bonnet and reveal his thinning red hair.

"Look, your majesty! You've got a Cromwell." I pointed to the obsequious knave in the pack. A man who would do a king no harm, and perhaps some service.

The king flashed his tiny blue eyes at me. "Go entertain the queen."

Kissbreech passed me a triumphant look. The French king would not stop until the world and history knew my master only as a dreadful monster from legends.

I scampered over to the window where the company of young people admired the gifts that arrived from all over Europe. The king's armorer, Tom Culpepper, sat close to the new queen. The two had their faces pressed together, admiring themselves in a mirror. "Mark this! The looking glass comes from my Lady of Cleves!" She should have shown the piece to the assembled crowd. Instead, Katherine, the two-hour queen, stared only at herself and Culpepper.

The Howard girl was not long for this world.

Sand was trickling through the hourglass. Cromwell's letter from the Tower should arrive any moment. If my master were to be remembered for the good he had done—rather than the wives he killed—Cromwell needed to live and smooth the way through this inevitable divorce.

I grabbed the mirror from the queen and danced over to where the king and the Frenchman played piquet. I pushed the glass under Kissbreech's nose and declared to Old Harry, "Froggy Marillac has only a false face! Nothing true appears in the mirror. You should *reflect* on that, your majesty!"

The king held my gaze for a moment, a faint smile on his pudgy face. Did I see a half nod?

A courtier, bearing a letter sealed with Cromwell's ravens and rose, interrupted us. The king broke the seal on the letter with one of his sausage-sized fingers. After reading it, he handed it to Marillac.

The ambassador broke into a large smile.

I was nearly out of time.

I threw the mirror to Culpepper. He was so distracted whispering in the queen's ear, he did not catch it in time.

The shattering glass made the king turn. "How fares the queen?" he called to her by her window seat. She did not look at him, but stared into Culpepper's eyes.

The king's beady eyes narrowed. "Already inattentive, my lady?" he accused. "Even my fool is beside me on my wedding day." He tried, but failed, to sound courteous.

"The highest heavens descend unto the hells!" I cartwheeled away to the center of the room. *No, we'll get no Duke of York from this lass.* Then I saw Culpepper's face flush. *Unless it is the armorer's bastard.*

With a flourish of my harlequin sleeves, I pointed toward the king. "This way to kill a wife with kindness!"

A lady-in-waiting nudged the queen. Queen Katherine blushed and rushed quickly to the king's side. She knelt like a beggar, pushing her arms together, displaying her lily-white breasts. "Somers rules you with his wit. How could I compete?"

Old Harry looked into the chasm of her breasts as if it contained his next meal.

Cromwell is lost.

And so is my Harry.

With a nod to Marillac, the king signaled the courtier to come to him. I watched him mouth "proceed."

Cromwell would die. The world would know Old Harry as a monster. The good he did for the country would be interred with his bones. *How can the king be such a fool?*

28 July 1540
Richmond Palace
Anne of Cleves

"HOW CAN SHE BE SUCH a fool?" Chancellor Cromwell had whispered, but I heard him anyway. He was not alone. Many at the Tudor court underestimated me.

Only King Henry suspected I was not the fool I played.

My sometime husband, now adopted brother, married my former lady-in-waiting that morning. My sometime stepdaughters, Lady Mary and Lady Elizabeth, now my nieces, were with me. "Keep them about you on that day, Anne," the king had commanded. "The Lady Mary is older than my bride. Her dour face will mar the festivities. And Lady Elizabeth is too young."

I looked at twenty-four-year-old Mary as she sat beside me, squinting at the sun setting on the silvery river. Her face was not dour. Her blue eyes and set mouth carried the mark of a youth untimely cropped before it was grown.

Mary's face relaxed as she looked at her half-sister, six-year-old Lady Elizabeth. Red-headed Elizabeth sat with her governess in the shade, reading *Mirror of Simple Souls* in French. I knew Elizabeth was exiled from the wedding not because she was young, but because her lustrous black eyes would remind Henry of the woman he loved to death.

I was almost the second such woman.

King Henry took a violent dislike to me at first sight. He called me too tall, too blonde, and too wide. He desired, short, brunette, and slim. That kind of beauty was a commodity in the Tudor court, and I brought nothing to market.

I knew of his distaste, but I knew not what would become of me—alone in a strange land. So, I played the fool. Graciously, I entertained as queen, brought the king's daughters and little son to court, ignored his lustful gaze at my ladies-in-waiting.

Playing the fool worked. Courtiers said things in front of me, thinking I did not understand. Advisors left their papers unattended, assuming I could not read them. Conspirators came and went, believing I did not know their errands.

But the king was not fooled. He knew my English was improving, that I had political sense, that I shivered in the shadows of his disapproval.

Truly, I feared him.

One night while Henry snored, exhausted by his fumbling attempts at consummation, I rose and looked through the papers he had brought with him. I hoped to find a letter to my brother the Duke of Cleves, the French king, even Martin Luther for all I knew. In terror-sickness, pale and cold, I searched.

Instead, I found a letter from Chancellor Cromwell.

. . . your Grace committed the secret matter to me . . . . You declared the things which your Highness misliked in the Queen. I willingly seek a remedy for your comfort and consolation. I wish greatly your comfort, and I would spend blood for that object . . . .

I turned to Henry's snoring bulk in the bed.

Had he left this for me to find?

Terror strangled my breath. My mind flew to my stepchildren—*Mary, Elizabeth, Edward.* I thought of the promise I had made to God the day I met them. *You will not lose your fourth mother.*

201

I pushed down a scream into a void of dread. With trembling hands, I carefully placed the letter back in the pile.

In the coming days, I worked damage with that intelligence.

I agreed to every one of the demands Chancellor Cromwell put before me. Divorce? *Ja.* Be the king's sister? *Ja.* Tell my brother the Duke of Cleves I would stay in England? *Ja.* Convert to whatever religion Henry decided was true on that day? *Ja.*

Chancellor Cromwell had laughed at my easy capitulation. A brittle, hollow laugh of a man who intended to spill blood, but unintentionally got his way.

Had he laughed when Queen Katherine, Mary's mother, begged for medicine on her death bed? Had he laughed when Anne Boleyn had begged to see tiny Elizabeth before the French swordsman arrived? Had he laughed when Jane Seymour begged to kiss her baby as she writhed in her final delirium?

Cromwell was angry, but Henry was well pleased with my answers. His bloated pride swelled, believing I still wanted to be around him as his adopted sister, that I still wanted to be an aunt to my former stepchildren.

Lady Mary's mannish voice interrupted my thoughts. "Have you heard from your brother the duke? Will he demand you return to Cleves?"

"All my letters go to the king," I spoke slowly, the English rolling oddly in my mouth. "I am . . . *glücklich* . . . I mean content to do as the king wishes."

"Will you be sad not to see your mother and your sister?" Mary asked.

I shook my head. No one from my family had lifted a finger to help me when the Chancellor wanted me bare necked on Tower Green.

"It broke my heart to be separated from my mother," Lady Mary whispered. I put my hand over hers. She squeezed back.

Lady Elizabeth's face was impassive. If she thought of her captivating mother, Anne Boleyn, her headless body crammed into an arrow chest under the floor of the Tower church, her expression did not betray it. Her eyes continued to move resolutely over her book.

"Your father has been most gracious to me," I spoke slowly and could understand why the clever princess Elizabeth thought I was a bit of a dullard. "I hoped to be of good service to him, should the need arise."

Lady Elizabeth's governess snorted in her sleep. The lowering sun cast shadows.

"My lord Cromwell likely met his end today," a dutiful Christian, Lady Mary tried to hide the victory in her voice.

I said nothing.

Lady Mary leaned in so that Elizabeth could not hear. "They say my father meant to pardon him, but that someone convinced him to sign the death warrant."

"Who do you think might have done that?"

"He had so many rivals. It may have been Archbishop Lee, Marillac, the French ambassador acting for the French king, even the Duke of Norfolk."

"We must pray for his soul."

"He meant you no good." Mary leaned back in her chair. "Nor me, nor Elizabeth."

To dwell on death brought only melancholy. "Let us . . . *sticken*?" I mimed the movement of a needle through cloth.

"Truly Lady Anne, you must apply yourself better to learn English," Elizabeth admonished, shutting her book. "You are not as dumb as court gossips say."

"Elizabeth!" Lady Mary rebuked. "Lady Anne is excellent at piquet. I'll call for a servant to get the beautiful deck of cards you brought from Cleves. We can all play."

I smiled. My stepdaughter Mary loved to gamble at cards, and she was quite good at it. "*Nein*. I mean no. I left the piquet cards with the king."

Mary quirked a brow. "But we just played two days ago."

Elizabeth shook her head sadly, clearly rethinking her observation that I was not a simpleton. "If father has the cards, he will never give them back."

A flourish of trumpet interrupted us from the quayside.

"Men from the Tower," Mary rose quickly, unable to hide the terror in her voice.

Little Elizabeth dropped her book and turned to look. Three yeoman wearing the king's livery disembarked. I stood to see them more clearly.

"They have come for you!" Elizabeth's governess howled, pointing at me.

Lady Mary grabbed me about the waist. She had known this moment herself. Men from the Tower striding with purpose toward her.

"Mother Anne!" Elizabeth cried as she ran to me and pushed her face into my breast, a motherless six-year-old underneath the king's daughter facade. I trembled in Mary's embrace as I stroked Elizabeth's coppery head.

The guards held their halberds high, blades pointing away.

Behind the Tower guards, I could see Johann von Kleve, his red and silver hat bobbing.

Johann smiled.

I dropped to my knees, looking Elizabeth in her watery black eyes. In perfect King's English, I said, "Elizabeth, you will never lose me."

Lady Mary also saw Johann's smile and knew what it meant. I felt her body relax into mine. She looked down and touched her little sister's cheek, brushing the tears away. "Elizabeth," she whispered, "this is the mother we get to keep."

"Truly?"

"Truly," I replied, hugging her close.

A trust settled into the little girl's face. "Now," I said, "let us greet the herald from Cleves."

The evening twilight streaked the sky and there was a chill coming from the water.

As I pulled the cloak around my shoulders, Elizabeth looked at me with a mixture of compassion and planning.

"Mother Anne, we must get you a new cloak. You look like a man in that one."

NET PROFIT AND LOSS

JANE LIMPRECHT

"SERIOUSLY? THEY PHOTOSHOPPED THEIR DAUGHTER'S head onto another kid's body to get her into college as a volleyball star?"

The raspy-voiced woman seated to Maggie's right slurped her frozen piña colada and then ripped the orange slice from its peel with her teeth. Large gemstones in her gold rings glittered in the sunlight that filtered through the patio window behind her.

In early March, while the sun warmed Florida's Treasure Coast, Frankie's Lounge provided an air-chilled refuge for retirees, vacationers staying in the adjacent time-shares, and business owners who could close up shop in time for four o'clock happy hour. Noisy, middle-aged drinkers crowded around the bar, a square of eight-foot-long polished wooden counters.

Framed sports photos covered the barroom's hunter-green walls, and a captioned TV screen hung in each corner. One TV was silently tuned to football tryouts, one to pre-season baseball, and one to golf. The fourth alternated between the stock ticker and the news. Today's news broadcast featured the sentencing of a wealthy couple who cheated to get their privileged offspring into an elite college. After he got caught, the adviser who concocted the scheme flipped and agreed to wear a wire.

"That really galls me," the tanned woman said to no one in particular. She turned toward Maggie and unleashed a raucous cackle. "Number one—why didn't I think of it?"

Maggie swirled the straw in her banana daiquiri and looked at the woman. "Are you the parent of a teenager?" she said.

"I'm not talking about the parents," the woman replied, waving her empty glass at the curly-haired bartender. "The guy who advised them.

Brilliant idea." She clunked her glass down on the glossy wood and slumped her shoulders. "Of course, he got caught." Straightening up, she waved her glass again. "Another one, Natalia." The woman twirled her barstool to the left so she could extend her right hand toward Maggie. "Name's Rona Grafton. Pleased to meet you."

"Pleased to meet you as well. I'm Maggie Springfield and this is my husband, Ben." Maggie cocked her head toward the burly man on her left, who responded with a smile. "Every year we drive down from Virginia for a couple of weeks. Ben's family bought a time-share here in the 1980s. How about you, Rona? Do you live here?"

"Part of the year. I'm the CEO of Trillium Home Savers. Trillium is an internet-based company, so I can run it from anywhere."

"Nice set-up," Maggie said. "We're retired."

Rona leaned close enough that Maggie worried she might tip off her barstool. "Honestly, I might as well be retired. I work three or four hours online and give my employees their marching orders. Then I divide my time between the beach and the pool." Rona tilted her head back, shaking her glass so the last slushy gulp of piña colada slid into her mouth. "Around three thirty, I snag a seat here before the happy-hour crowd pours in. When Frankie's brings out the food, I grab a plate."

"What's on the menu? Our time-share unit's only fifty feet away, so we stop in at Frankie's every year for a couple of umbrella drinks, but that's the extent of our barhopping. Mostly we hang out on the beach or on our balcony."

"Chicken tenders and mini hot dogs on Mondays and Wednesdays. Meatballs on Tuesdays and Thursdays. Taco night on Friday." Rona ticked off the options on her fingers as she named them.

"Sounds tasty," Ben said. "Especially the meatballs. What kind of a business is Trillium Home Savers?"

"Just what it sounds like. People come to us when they can't keep up on their mortgages and need help holding onto the home life they deserve." Her emphasis on "deserve" sounded well-rehearsed.

"How exactly does that work?" Maggie said.

"Well, we watch the legal notices—all public information—and we contact people whose homes are facing foreclosure. We offer to help renegotiate their mortgage, so they won't lose their home. All they pay is a monthly fee. All done over the internet."

"Does that usually work?" Maggie said. "I mean, do you save their homes from foreclosure?"

In an instant, Rona transformed from merry, if obnoxious, tippler to suspicious drunk. She drew her head back and regarded Maggie with one eye squeezed nearly shut. "We do pretty well. As well as can be expected." Hooking her foot under the bar footrail, Rona swiveled back to center. She sucked her newly freshened drink through its melon-colored cocktail straw and waved yet again for the bartender's attention. "Make my next one a rum rummer—runner." She stabbed a skinny index finger toward Natalia, who was occupied with another customer. "And don't forget the pineapple slice."

Maggie watched as Rona slanted into the drinker who stood on her other side. "Three kinds of rum and two liqueurs, all in one tall orange drink," Rona said. "That's what I call a cocktail." The short, sunburned fellow quickly closed the distance between himself and Rona, smoothing his comb-over and placing a pudgy hand on her shoulder. Maggie rotated her stool to talk to Ben. He was already conversing with a gray-haired man in a pink Oxford shirt and loosened tie.

"Internet book publishing," Maggie heard Ben say. "What exactly is that? I've heard of companies that offer services for self-published authors. Editing and marketing and so forth."

"That's one model," the man replied, pushing his empty rocks glass toward Natalia and flashing bright white teeth. "Another martini, hon." He craned his neck to see around Ben, who had placed his hand on Maggie's forearm.

"Maggie, this is Steve Baldwin," Ben said. "He's in internet publishing."

Steve mimed a tip of a hat. "Pleased to meet you. Writers' Best Publishing, chief cook and bottle washer. We offer aspiring authors the chance to fulfill their dreams of publication. Our services are all online, so, wherever they may be situated, writers can grasp the opportunity they deserve."

"Aren't online services for writers fairly standard these days?" Ben said. "No need to visit an office to talk to an agent or editor or book designer. At least, so I've heard."

Steve held his hand up like a crossing guard, then took a healthy swig from the drink Natalia set before him. "True, in general, but Writers' Best offers unique services, hardly standard. We promise a successful launch for every author, with positive reviews in outlets like the *New York Times* and *Publishers Weekly*."

"How can you promise that?" Ben said, sipping his mai tai. Maggie placed her right elbow on the bar and leaned in a tad to hear Steve's answer.

"Connections, my friend. Connections. That's what makes a contract with Writers' Best so valuable." Steve picked up his martini, peeled off the sodden paper coaster, and rose from his seat. "And now I note that the cocktail weenies have arrived. The chicken tenders can't be far behind." He extended his right hand to Ben. "Good to meet you, Dan."

"Ben."

"Right." Steve peered down the low-cut blouse of a brunette who was clearly angling for his barstool. "Ben."

TWO KITES SWOOPED OVER THE beach that evening as the setting sun glinted off the ocean. Maggie and Ben watched from the narrow balcony of their second-story time-share, occasionally glimpsing the small boy and girl who trotted backward to keep the kite strings taut.

Crammed into Frankie's Lounge, you'd never guess a brilliant blue sky sparkled over the ocean less than fifty yards east of the sheltered patio. Between Frankie's and the beachfront, five two-story buildings housing sixty modest time-share units clustered around an outdoor pool. Lush plantings of manzanilla, wax myrtle, and palm zigzagged through the property, which was elevated eight or ten feet above the beach, creating a sense of privacy and maybe even an illusion of upscale resort splendor.

From their ocean-view unit, Maggie and Ben could see a sizable stretch of ocean. The blue-and-green-striped kite soared over the waves, barely fluttering, while the purple dragon-shaped kite wavered, and then dove into the sand. A teenaged boy ran to rescue it for the little girl who clutched the string; she bounced on her toes as he lofted it back into the air.

"Want some avocado?" Maggie asked Ben. Plates and bowls of taco fixings covered the round glass-topped table between them: spicy ground beef, chopped tomatoes, shredded lettuce, grated cheese, avocados, sour cream, and even diced radishes. Maggie leaned over the table as she crunched into her taco. "Mm, can't beat tacos and an ice-cold Corona. Why wait until Friday?" she added, poking her thumb over her shoulder toward Frankie's.

"You did a fine job rustling up the ingredients," Ben said. "It's not as easy when we're away from home. I probably would have forgotten the taco shells."

Nodding a thank-you, Maggie stretched one leg to brace her foot against the balcony rail. She tilted her chair back, holding her taco with one hand and her plate under it with the other. For a moment, she watched the kites hover in the fading sky; then she chomped another bite. "About Steve and Rona, in Frankie's," she said. "Are you thinking what I'm thinking?"

Ben remained silent long enough to consider Maggie's question. "If you're thinking that they seem kind of dodgy, then, yeah."

"Dodgy?" Maggie halted the progress of her taco halfway back to her plate. "Con artist is more like it. Rona's company sounds like what we called a loan modification or foreclosure rescue scam when I worked in consumer protection. The scammer takes a monthly fee—like, a thousand dollars or more—and promises to negotiate with the mortgage lender. Supposedly to reduce or stretch out the payments."

"I remember you talked about that," Ben said. "And the scammer pockets the payments without doing anything?"

"Yep. Nobody contacts the lender, the foreclosure process moves forward, and the homeowner loses the house. The details are more complicated, of course, but that's the gist of it."

"Maybe there's a legitimate loan mod business somewhere, but I don't think it's Trillium Home Savers," Ben said.

"The very first thing I heard Rona say, about the student admissions scam, set off alarm bells for me." Maggie waggled her head and frowned. "Granted, I thought she might have been joking."

"Fueled by too many piña coladas."

Maggie snorted. "And rum runners and who knows what else. At least she consumes her daily recommended allowance of sliced fruit. But tell me what you think of Steve. Do you know anything about internet publishing?"

"I learned a little from my theater students. A few were into creative writing as well as drama. They were so eager to be published, or simply to have their work recognized." Ben shook his head. "And plenty of scam operators were waiting to pounce."

"What were the scams?" Maggie said.

"Oh, different ones. A lot of marketing come-ons. 'There's an important book fair in New York City and for six hundred dollars, you'll claim a choice location on the conference center floor.' The writer pays six hundred bucks and ends up with thirty brochures to stack on the corner of a shared table. After shelling out for travel and a hotel."

Maggie flinched. "Travel and lodging add up fast in New York City."

"Exactly." Ben tapped his fingers on the arm of his wicker chair. "Ah, they also targeted self-published authors. 'We read your e-book fantasy trilogy, and we believe in your potential as the next great American novelist.' They dangle the lure of publication by a major publishing house. All you need to do is pay for an exclusive introduction to well-known Literary Agent X, who's allegedly searching for talent."

"Sure," Maggie said, squeezing lime juice into her beer. "Well-known Literary Agent X awaits your masterpiece."

"There are organizations and web sites that expose these scams. But a lot of writers who've been cheated chalk it up to experience and move on. Individually, they don't lose enough money to justify a lawsuit. Or they're embarrassed. Or the company that defrauded them shuts down and disappears."

"Like the loan mod and foreclosure rescue operations," Maggie said. "We used to call it whack-a-mole. That game where you conk a mole on the head, and another pops up from a different hole. Get an enforcement order to shut down one business entity, and the scam operator pops up with another."

Maggie stood to open the balcony's sliding door. "Did you notice how Rona and Steve both use the word 'deserve' in their spiels? Playing on the emotions. 'We'll protect the home you worked and saved for. We'll deliver that big break you always dreamed of.'" She paused to watch a half-dozen pelicans skim the building's roof as they flapped northward to the wildlife refuge. "I almost feel like we should report both of them to . . . somebody."

"Me too. But I don't know if we'd be taken seriously or viewed as a couple of cranks."

Grasping the door handle, Maggie tugged sideways. "Well, enough of this. I feel like I'm back at the office. We're retired."

"And on vacation," Ben said. "Let's walk to our favorite bench, where I can sit with my beautiful wife and watch the moon rise over the sea."

"Very romantic," Maggie said, glancing at Ben, at the leftovers that cluttered the tabletop, and back at Ben.

Ben gave her a thumbs-up sign. "After we put away the leftovers, of course."

Maggie blew him a kiss. "I love how we think alike."

FIFTEEN MINUTES LATER, MAGGIE SHIVERED as she locked the balcony sliding door from the inside. "It's getting chilly, isn't it? I'm going to put on something warmer. Do you want to go ahead and grab our bench?"

"Sure, I'll meet you there in a few minutes," Ben replied. "Watch your step in the dark."

The beach cooled down quickly this time of year. Daylight Saving Time wouldn't arrive for another two weeks, so the sun set by six thirty and darkness fell by seven. With turtle nesting season underway, curtains were pulled shut so as not to disorient the protected reptiles. Here and there, a sliver of light escaped from a building along the beachfront.

After changing her clothes, Maggie followed the amber turtle-friendly lanterns that bordered the sidewalk leading to the resort's eastern boundary. The walkway meandered from Maggie and Ben's time-share unit past a covered picnic shelter, a tot lot, and a three-hole minigolf course, then forked right and left in a T at the metal railing that overlooked the beach. Three yards to Maggie's right, a wooden picnic table caught the ocean breeze; twenty yards to her left, a blue-painted metal bench provided early birds a spot to view the sunrise and night hawks a place to watch the waves gleam in the moonlight. Between Maggie and the metal bench, Ben stood with his elbows propped on the railing. Someone had claimed their favorite evening perch.

Before Maggie veered left to join Ben, she noticed a glow to her right: a laptop screen flickering to life on the picnic table. Maggie squinted at the face revealed by the computer's harsh light. "Rona? Hey, it's Maggie."

Rona jerked her head around when Maggie spoke.

"Sorry to startle you," Maggie said. "We met at Frankie's. Catching up on work this time of night?" Maggie was surprised Rona could sit upright after knocking back two piña coladas and a rum runner on an empty stomach, not to mention whatever she imbibed after the happy-hour snacks appeared.

"Work pays the bills," Rona said. "Writing novels is my passion. Romance novels, specifically."

"Interesting. Should I check for your romance novels in the bookstores?"

"Not yet, but I expect to finish my debut novel within the next month, and then cast it on the waters. You know, find an agent, get published, embark on a book tour. It can't be that hard."

For a moment Maggie didn't know what to say—she thought it actually might be that hard—so she focused on buttoning up her sweater. "I'll keep an eye out. What's the name of your book?"

"The working title is *Mojitos at Moonrise*." Rona lifted her face to the sky and breathed deeply, apparently channeling moonlight for inspiration. "I've planned a five-book series. My second book is tentatively titled *Daiquiris at Daybreak*. Or perhaps, *Daiquiris at Dawn*."

"A cocktail theme," Maggie said. "Write what you know, and all that." She waved goodbye with a quick salute. "I'll be on my way. Best of luck to you." Maggie continued along the sidewalk to join Ben. Before she could say anything, he placed his hand on her arm and inclined his head toward hers.

"Don't look now, but that's our friend Steve on the bench," he whispered. As Maggie peeked around her husband, a tall man pushed himself upright and strode, head down, toward the buildings on the other side of the pool.

"Grab that seat," Maggie said, her voice low. "I want to tell you something." With her back to Rona, she jabbed her thumb toward the picnic table and held a finger to her lips.

Ben took her hand as they followed the sidewalk to the bench. "I have something to tell you too. I got an earful listening to Mr. Internet Publishing talk on his phone."

"From this far away? I'm surprised you could hear his voice over the waves."

"My new hearing aids," Ben said, tapping his right ear.

"Told you they'd make a difference," Maggie said with a grin. "Perfect for eavesdropping."

"I prefer to call it sleuthing. To tell the truth, he ranted so loudly I worried that he'd scare the turtles." Ben moved his head close to Maggie's. "His publishing company may be internet-based, but he also runs some sort of bricks-and-mortar business out of his house. The company's deep in the red. And his home is about to be foreclosed upon." Ben sat back, raising his eyebrows. "How about that for intel?"

"Excellent job, Inspector Clouseau. Here's what I wanted to tell you. That's Rona at the picnic table. She's writing a romance novel. A series, in fact. And she's looking to find a book deal, which she assumes will be a piece of cake."

"Mortgages and manuscripts." Ben steepled his fingers, twiddling them in Snidely Whiplash fashion. A smile spread across his face. "Mortgages and manuscripts. And meatballs."

Maggie's hand flew to her mouth. "Are you thinking what I'm thinking?"

"I'm thinking we know a company that claims to offer unique services to authors who deserve to be published," Ben said.

"And I'm thinking we know another company that claims to help homeowners protect the home life they deserve," Maggie added.

"Perhaps we could introduce the two company CEOs tomorrow, on Meatball Tuesday. They could . . . help one another."

"What a marvelous idea." Maggie clasped Ben's warm hand. "I can't think of two more deserving people."

PERFECT PARTNER

VINNIE HANSEN

MONEY. HE NEEDS MONEY. IN another minute, he's going to follow up his text to me with an ask.

I've been an idiot. A complete moron. Heat crawls up my neck. I nip at my embarrassing nub of a fingernail.

Right now, Adam is waiting for my response. Poor Adam, arriving at the airport to discover he has his ticket and passport, but his wallet—his cash, his bank card, his credit cards—gone. Lost or stolen.

Right.

I could tuck my phone in my pocket. End the communication right now and go on with my Santa Cruz life. But I don't think so.

I text him *OMG* and a pile of poop emoji. If he were in front of me, I'd grab a handful of his dark, wavy hair and push his head into that poop. Except after two months of interaction, it's dawned that I have no idea what he looks like. He could be a 200-pound Russian gorilla. If he's a "Nigerian Prince," he's avoided any weird, telegraphing syntax.

At the roar of the espresso machine, I look up. The barista gives a headshake that sends her large skeleton earrings dancing and lifts an index finger to indicate one more drink before my latte.

A new text pops up.

Adam: I'm in a bind here, Blanche. This chip deal will make or break my start-up.

Ah, yes, the chip deal. With the global-supply-chain issues, Adam's trip to Geneva is an opportunity to scoop up a secret cache of cut silicon wafers to save his company, a Fitbit competitor making monitors in hip shades of mauve and neon orange. A "business" he no doubt tailored to my profile interest in "well-being."

I write back:

Me: At hospital with Mom.

A preemptive delaying tactic. My mom is seated at her home computer fretting away with worry about her future given the crushing cost of residential-care facilities. I wonder if fears for my mom's early onset dementia flagged me on Perfect Partner as a vulnerable mark. I still am, I suppose.

I tap on Perfect Partner, a dating website, its logo two Ps, the second one reversed, each letter anthropomorphized with an arm and hand reaching to join the other's. Clever with the non-gender-specific figures. *Cute.*

In 20/20 hindsight, too cute for someone with a profile like Adam's. *And Adam.* How had that name not tipped me off? *Adam Williams.* The name should have semaphored red flags. It was the kind of name attached to photos of clean-cut military men on otherwise blank Facebook accounts to lure lonely, middle-aged women into "friendships." How pathetic that I, a thirty-eight-year-old, have fallen into the trap. A hot flash of embarrassment sears my cheeks.

But there'd been my break-up after a five-year relationship because of an ego-bruising, twenty-five-year-old *other woman.* Then the move to a new apartment. My mom's declining mental health. . . .

I try to cut myself slack. Adam was slick. And I had taken precautions. I'm not Blanche Dubois, and this professional scammer missed the reference—hadn't raised a virtual eyebrow at the name.

That lack of curiosity should have tipped you off, Maya. Except my peers can be shockingly ignorant of masterpieces like *A Streetcar Named Desire.*

While I've moved over to Shutterstock to search the images for *dark wavy-haired male,* he's responded with a care emoji. Asks about mom's prognosis.

Me: Not good.

I relish the idea of "Adam" squirming, reformulating his angle to ask for money. But is he even breaking a sweat? Patience has been his modus operandi from the start. He has his fish. He'll take his time to reel me in slowly.

Works for me.

His next message says how sorry he is, how much he wishes he could be there for me.

Adam: But . . .

I don't need to read. He's spent the last two months grooming, setting parameters, making any hook-up contingent on finishing this deal. Until then, he has to devote 24/7 to "rescuing his company."

Yet, he's always had time for me online. Why had I never questioned the inherent contradiction? When you think you've found a soul mate, logic flies out the window.

Adam circles back to his flight. And then . . . the need for cash.

Me: When's your flight?

Adam: One hour.

Me: I know how important this is but can't leave mom. Later flight?

I smile. *Sure he can. He's not at the friggin' airport, anyway.*

Adam: Love ya, Babe. See what I can do. You're the best!

At the hiss of steamed milk, I raise my head. The barista nods and sprinkles chocolate powder on my drink. I fetch the ceramic mug. She slides a carrot across the counter, winks, and says, "For Pudgy." I scurry back to the tiny corner table, bend down to open the top of Pudgy's carrying cage, and run a hand over the soft head and long black ears of my rescue bunny, calming myself. I poke the carrot through the grilled front toward Pudgy's quivering nose.

I sip my latte. Despite my fake name and vague employment as "customer service rep," elements of my real self—my comfort animal, for example—had slid right into my profile. *No kidding? He had a pet rabbit as a child.* At the mention of my hobby of playing ukulele, he'd launched into a rhapsody about the famous uke master Israel Kamakawiwo'ole's version of "Somewhere Over the Rainbow."

I'd broadcast myself as easy prey all right.

Now what?

As I finish my latte, I move from Shutterstock to Unsplash images and no friggin' way. There's "Adam," or rather a guy who likes to model for photos. No surprise Adam helped himself to free images, but the ease of the discovery burns my ears with humiliation.

I don't have time to roll around in self-pity. A new text arrives.

Adam: New flight but plane packed, only seat available is in first class!

Hah! The guy is merciless.

But, if I play along, it gives me more time, especially if he thinks he has me duped, with more money to come.

Me: By when? How much?

Adam: $3282. New flight in 3 hrs.

Me: On it soon as I can leave hospital.

Adam: Western Union, international terminal.

I may have been a sucker, but this guy is a rube.

Me: I'll need your email.

I don't know if that's true; it's worth a shot. All our communication has been via text. An email will give me vital information to work with.

He sends it without hesitation. Blinded by greed, I suppose, or maybe the rush of landing his fish.

Me: On it, asap.

I slip my phone into the pocket of my jeans, stride out to my turquoise cruiser bike on the sidewalk, and strap Pudgy's carrier into the basket. Pudgy snuffles like he thinks there may be another carrot in the offing.

"Dream on."

I pedal furiously the four blocks to Surf the Web Computer Repair. An ancient Commodore PC props the door open so our clients can more easily lug in their hardware.

Two desks face the door. At one, a gray-haired man clutches a cell phone in a liver-spotted hand as my co-worker Tobias leans across the desk to help the guy. Behind Tobias's desk are shelves full of phones and a pegboard with hooks dangling packages of charging cables and SIM cards.

On the other desk, a large computer screen plopped down by a female customer hides Kevin.

A senior citizen (like most of our clients), the woman is telling Kevin, "This thing is running slower than a banana slug."

Tobias glances at Pudgy's carrier, his eyebrows threatening to fly off his face like a couple of crows. "You let that cable-eater out, he's stew."

"Rabbit stew is delicious," the old man says.

"What a gorgeous bunny," the female customer trills.

Kevin's muscles and tight CrossFit tank top rear above the thirty-inch screen on his desk. "What are you doing here?"

"Checking on a data transfer." I waltz behind Tobias's desk and unhook a SIM card package. "Explain later," I say.

"Pay later," he mutters.

Swinging the carrier, I scurry between the two desks to the inner sanctum, a room lined with counters covered with computer hardware and twining cables.

Plopping into the desk chair at our company computer, I place the cage on the floor. I take a moment to center myself by sliding a palm along Pudgy's silky fur.

Time to spring into action. I rummage in the drawer for an old demo phone and come up with one, the screen liberally smeared with fingerprints.

As an authorized cell phone dealer, Surf the Web Computers can access phone numbers. I look up "Adam's" number. It's under the name Will Smith. *Indeed.*

On the other hand, he uses the same service as I do. A surprise even though it dominates the U.S. market. I'd anticipated something foreign.

I pull out my cell and text Adam.

Me: Leaving hospital.

He sends flowers and hearts. Seals them with a kiss.

For one crazy second, I wonder if my scammer could be a woman.

My heartbeat thrums. If Adam tries to text me in the next few minutes, the whole game could be off.

I send him a final message:

Me: Sit tight. Get back to you as soon as I'm at Western Union.

I wait for his response because he's the master of solicitude.

Adam: I knew from the start you were the one.

I bet you did.

This is the tricky part. I flip over an invoice and jot down the Integrated Circuit Card ID, the unique identification code for Adam's current SIM card.

I assign the new subscriber identity module to Adam's phone number, then, fingers trembling, insert the delicate wafer into the demo phone. Press Activate SIM.

Presto. That simple. Adam's phone data is now mine, filling the screen of the old demo phone.

The minute changes on the computer clock. My heart races. Time is short. Even if Adam is off to a Western Union somewhere, his phone is his livelihood. He won't be off it long.

If he tries to use it now, it's not going to work. Will he become suspicious and abort the mission? Or will his ego rationalize the problem as a service glitch?

The demo phone is chock-a-block full of icons. Adam maintains pages of apps—could obviously have paid for almost anything—if any of his scenario were real. My eyes land on the familiar blue P of PayPal.

I open it, enter his email as the username, and click the Forgot Password link. Another minute flips over on the computer clock as I wait for PayPal to call Adam's phone with the code for the password change.

Despite the expected ring, my heart jumps at the sound.

Entering the code, I create the new password: F**kingScammer.

I confirm it.

The phone in my hand whooshes. I drop it on the desk. But the sound is only for an incoming text from a woman named Gabriella. It's disconcerting to receive a text not meant for me.

Gabriella: Babe, are you at the airport? Can't wait for this deal to close so we can meet. I totally fantasize our first date of catching Chris Stapleton live.

Gabriella's message is followed by a parade of emojis—hearts, kisses, and musical notes.

Sheesh. What did I expect? Scammers aren't monogamous.

But, yeah, Adam is not going to be off his phone long. God only knows how many women he's stringing along.

I open his PayPal account with the new password. For a second, I consider sending money to my mom, providing a modicum of relief to her worries. But if any part of this goes sideways, she can't be involved.

Pudgy sighs and turns around in his cage.

That's it.

I Google the Santa Cruz Animal Shelter, click their "get involved" page and select Donate. Like any smart organization, they've made it easy-peasy to send them money. On Adam's PayPal, I type in $3282.00. I hope when he receives his PayPal notice, he recognizes the amount.

After the money is on its way, I pause a second.

Then I quickly make another payment—twenty dollars to myself to cover the cost of the SIM card. *Only fair.*

Hands shaking, I reverse the process, reassigning Adam's phone number to his original SIM card, using the Integrated Circuit Card ID written on the back of the invoice.

I take one second to draw a deep breath.

Picking up my own cell, I text Adam:

Me: Money on its way.

I can't resist. I add a smiley face.

Shoving the old demo phone back in the desk drawer, I snatch up Pudgy and swing my way to the front. Tobias and Kevin are busy with the same two customers. I slap a twenty on Tobias's desk and mouth, "For the SIM card."

When I walk out the door, the snappy sea air of Santa Cruz revives me. My step is buoyant.

I strap Pudgy into my bike's basket and jam. The sun is bright. The sky is blue. Revenge *is* sweet.

I head to the beach, exhilarated, the lightest I've been in months.

Maybe Adam was the perfect partner after all.

CHANGELING

ANN MICHELLE HARRIS

SHANE SHIFTS HERSELF UP FROM the cot. The cavernous room echoes with sounds of breathing, heavy and loud, soft and tentative, floating like waves of water around her as she drags herself to her feet. It's six a.m. She stares out at the sea of bodies around her, then squats back down.

"I'm taking her." Shane keeps her voice low and picks up the little girl curled beside the unmoving woman.

"I need her back by tomorrow," the woman grumbles sleepily. She doesn't lift her head. Shane pulls fifty dollars from her pocket and shoves it under the woman's pillow.

In the bathroom, Shane washes up, brushes her teeth with soap, and runs her soapy fingers through her tangled hair. She needs a balance of looking shabby but not dangerous. Or grotesque. Disheveled is okay; revolting is counterproductive. She doesn't linger on the reflection in the metallic mirror. Her face is helpfully unremarkable, a balance of all things familiar and forgettable at the same time. She wets a paper towel with soap and water and washes the child's face. She helps her onto the toilet and fixes her clothes, securing the Velcro straps on the pair of tiny white sneakers. The child endures all of this without speaking or crying. Soundless. Shane tugs the child onto her hip and exits the women's shelter. She hates coming to this place, but it always has the prop she needs.

The weather outside is bracing, cold and bright in the early morning. The child shivers wordlessly in the chill air. For the first time, Shane hesitates. This is the first emotion the child has shown. The sliver of tension shivering from her little body sends a brush of guilt across the back of Shane's thoughts. She tugs the child closer to her, warming the little girl with her body heat. She should have brought a coat. What kind of parent would have their child out without a coat in this weather? She will have to think of an explanation for that. It's not really Shane's fault. She barely knows this kid, and the donation bin at the shelter never has anything close to a child's size.

A block away is the Ellis Hotel. It looms tall and majestic in old-fashioned splendor. The ornate designs of the entryway are carved in stone and marble and stand out in sharp contrast to the sleek, angular, glass buildings around it. The hotel guests here are decidedly old fashioned, un-savvy. Willfully so. She steps out from the cold morning into the wood-paneled lobby. It's filled with velvet furnishings. A good-looking man in a navy blazer greets her at the warm check-in section. He seems to be about her same age, young but sweet in a way that matches this old space. Perhaps he is the owner's grandson.

"Welcome to the Ellis."

Shane gives him an embarrassed smile.

"I'm not checking in," she says. "I just needed a place to get out of the cold. My taxi driver said he needed us to step out of the car for a minute so he could check the tires. Then he just took off with my purse and her coat." Shane tugs the child closer, using her hand to push the child's head against her shoulder. The child complies as always, leaning silently against the body of this stranger who drags her through midtown once a week. Shane keeps her eyes locked on the man's face. His eyes are kind. She relaxes a bit. "We just need to warm up for a moment."

"Of course," he says. He points to a sofa near the oversized marble fireplace. Thick logs crackle in the enclosure. "You can both sit over there if you like. The screens are in place. They're very secure, so she'll be fine." He stares at Lia. Lia is the child's name Shane recalls. She can tell he is smitten with the little girl, by her ordinariness and her silence. A gust of wind signals the presence of new customers. Shane hesitates, waiting for the new arrivals to draw closer to her. She bites her lip, looking up at him again.

"Could I borrow your house telephone, please? I just need to call for a taxi." The young man frowns at her.

"How will you pay for another taxi without your wallet?"

Shane steps back a bit as if she has been struck. Tears form in her eyes.

She blinks them back, but one slips free. "We're stuck in this town," she mumbles. "He just abandoned us."

She bites her lip again. Behind her, the elderly couple whisper to each other.

"I'm sorry," Shane says, turning to them and ducking her head. "Sorry for holding up the line." She kisses the child and turns toward the little alcove with the fireplace.

"Excuse me." It's the voice of the older man. She turns back to him, trying in that moment to become his daughter, his granddaughter, his long-lost sister, his own mother on hard times decades ago. Shane exhales a shaky breath. His mother, probably. Yes, there's an ancient family story there. She can see it in his eyes. She imagines his mother abandoned in a strange city, clutching her small son. Beginning life anew, surviving on the kindness of strangers. His wife stands behind him; she knows the story too.

"Here," he says. In his hand is a cluster of twenty-dollar bills. Six bills, a hundred twenty dollars. Shane counts quickly in her head. But she doesn't accept the money.

"I can't take that." She grinds the words out. "I might not be able to pay you back."

"It's fine." He means it. Wrinkles crease around his eyes. His wife hands her another few bills. The wife's gaze is firm, not sentimental like the husband's.

"There's a store down the street." The wife stares at her. "Get the child a coat."

Two hundred total. Shane can count by sight.

"Thank you," Shane says, relenting. The husband gives her a sad smile and drifts away with his wife. Shane makes her way to the little sitting area by the fireplace. As she sits down, a hotel attendant appears with a small plate of sugar cookies and a paper box of juice. The child settles down on the sofa and eats the cookies, chewing and swallowing silently. The door opens and the child shivers again, tensing against the cold before returning to the plate of sweets. Another couple walks over and strikes up a conversation with Shane. The child reminds them of their little granddaughter.

"She's so quiet." The woman says it with a mixture of concern and sadness. A quiet toddler is a rare find, magical.

"It's been a difficult morning," Shane says.

It's nine a.m. and she already has four hundred dollars. Much more than normal. She will be at two thousand by lunchtime. It's the shivering Shane decides. The child does it every time the door opens. The shivering is the one authentic thing in a sea of lies. Shane thinks about this as she stands near the hallway, refocusing her attention on the gentleman talking to her. She doesn't even remember walking up to him.

The antique clock in the hotel entranceway announces noon. Shane takes the child to the lobby bathroom. The child walks carefully over the marble floors, staring down at the broken pattern as though it is a night sky full of stars. Shane washes the child's hands and heads for the exit. She is well past two thousand dollars, enough for now. Some of the crisp twenties are fresh from the hotel's ATM. The bills are folded flat and fit neatly into her various pockets. No one has noticed the skimmer. She is certain none of these people even know what a skimmer is. They keep their money at banks that grudgingly forgive the fraudulent charges destined to sneak through their accounts in the next few days. It all feels a bit like overkill now.

"Excuse me," the young man at the check-in desk calls to get her attention. She curses silently and wonders if he remembers her from the last time. David. The letters are carved into his nametag. He finishes with the current customer and then beckons to her. She strokes Lia's head like a talisman and carries the child with her to the front desk. The man whispers to her that she can have one of the empty rooms tonight if she wants to take a break with the child. Free. The manager has approved it. He assures her of this solemnly and hands her a key. For a moment, she feels bad for him. He will never survive in this city, in this life. He was born in the wrong era. But she accepts the key. She has always wanted to stay at this fancy old hotel. And this way Lia can have a night of walking on marble floors. The front door opens and the child shivers again. Shane has a fleeting image of a family, a young father with kind eyes, a little girl searching the floor for stars, and a sharp-eyed mother protecting them both. This afternoon, she will buy a proper coat for Lia. But for now, she takes the key from the young man and walks away.

RESTITUTION

A. W. POWERS

MADAME VARNA, WEARING FADED JEANS with a grass stain on one knee and a Minnesota Lynx sweatshirt with a frayed collar and sleeves pushed up past her elbows, opened the door. The young couple on the front steps stared at her. "I know. Not what you expected," Varna said. "The people who dress up are into theatrics. Makes it easier to hide the fraud." She smiled. "I'm no fraud." Her sandy brown hair was pulled back and tied into a two-inch ponytail. She was in her early forties, wore no makeup, and was about ten pounds overweight, with most of it clinging to her middle.

"I'm . . ." the young woman said.

"I know, Hope," Varna said. "I've been expecting you."

Hope's mouth dropped open, and she looked at her friend. "I never told her my name," she said. Hope had called and asked to schedule an appointment. The woman who answered said, "Tuesday at 7 p.m. See you then," and hung up.

"That's a good sign," Hope's companion said. He held out his hand. "I'm John."

"Of course you are. Hi, John. Welcome." Varna stepped back and opened the door further. "Please come in." Hope walked in. She was in her early twenties, a petite black woman with natural hair about two inches long. Her makeup was impeccable and called attention to her eyes. Her jeans and boots suggested she was a savvy, yet fashion-conscious, shopper.

John stepped to the door and stopped, leaned forward, and looked around. He was about six foot four, thin and pale. His dark brown hair stuck out at peculiar angles, as if either he'd just woken, or the wind had circled his head lifting tufts. He wore jeans and a flannel shirt under his

227

open coat. John looked at Varna, flashed a quick smile, and stepped into the house. "This is a great house," he said.

"Thank you. A friend, who was a fan of my work and a believer in my mission to help people, left it to me when she died. I miss her, but I welcome people here to honor her." Varna closed the door behind them. "Let me take your coats." She extended her arm, open palm up. Hope had already shrugged off her heavy winter coat. John looked at Varna's hand, then slid his coat off too. Varna took them and hung them on hooks behind the door. "We'll be in the dining room." She gestured through the nearest doorway.

Hope turned and led them into the living room, then through an arch and to the dining room table. She moved to the far side and glanced into the kitchen.

"Please, have a seat," Varna said. She moved to the chair at the far end of the table. Hope took the chair closest to her and John sat opposite Hope.

"You know I'm a medium as well as a psychic," Varna said. "You're here to communicate with the other side. If the spirits are willing, I will be your guide and conduit. If the spirits are not willing, we'll have a nice visit, and you can leave with your questions and your money, but no answers." She smiled. "Unlike others, I only charge when the spirits play along."

"How often do people leave with their money?" John asked.

"Not often, but it happens," Varna said. She looked at him as if trying to get inside his head. "But you, you're a believer. You expect something to happen."

"I am a believer," John said. "So yes, I do expect to see and hear something special."

"Well, spirits willing," Varna said. She chuckled. When the lights suddenly faded, then glowed brighter than before, then faded again, to a level some people would consider romantic, she said, "I guess they are."

John's eyebrows rose. Hope bounced a little in her chair and smiled toward Varna.

Varna's back arched and she looked toward the ceiling. "I am here," she said in a voice that wasn't hers. "Who seeks the counsel of Chekov?"

"I do," Hope said.

"Ah, Hope Brannigan, it is your time."

Hope leaned and whispered to John, "She knows my last name too." Her eyes were wide and bright. "This is so cool."

A faint smile formed on Varna's lips.

"There is one here who wishes to speak with you," Chekov said. "She says love will find you soon."

"I hope so," Hope said. "I'm ready. I've been alone too long. Do I know her?"

"He . . . she is not someone you know," Chekov said. "Yet. But be patient. It will be worth the wait."

"This is so cool. What else?" Hope said. She took a deep breath. Her eyes widened, stared off into the distance. She leaned back. "No. Don't. What are you doing? Stay away," she called out, fear creeping into her voice. A scream tore from her throat and was instantly cut off. She thrashed back in her chair, then flung herself forward, her head hitting the table hard.

Hope sat up in her chair as if she didn't have any bones, just rolled up and into position. In a deep and gruff voice, she said, "I am Feklar. I bring greetings to the one named John Thompson." Her head, as if mounted on a rusty gear, rotated in his direction. "Your sister says, 'Stay the course, protect your friends. Their troubles are not yet over.'"

"You know Rachel?" John asked.

Hope thrashed forward, hitting her arms and head against the table with a resounding bang, then flung backwards, tipping the chair and crashing to the floor. She lay still for a moment, then rolled onto her side, cradling her head. John pushed his chair back, circled the table, and crouched next to her.

"What . . . what . . . what just happened? What was that?" she asked.

"I think you channeled a spirit," John said. "Have you ever done that before?"

"No . . . no, I've never experienced anything like that," Hope said.

"Are you okay?" John asked.

"Yeah, I think so," Hope said. "Help me up." John helped her to her feet, then righted her chair and positioned her and it so she could sit.

Madame Varna sat paralyzed, staring at Hope. She had lost all color, her eyes were wide, perspiration formed on her upper lip, which now had a bit of a twitch.

"Madame Varna, is that you?" Hope asked. "Or are you still Chekov?"

"Chekov is gone," Varna whispered.

"Are you okay?" Hope asked.

Varna nodded and pointed at Hope's forehead. "You're bleeding."

"I'm okay," Hope said. She touched her head with her fingers, brought them down and looked at them. "It's not much. I'll be okay."

John examined her forehead near her hairline. "Maybe we should get you checked out."

Hope smiled at him. "No, I'll be fine," she said. "Let's continue."

John nodded and returned to his seat. Hope smiled. "Well, that was something I never expected." She smiled and looked between Varna and John. "A session with a psychic. A little harmless fun. What could go wrong?"

"So, nothing like that has ever happened before?" John asked. "Have you ever experienced anything that would be considered paranormal? Channeled or been possessed?"

"No. Never," Hope said. She looked at Varna. "What happened to Chekov?"

"I don't know," Varna said. "He left."

"Can you get him back?" Hope asked.

"I . . . I don't know," Varna said. "Nothing like this has ever happened before."

"Ever?" John asked.

"No. Not once," Varna said.

"Maybe being with you makes it possible for Hope to channel too," John said. "Maybe you've opened a doorway."

"I . . . I don't think so," Varna said. "I think maybe you should leave. I won't charge you."

Hope nodded. "If you think that's . . . " She thrashed in her chair, then slammed to the table once again. With a smile, she turned and looked at Varna. "Paulette, it is so wonderful to see you again." The voice was higher, rather musical.

"How do you know my name?" Varna asked. "I've never told you my name."

"Don't you recognize me? I'm Claudia. We're friends," Hope said.

"Claudia . . . um . . . wow, is it really you?" Varna asked. There was a tremor in her voice.

"Yes, silly, it's really me. Did you think I'd leave you?" Claudia asked.

"Well, no," Varna said.

"I love what you've done with the kitchen," Claudia said. "Especially the island. I should have put one in years ago. It gives you so much more room to work."

Varna looked through the doorway and into the kitchen. "Yeah, it's been nice," she said. "It was a little cramped before."

Hope leaned forward in her chair. "There are some things we need to discuss," she said in Claudia's voice.

"There are?" Varna asked.

"Yes. Things friends discuss, things friends can discuss," Claudia said. "This is so unpleasant." She cleared her throat. "Why did you put me in that home?"

"You needed care," Varna said. "Care I couldn't give you."

"I'm not so sure," Claudia said. "I thought I was okay. I mean, I wasn't perfect, but I was fine until I got there. Then I was drugged and sat in a corner, waiting to catch a disease." She shook her head. "It was sad. I was sad."

Varna said nothing.

"Being sad and trapped makes you want to die," Claudia said. "And I did." She frowned. "I did want to die. I did not have my home, my belongings, only my memories." A tear fell onto Hope's cheek. "And I was sad, so very sad. So, I died."

"Why did you die?" John asked. "Were you sick?"

"My heart was broken," Claudia said. "No one, absolutely no one, came to visit me." She narrowed her eyes. "You put me there and abandoned me. You never even told my family where I went."

"I didn't abandon you. I made sure you were cared for," Varna said. "And your family already didn't come see you. They didn't care."

"They weren't the most attentive, but they did care. They didn't live close. Their distance and absence made it easy for you to become my friend," Claudia said. "I gave you everything. I signed over the house, put you on my bank accounts. Everything you suggested so you could help me. So I wouldn't be alone. And what did you do?"

Varna shook her head. "I didn't do anything wrong," she said.

"I know," Claudia said. "You convinced me we were friends, that you were there to help me, that you would make sure I was taken care of for the rest of my life."

"We were friends. You were taken care of," Varna said.

"Then why are you living alone in my house and I'm dead?" Claudia asked. "I should be angry. I should be haunting you day and night."

Varna shook her head faster.

"Instead, I waited until this lovely young woman came to visit you. She didn't even know she could let me in. But she did. As soon as she walked in the door, I knew she was my way to talk to you." Claudia laughed. "Maybe I'll have her set me free and stay here after all. We can be roommates again. Or maybe I will have my friend Feklar possess her and murder you in your sleep."

"No, please, you can't," Varna said.

"Why can't I?" Claudia asked.

"Because none of this is real," Varna said. "It's all a fraud. I'm a fraud."

"I'm real," Claudia said. "Don't you believe in me? Don't you believe what you are seeing and hearing?"

Varna nodded slowly. Her eyes were filling with tears. "You don't want to hurt me. That's not who you are," Varna said.

"Maybe . . . after what you've done . . . I've changed," Claudia said. "I am dead, after all. Dying changes things. Death makes you see lots of things differently." The table vibrated and bounced for a couple of seconds.

Varna watched the table. No one seemed to be touching it. She returned to shaking her head. "It's not you," she said. "Even after what I've done, you're not a killer. You don't want to kill me."

"I could," Claudia said. Hope's body leaned forward. "I could get away with it too."

"Please . . ." Varna said.

"What are you willing to do to save your life?" Claudia asked. The table bounced again, a little higher this time.

"I . . . I could . . .I could sign the house back to your family," Varna said. "I . . . I could give back the rest of the money. I still have most of it."

"You should do that," Claudia said.

"I can help," John said. He pulled a piece of paper from his pocket, unfolded it, and lay it on the table. Then he produced an ink pen and set it on top of the paper.

"Why do you have that?" Varna asked.

"I came prepared," John said. "A friend told me how this was going to go."

"How could he know that?" Varna asked.

"He's a real psychic," John said. "He also hacked into your computer, searched your browser history, and knew how you played your subjects. But he knew you would do the right thing in the end."

Varna stared at him, then looked at Hope. The blood had trickled a little further down Hope's forehead. Varna reached for the pen.

The paper was a quitclaim deed, like Claudia had signed while alive. The top portion was already filled in. Varna recognized the names as the children of Claudia, who Varna had never met and never tried to contact. She sighed and signed.

"Thank you," Hope-as-Claudia said. "But what of the others you swindled?"

"No . . . I never . . ." Varna said. Tears slid from her eyes.

"We've been working with the police," John said. "We know of three others you conned." He paused. "Not to mention all the people who came to you for a psychic experience, gave you money, and went away thinking they had talked with the dead."

"But . . ." Varna said.

"The police are outside," Hope said. She pulled a tissue from her pocket and wiped away the blood on her forehead. She turned the tissue to Varna. "Stage blood. Claudia wasn't here, just like Chekov and Feklar don't exist."

"Why did you do this?" Varna asked. The words were choked and broken.

"Did you know Claudia took in foster kids?" Hope asked. "I was one. My family was in a bad spot. I was trouble and we were a mess. Claudia took me in, treated me like her own daughter, and loved me. She taught me things could be different, that I could change my family. I was here almost six months, then I went home and worked to fix my family." She smiled and nodded. "Thanks to Claudia, we're okay. We are a family." Her smile left. "Claudia was part of it. Until you came along."

"I . . . I . . . I . . ." Varna said.

"I know, you're sorry," Hope said. "Claudia was the type who would forgive you. But I'm not, so I found John. He studies psychics, wants to believe they're real. But our research and his friend said you weren't the real thing, so we worked up this plan and came after you."

"But you had Claudia's voice? I heard it, recognized it. How?" Varna asked.

"I'm an actress. I specialize in voices," Hope said. "I learned to do her voice when I lived here. I would practice talking to her as her. She thought it was funny. And I loved to make her laugh. Did you ever make her laugh?"

Varna wiped the tears from her cheeks.

"I'm sure Claudia loved you. She could love everybody, no matter their faults," Hope said. There was a knock on the door. "That would be the police, right on time." John got up and went to the door. "You can make restitution through the courts. I'm good with her family having the house back."

John and Hope watched the Minneapolis Police put Madame Varna in cuffs and take her out the door. "Nicely done," John said.

"I couldn't have done it without you," Hope said. "Are you going to continue going after fraudulent psychics?"

"I'm going to continue looking for real ones. That's what a parapsychologist should do," John said. "But if I debunk a couple of frauds along the way, I'm okay with that."

"I'm okay with it too," Hope said. "If you ever need help . . ."

"I'll keep that in mind," John said.

"I've got to say, I was impressed with your performance," Hope said. "Are you sure you've never acted before?"

"Thanks. I've never acted, but I was on the debate team. No matter which side you're on and what you believe, you've got to look like you believe in your argument," John said. He smiled. "I've got to say, the vibrating and bouncing table was a nice touch. How did you do it?"

Hope looked at him. "It wasn't me," she said. "I thought it was you . . ."

THE BUDDY SYSTEM

KATE FELLOWES

BENNETT, AGE TEN-AND-A-HALF, GROANED INWARDLY when his new teacher, Ms. Shepard, presented him to the class.

"Bennett just moved to Mapleville, class. Please help him out, answer any questions he might have. Show him around our school. Let's all make him feel welcome."

On cue, the entire class of twenty chorused, "Hi, Bennett."

This was always the worst part of being the new kid. He should know, he'd been to five different schools since kindergarten. "When your dad is in the military, you move around a lot," Dad had told him more than once, as if he should just get used to it. Well, he wouldn't. Not ever.

Now, he smiled his biggest smile, the one that looked fake, and gave a half-hearted wave.

"Why don't you sit there, in the back, next to Max?" Ms. Shepard suggested, pointing to a desk in the far corner, near the sink and alongside the window.

The kid who had to be Max must have been held back a grade or two. He was bigger than the rest of the kids. Taller, heavier, older. Bennett felt a little shudder as Max gave him a smile. It was just as fake as his own, but in a scary way. None of the other kids said anything as Bennett walked down the aisle to his desk, but he thought he saw pity on a few faces.

Sliding into his seat, Bennett put his backpack on the floor and fussed with the zipper as Ms. Shepard began the first lesson. He took a long time finding his pencil and pulling out a notebook. Max's eyes were drilling into the side of his head. He could feel it, and knew if he looked that way, he'd get another fiendish smile. Why couldn't his dad have been a mailman?

He managed to stare straight ahead nearly all the way through class, bending his head once in a while to write carefully in his notebook as the teacher talked. On the playground for recess, he watched his classmates scatter among the playground equipment, feeling no need to push his way into any of the groups.

"Hi, I'm Savannah." The high-pitched voice beside him jerked him from his musings.

He turned, spotting a brown-haired girl just his height. In jeans and a tee shirt, she held her hand out for a shake. Solemnly, they shook.

"Hi."

"You'll like Ms. Shepard. She's really nice," Savannah told him. "Everybody in class is mostly okay too." She looked to the basketball hoops, where Max was wrestling the ball away from a kid half his size.

"Except Max," Bennett said. "Right?"

She gave a big sigh, shoulders coming up to her ears. "Mom says he's just misunderstood. That it's because he lost his Mom when he was so little. I don't know."

They watched Max make a basket while the kid he'd shoved fell to the ground.

Bennett thought of his own mom, who worked just as hard as Dad, but always had time to read a book with him, or play a game, or listen while he spelled words for vocabulary.

"I would miss my mom if she died," he said.

"Me too," Savannah said.

Bennett ran off, scooping up the basketball as it rolled off the court and headed his way. He dribbled it back to Max and passed it the way he'd learned in gym class—both hands, chest high, and push. He knew he wasn't really athletic—he was 'academic' Mom said—but the throw wasn't a bad effort. Max caught the ball, dribbled in a quick circle and chucked it back at him. If he hadn't been paying attention, the ball would have hit him in the head or knocked him flat. But, because he'd watched carefully, he could see the ball coming. It knocked the air out of him, but he held fast, then bounced the ball a time or two, first with one hand, then with the other.

The bell rang just then, signaling the return to class. Good thing, because that dribbling bit was the end of what he knew about basketball.

Dribble, pass, make a basket. Max didn't look like he would ever let anyone else make a basket, unless maybe in gym class, when the teacher was there to enforce the rules. Max didn't seem like a kid who followed rules unless someone made him.

Back in class, Ms. Shepard announced the plan for the annual fundraiser for the school library. Students were to team up with a buddy to sell candy bars in the community and among their family and friends.

"Everyone choose a buddy now," she sang out.

Bennett's spine stiffened. Would Savannah turn to look over her shoulder at him, way off in the corner of the room? Or would—

"We'll be buddies," Max announced, leaning across the aisle between them to chuck him hard on the shoulder. "Okay?"

Nodding, Bennett felt resigned. Of course he'd get stuck in the back of the room next to the class bully and now be expected to trail around their neighborhood with him after school and on weekends. Of course. He sighed.

"MAYBE HE REALLY NEEDS A friend," Mom said that night at dinner. "Maybe he can tell how nice you are, and what a good friend you could be."

"Maybe," Bennett said, not believing it. "I think he just knew I didn't have a friend, and neither did he."

"Just give him a chance," Mom said, kissing the top of his head on her way to the sink. "You never can tell with people. They can always surprise you."

That Saturday, the two boys went off to knock on doors and sell candy bars from cardboard boxes with handles. Max ate two of the bars as they wandered from block to block.

"Don't do that," Bennett said. "Who's going to pay for those?"

"My Uncle Rick will pay," Max said, crumpling up the wrapper. "We can stop by my house last. You'll see."

"Your uncle lives with you?"

Max shook his head. "Not really. It just seems like it because he's there so much. He's not really my uncle, either. Just a friend of my dad's. They've known each other since grade school. Hey," as a thought occurred to him, his voice brightened, "maybe we can be like that when we're ancient."

They both laughed at the idea. Bennett couldn't imagine being actual friends with Max any more than he could imagine being ancient.

As they wandered, they talked. Bennett answered all of Max's questions about life in a military family. Yes, he really had lived in five different states. No, he'd never shot a gun. Yes, his dad had one, but so did his mom, because she was a police officer. No, he didn't want to be a policeman when he grew up.

By the end of several hours, they'd managed to sell fourteen candy bars, which was nearly a whole box. Well, Bennett managed to sell them. Max had mostly waited back on the sidewalk, but it was a system that worked.

They walked blocks and blocks to get to Max's house, which was a little place tucked between a car repair shop and a tavern. Max led the way around to the back door, which had peeling paint and a doorknob thick with grime.

Before they entered, Max turned to Bennett. "Listen, don't mention that your mom is a cop, okay? Uncle Rick, he . . . he's been in trouble a few times, so he doesn't like cops much. How about you say your mom does something else?"

Bennett frowned. He didn't want to be a police officer, but he was proud of his mom. "I can't do that."

Max leaned closer, his face suddenly inches from Bennett's. "Then don't say anything." It wasn't a suggestion. "Uncle Rick says he was railroaded. Dad says it was an accident."

"What was an accident?" Bennett asked.

Max shrugged. "Whatever happened. Dad says Uncle Rick didn't mean it."

Understanding dawned. Bennett said, "He was misunderstood."

"I guess so." Max said, pushing open the door.

A great big dog, brown with long ears, charged at them the minute they stepped inside the kitchen. Bennett was very glad he was standing behind Max, who crouched low and took the dog in his arms.

"Hiya, Luke," he said, ruffling the long ears. "This is Bennett." To Bennett, he said, "Hold out your hand, so he can smell you."

Hoping the dog wouldn't bite it off, Bennett did as Max said. Luke sniffed his hand, his wet nose leaving a trail across Bennett's skin.

"He likes you," Max said, and Bennett smiled as Luke's tongue stroked his fingers.

"C'mon." Max headed for the front of the house, where a TV blared a basketball game. Two men sat watching, one from a couch, one from a chair.

"Hey, Dad. Hey, Uncle Rick. Guess how many candy bars we sold," Max said.

"Three and a half," the middle-aged man, in tee shirt and ripped jeans, quipped from the couch. He held out a bowl of potato chips and Max took a handful. Bennett shook his head.

"Dad, that's not a real guess. Guess again."

"Ten," his dad guessed low.

"Twenty," Uncle Rick guessed too high.

"And how many did you boys eat?" Dad, again.

"Max ate two," Bennett said. "I didn't eat any. I'm Bennett," he introduced himself.

"Welcome, Bennett. Max's talked about you. Sit down. Watch the game," Max's dad suggested.

"We sold fourteen," Max said, sitting beside his father, leaving no room for Bennett, who went to sit on the radiator cover instead.

"And you ate two, so that's sixteen," Uncle Rick said. "How much are they?"

"Two dollars apiece," Max said, reaching into his box for the envelope stuffed with twenty-eight singles. Pulling out the wad of cash, he fanned it. "Look at that!"

"I'll pay for the ones you ate," Uncle Rick offered, standing up to pull a battered wallet from his back pocket. Looking up at the ceiling, he did math out loud. "Let's see, that's two dollars time two candy bars. That's four. You have twenty-eight dollars, plus four, that's thirty-two."

He held out two brand new twenty-dollar bills. "Give me four more bars and we'll be even. We can eat them now."

Bennett looked at Max, who shrugged.

With an impatient sigh, Uncle Rick explained, "I'll take all those singles, and you take these twenties. I can always use singles at the bar."

Max had told Bennett Uncle Rick used to have a good job at the factory in town before it closed. Now, he worked in the tavern next door and bought too many lottery tickets.

"Okay," Max said, and the exchange was made.

The pattern was set. Every Saturday, the boys stood outside a store selling candy, or walked down a block they hadn't walked before. They always ended their shift back at Max's, where Uncle Rick paid for the candy they had eaten as they worked, and then rounded up to the next twenty. Max kept the envelope full of money in a coffee can on the kitchen counter.

"Don't tell anyone where we're putting our money," he warned Bennett.

Bennett, who was becoming used to Max and Max's house, said, "Luke won't let anyone steal it."

The dog, asleep on a rug across the room, didn't look very ferocious just then, so they both laughed.

As he walked back to his own house, Bennett thought maybe he and Max were becoming like real friends. All this time fundraising, all their time at school, they were together a lot. And while Max had seemed scary and mean at first, he didn't anymore. Sometimes, he was funny. Sometimes, he seemed sad. Bennett never forgot about the fact that Max didn't have a mom, only his dad and Uncle Rick. Then, he'd feel sad too.

"You're a good friend," Mom said, when he told her one day. "You have a sympathetic heart. That's good. At least Max has his dad and his uncle and Luke to be a family."

Bennett explained about Uncle Rick not really being a family member. Then, just because, he told her about the man's generosity, always paying for what the boys ate, and then buying extra bars to round up to twenty dollars. Stiff, new twenty-dollar bills.

Mom made her thinking face. "That's very interesting," she said.

"Why?" Bennett asked, and she told him a story.

THE NEXT SATURDAY, WHEN THEY were at Max's house, Bennett said, "My mom's picking me up here today. I'm going to the dentist." He stuck out his tongue in anguish.

Max's eyes widened, but Bennett shook his head, just a little. It was okay. Mom wouldn't be wearing her police officer's uniform or anything like that.

On the stroke of three o'clock, a sharp knock came on the front door. It creaked open when Max went to answer it, and Bennett thought that door probably never got used. This family didn't get many visitors.

Mom looked pretty, in a bright green jacket and jeans. Bennett saw Uncle Rick sit up straighter as she stepped into the room, and Max's dad gave his tee shirt a tug over his beer belly.

"I've heard so much about you," Mom said after Bennett had introduced everyone, even Luke. "All of you, I mean. It's so nice knowing Bennett has a friend in our new town."

Bennett's face flushed with embarrassment. "Mom," he drew out her name with a groan and everyone laughed.

"So, the fundraiser is just about finished now," Mom said. "And I know you boys have a lot of money to turn in, right?"

"Three hundred dollars!" Max said. "We sold about a million candy bars!" Pride shone from Max's eyes. He and Bennett had worked hard and really achieved a success. They high fived, then Max ran for the coffee can to show off.

"That's a lot to be responsible for," Mom said, looking at all the twenty-dollar bills.

"Weren't you supposed to turn them in a little every week?" Uncle Rick asked, leaning forward. He looked at Max's dad, who was watching TV again.

"We wanted to take it in all at once, so it looks even better," Max said.

"Well, here then." Mom pulled her wallet out. "I just went to the bank this morning, so I have some big bills. Let me give you those, in exchange for all those twenties. It will be less to carry."

"And it'll look so cool!" Max said, eyeing the hundred-dollar bills in Mom's hand.

"I'll drive you boys to school on Monday, if that's all right with your dad," Mom said, glancing at Max's dad. He gave a distracted nod. "Just so you get the money there safely." She put the bundle of twenties in her purse as she spoke, then steered Bennett toward the door. "It was nice to meet you," she said.

Uncle Rick smiled a big smile, but his eyebrows were drawn together. Max's dad lifted a hand.

"See you Monday," Bennett told Max, and they high fived again.

Monday morning, Bennett and Mom drove to Max's house. He came out before the car had even stopped in the gravel driveway. He clutched a long white envelope in his hand and his backpack dangled off one shoulder. From the look on his face, Bennett knew something had happened. He hoped it was something good and not something bad.

"Good morning, Max," Mom greeted him as he climbed into the back seat beside Bennett.

"Hi," Max said, his eyes on Bennett. "You'll never guess what. Just guess. You'll never guess." He looked fit to burst.

Bennett looked at the back of Mom's head, trying without success to see her eyes in the rearview mirror.

"What?" he said.

"My Uncle Rick's working for the police!" he said. "Like an undercover agent!"

"Really?" Bennett asked, amazed. "Doing what?"

Max turned his head in both directions, as if checking to be sure they were alone in the car and wouldn't be overheard. "Turns out those twenty-dollar bills he gave us were fake! Counterfeit, it's called. He kept getting them from some guy at the tavern and had no idea!"

Bennett saw his mom's eyes now, glancing in the mirror to catch his own.

"Gee!" he said. "He could have gotten into real trouble."

"Yeah, but he didn't know," Max said. "So, now, he's helping the police, telling them about the guy and when he comes to the tavern and stuff like that. So they can catch him and stop him from using fake money. Isn't that something? Uncle Rick's like a hero."

"Like a crime fighter. Like Batman," Bennett said.

"Can you see Uncle Rick with a cape?" Max asked, and the two boys cracked up laughing.

At school, Max got out of the car first, clutching the white envelope full of real money so tight, it crinkled.

Mom put down her window as Bennett came around.

"Thanks for your help, Bennett," Mom said. "And for your good suggestion about using Uncle Rick to help us, rather than putting him in jail."

"He's misunderstood. That's what Max says," Bennett told her.

"People can always surprise you, honey," Mom said. "Have fun at school."

As he raced to catch up with his friend, Bennett thought about what Mom said. Max had surprised him, that was for sure. He'd seemed scary, at first, but now Bennett knew he wasn't scary at all. He was just a kid, just like him, except without a mom.

Bennett wondered if Max guessed Uncle Rick really had known those twenties were fake. If he knew Uncle Rick was part of the gang circulating them all over town.

Probably not, he decided, glad Mom had agreed to his plan. Max needed his family the way Bennett needed his.

"Wait up!" he called out, running faster.

Max stopped at the door to school, and they walked in side by side.

Just Another Shot in the Dark

M. A. Monnin

RAYMOND SNAPPED THE COVER DOWN on his beaten-up flip phone. Any scam was a shot in the dark—it all depended on who the mark was, how savvy, how lonely. Seth said the new one would be a real winner. He'd show up any minute with the details.

The last con they'd worked had been his own and earned them a steady income until the cops and social workers got wise. They got the word out to report calls about paying $15 to talk to a depressed veteran, and the suckers had stopped falling prey—er, sympathizing—with their finances.

"Raymond, where are you? I think we're going to need to call them again."

"Right here, Dad. What's the matter? Is your blood sugar low?" Ray plucked a ripe orange off the tree beside the front door. That was the beauty of living in Upland, California. Fresh fruit always within arm's reach, and plenty of fresh marks no further away than a phone call.

He walked into the house to the dark, low-ceilinged living room. Dad was sitting in his plaid Herculon recliner, as always, his feet propped up on the extended footrest.

"It's not my blood sugar. It's this sore on my leg. I think it's infected."

Raymond bent down and peered at his father's calf. What had been a tiny pinprick was now the diameter of a Coke can and just as red. "Jim said it was a bedsore. Looks like it's infected. You need to get up and walk around more, Dad. Go ahead and call them."

Ray stood back as his father picked up the telephone on the fake oak end table and called 911 on the landline. When Dad finished explaining

245

his emergency and hung up the black plastic handset, Ray reached down and unclasped the sterling silver bracelet his father always wore. It was biting into the flesh, the skin around the links red and swollen, with angry abrasions.

"Looks like this is chafing, Dad." Ray dropped it on top of the bookcase by the foyer, watching out the front door for Seth while he talked. "Might be infected too. When Jim and Donell get here, they'll fix you right up."

The San Bernardino County EMTs were used to Dad calling, and they were good to him too. They understood an old man sometimes needed someone to talk to, just as much as a heart attack victim needed CPR.

It was a shame Dad got that bedsore from sitting in the recliner hour after hour, day after day. He could walk with the walker, the metal aluminum one with tennis balls on the bottom of the legs to keep them from getting caught in the beaten down, forty-year-old shag carpet. A new con would provide a steady income. Probably enough to buy Dad a new walker.

"Hey Dad, how'd you like a new walker? One of them fancy ones, with a seat?"

"Dark red? Annie 'cross the street has one in dark red. The sun shines on that thing, I got to squint."

"Any color you want," Ray said. "They got brakes too, case you and Annie race and get going too fast."

Dad laughed. "Raymond, you're a good boy."

At a knock on the door, Raymond left his father in the living room.

"Seth, where'd you park?" he asked, scanning the street for Seth's black Ford Taurus.

Seth, big and burly, came in, but stayed in the dark foyer. He looked over his shoulder past the citrus trees in the front yard.

"Around the corner," Seth said. "I know how your dad is always calling 911. I expected to see the ambulance here."

"Yeah, if they ever come and it's a real emergency, they won't know what to do." Raymond lowered his voice. "So, what's this new game plan? Not vets again, is it? We need to let that well fill up before we dip in again. Newly bereaved? Selling memorial posts on Facebook? Contributions for

Ray and Seth's Home for Wayward Cats?" There was really no end to the generosity of people who wanted to make a difference.

Seth grinned, revealing a mouth full of surprisingly white teeth. A front tooth was chipped, a souvenir from the grandson of one of their marks who took exception to Seth's romantic neediness.

"This one can't lose. We're moving up in the world. You know what a racket the pharmaceutical market is."

"I ain't doing drugs, Seth," Raymond said, disappointed. He'd already been planning on a new cell phone with the earnings.

"Not that kind. Legitimate drugs. The kind people need but can't afford."

"Yeah?" Raymond heard the siren in the distance. Jim and Donell coming to take care of Dad. He opened the screen door and slid the brace to hold the door open, more to let in the warm sunshine than anything else. Jim and Donell were so used to Dad's calls, they didn't bother to bring the gurney up anymore. "What do you mean?"

Seth cocked an ear, his eyes brightening with anticipation. "EpiPens. They're selling for hundreds, and people need 'em. Bee stings, peanut allergies. Moms can't afford 'em, but they got to have them."

"EpiPens. Yeah, I've heard of 'em. Never seen one. But I know those drug companies gouge patients like Dad." Raymond leaned in. "Where do we get 'em?"

Seth nodded backwards toward the sound of the approaching sirens. "Ambulances. They all have them. Kept in a cooler. Like beer."

"Like beer." Raymond laughed, then got serious. "The cooler will be locked."

Seth held up his leather case of lock picks. "Taken care of."

"We can get what? A hundred bucks a pop? Two hundred?" A couple hundred every week would buy a lot of beer. And a walker, and a smart phone.

"At least that. I know a guy that'll buy 'em. Brett's got a nice little pharmaceutical business of his own on the side."

Ray smiled. "The ambulance crew refills their stock at the end of the day. They'll never know where they lost them. I like it." His mind churned, ticking off the possibilities. "Between the nursing homes and all Dad's old cronies, we can make a killing." He nodded at the brilliance of Seth's scheme. "A killing. Cell phones ain't cheap."

Seth grinned. "The more the merrier. You distract them while I get the goods." With a hand on the battered oak-framed doorway, he leaned into the dim living room, where the TV blared out *Rockford Files* reruns.

"Hey, Lester. What's Rockford up to this time?"

"The damn police are hounding him again." Dad pointed the remote at the television and turned down the volume. "What are you up to?"

"Got a new con," Seth said.

Raymond listened to their conversation while he checked for the ambulance.

"Not veteran's widows, is it? Linda's death wasn't my fault," Dad said defensively. "It was her choice."

"Nothing like that," Seth said. "But you gotta contribute if you want a cut."

At the sight of the ambulance coming up the road, Raymond turned back to his partner.

With his hands in his pockets, Seth grinned. "Lester's gonna contribute too."

"The more the merrier," Raymond said. "He'll call his cronies. They'll help."

Seth frowned. "They'll want a cut."

"Doesn't have to be much." The monthly bill for a smart phone would be a lot more than he was paying now.

"There's other ways to contribute. Maybe a little something that Brett can fence," Seth said. "The more the merrier."

The ambulance sirens blared, then abruptly cut out as the ambulance pulled up in front of the house.

Raymond waved Seth away. "Go out the back door so they don't see you, then leave as soon as you get the pens. If they don't know you're here, and see me the whole time, they'll never be able to pin it on us. Call me when you sell 'em. I got plans for that money."

While Seth dashed out the patio door to the backyard, Raymond went to the front and waited for the EMTs. This one's for you, Dad, he thought. This one's for you.

Sure enough, Jim got the gurney out, but left it on the sidewalk near the ambulance. The EMTs strode calmly up the walk, as they always did, approaching each emergency with calm rather than panic. Jim was with a woman this time, a newbie by the look of her.

"What's going on with Lester today?" Jim asked.

"That bed sore on the back of his calf you told us about. It's infected. Looks real bad."

The paramedic shook his head. "I told him he needs to get off of that chair and walk around."

"Working on it," Raymond said with a smile. "Where's Donell? He get tired of beautiful downtown Upland?"

"He's flexing his muscles at the state EMT competition. This is Amanda."

"Hi Amanda," Raymond said. "Hey, take a look at Dad's wrist too, would ya?"

Jim and Amanda would clean up the wounds, swab 'em with a little alcohol, and Dad would be happy. They would all be happy.

Raymond glanced at the ambulance. Seth peered out from the far side. When Jim turned around in the doorway, rather than entering the house, Raymond stepped forward, blocking Jim's view of the vehicle.

"I'm letting Amanda take care of Lester," Jim said. "She can get to know him."

"Sure. He'll probably flirt with her." Raymond fidgeted with his phone, opening and closing it as anticipation flooded his veins with adrenaline.

Amanda called from the interior. "Jim?"

"You better go see what she wants," Raymond said. He didn't worry about Dad. There was no emergency, just a lonely old man. And why shouldn't insurance pay for them to come see him? He was entitled to it. He'd paid into Medicare when he worked.

When Jim went inside, Seth jumped out of the back of the ambulance, grinning and holding up four thick pens. "Got 'em all," he mouthed.

Raymond gave him a thumbs up. As he entered the house, the loud engine of Seth's Ford Taurus reverberated in his chest, giving release to his silent glee. Done! And it had only taken seconds. The paramedics would never know it happened here.

Amanda spoke to Jim in the hallway.

"That infection on his calf was inflamed. The one on his wrist too," she said. "I cleaned them up and gave him a shot of penicillin." She smiled at Raymond. "The swelling should go down before long."

Raymond went cold. "Not penicillin. You saw his bracelet, right?"

Amanda looked from Raymond to Jim. "He didn't say anything, and he's not wearing a bracelet."

Raymond had taken it off himself, put it on the bookcase. He rushed past her. The bracelet was gone. *That's what Seth meant about Dad contributing.*

"He's allergic!" Raymond swung around to the paramedics, but Jim was already in action.

"No problem. We always carry EpiPens." Jim took the tackle box Amanda carried. "Lester is going to be just fine."

Amanda looked stricken as she hurried to the ambulance. "I used it on our last call and didn't restock the box."

Raymond ran into the living room. "Dad!"

"There's nothing to worry about, Ray," Jim said, maintaining professional calm. "We've got four more in the ambulance. Ray, why are you crying? Ray?"

ABOUT THE AUTHORS

Sandra Benson abandoned her initial dreams of being a world-famous author when she landed a spot in law school. She spent the next thirty-odd years as a writer of contracts, which never seemed to have enough character development. Now that she's retired from law, she's returning to her first love and is working on her debut novel. She lives near Victoria, BC, with her partner and a very pushy cat.

C. N. Buchholz is a freelance writer and former anesthesia technician. Her writing has been featured in *Minnesota Not So Nice: Eighteen Tales of Bad Behavior, Cooked to Death: Volume II,* and *Festival of Crime.* She and her cohort in crime, William J. Anderson, had their manuscript, "In Too Deep," place as a top finalist for the 2017 Freddy Award for Writing Excellence (FAWE) competition sponsored by the Mystery Writers of America, Florida Chapter. C. N. Buchholz lives in the Land of 10,000 Lakes with her husband, her pony-size puppy, and five house cats.

Lida Bushloper's short stories have appeared in *Kings River Life, Flash Bang Mysteries, Mysterical-e,* and numerous confession magazines. Her story, "The Wannabe," was included in *Fishy Business: The Fifth Guppy Anthology.* She has published poetry in *The Lyric, Light: A Journal of Light Verse,* and *The Formalist.* She also writes and publishes essays and anecdotes. She is the author of the poetry collection *Fault Lines.* Visit her blog at lidabushloper.com.

Judith Carlough has written professionally as a Boston radio and TV personality. Her mystery novels are set in Savannah and her historicals set during the Civil War. This is Judith's first published fiction, aside from winning a NY Times competition. She belongs to SINC (proud Guppy), MWA, SCBWI, and many, many museums and historical societies. Judith attended Middlebury College and Boston University and lives west of Boston.

Kait Carson writes two series set in the steamy tropical heat of Florida with a third on the way. The Catherine Swope series is set in greater Miami, and the soon to be released Hayden Kent series is set in the Fabulous Florida Keys. Two new series are scheduled for release in 2023: Southernmost Secrets, set in and around Key West, introduces nurse practitioner turned innkeeper Hank Wittie. A second series, set in the mountains of New Jersey, features Sassy Romano, a newly divorced forty-something, trying to put her past behind her while she creates a new future. Now, if only those pesky bodies would stop dropping. Like her protagonists, Kait is an accomplished SCUBA diver, hiker, and critter lover. She lives with her husband, four rescue cats and flock of conures in the Crown of Maine where long, dark nights give birth to flights of fictional fantasies.

Susan Daly writes short crime fiction as her way of crusading for social justice. Her stories have appeared in a surprising number of anthologies, and "A Death at the Parsonage" won the Arthur Ellis Award for best short story from the Crime Writers of Canada. She lives in Toronto and hangs out with Sisters in Crime, Crime Writers of Canada, and other known criminal types. She can be tracked down at https://susandaly.com/.

M. R. Dimond knew from fifth grade that she wanted to be a writer, so naturally she majored in music for her first college degree and business for her graduate degree. After stints in professional orchestras, law firms, cat rescue, chemistry labs, bookkeeping, and technical communication, she returned to that dream of writing fiction, which has turned out to be about musicians, lawyers, veterinarians, accountants, and cats. She's published science fiction short stories, most recently "Blessed" in